PENGUIN BOOKS

SLAM

'Truthful and funny' *Sunday Times*

'Hornby takes the raw ironies of life and gently rubs away at them to reveal gems of bittersweet truth' *Observer*

'A moving read for anyone' *Elle*

'Touching, very funny' *Guardian*

'Hornby gets his point across with the subtlety and skill of a born novelist who always deserves to be read' *Independent*

'Warm, witty and wise' *Arena*

'Very funny . . . very real' *Telegraph*

'Hornby's writing is hilarious' *Cosmopolitan*

'A funny, sensitive story' *Heat*

ABOUT THE AUTHOR

Nick Hornby was born in 1957. He is the author of five novels, *High Fidelity*, *About a Boy*, *How to be Good*, *A Long Way Down* and *Slam*; three works of non-fiction, *Fever Pitch* (winner of the William Hill Sports Book of the Year Award), *31 Songs* (shortlisted for the National Book Critics Circle Award) and *The Complete Polysyllabic Spree*; and a Pocket Penguin book of short stories, *Otherwise Pandemonium*. He has also edited two anthologies, *My Favourite Year* and *Speaking with the Angel*. In 1999 he was awarded the E. M. Forster Award by the American Academy of Arts and Letters. In 2002 he won the W. H. Smith Award for Fiction, and in 2003 he was honoured with the Writers' Writer Award at the Orange Word International Writers Festival. Nick Hornby lives and works in Highbury, north London.

Slam

NICK HORNBY

PENGUIN BOOKS

PENGUIN BOOKS

Published by the Penguin Group
Penguin Books Ltd, 80 Strand, London WC2R ORL, England
Penguin Group (USA) Inc., 375 Hudson Street, New York, New York 10014, USA
Penguin Group (Canada), 90 Eglinton Avenue East, Suite 700, Toronto, Ontario, Canada M4P 2Y3
(a division of Pearson Penguin Canada Inc.)
Penguin Ireland, 25 St Stephen's Green, Dublin 2, Ireland (a division of Penguin Books Ltd)
Penguin Group (Australia), 250 Camberwell Road, Camberwell, Victoria 3124, Australia
(a division of Pearson Australia Group Pty Ltd)
Penguin Books India Pvt Ltd, 11 Community Centre, Panchsheel Park, New Delhi – 110 017, India
Penguin Group (NZ), 67 Apollo Drive, Rosedale, North Shore 0632, New Zealand
(a division of Pearson New Zealand Ltd)
Penguin Books (South Africa) (Pty) Ltd, 24 Sturdee Avenue, Rosebank,
Johannesburg 2196, South Africa

Penguin Books Ltd, Registered Offices: 80 Strand, London WC2R ORL, England

penguin.com

First published 2007
Published in this edition 2008
3

Quotes from *Hawk – Occupation: Skateboarder* copyright © 2001 by Tony Hawk, used by
permission of the publisher, HarperCollins Publishers, New York, NY.

Set in Sabon
Typeset by Palimpsest Book Production Limited,
Grangemouth, Stirlingshire
Made and printed in England by Clays Ltd, St Ives plc

British Library Cataloguing in Publication Data
A CIP catalogue record for this book is available from the British Library

ISBN: 978-0-141-32449-4

www.greenpenguin.co.uk

Mixed Sources
Product group from well-managed
forests and other controlled sources
www.fsc.org Cert no. SA-COC-1592
© 1996 Forest Stewardship Council

Penguin Books is committed to a sustainable future
for our business, our readers and our planet.
The book in your hands is made from paper
certified by the Forest Stewardship Council.

For Lowell and Jesse

Thanks to Tony Hawk, Pat Hawk,
Francesca Dow, Tony Lacey, Joanna Prior,
Caroline Dawnay and Amanda Posey

1

So things were ticking along quite nicely. In fact, I'd say that good stuff had been happening pretty solidly for about six months.

– For example: Mum got rid of Steve, her rubbish boyfriend.

– For example: Mrs Gillett, my art and design teacher, took me to one side after a lesson and asked whether I'd thought of doing art at college.

– For example: I'd learned two new skating tricks, suddenly, after weeks of making an idiot of myself in public. (I'm guessing that not all of you are skaters, so I should say something straight away, just so there are no terrible misunderstandings. Skating = skateboarding. We never say skateboarding, usually, so this is the only time I'll use the word in this whole story. And if you keep thinking of me messing around on ice, then it's your own stupid fault.)

All that, and I'd met Alicia too.

I was going to say that maybe you should know something about me before I go off on one about my mum and Alicia and all that. If you knew something about me, you might actually care about some of those things. But then, looking at what I just wrote, you know quite a lot already, or at least you could have guessed a lot of it. You could have guessed that my mum and dad don't live together, for a start, unless you thought that my dad was the sort of person who wouldn't mind his wife having boyfriends. Well, he's not. You could have guessed that I skate, and you could have guessed that my best subject at school was art and design, unless you thought I might be the sort of person who's always being taken to one side and told to apply for college by all the teachers in every subject. You know, and the teachers actually fight over me. 'No, Sam! Forget art! Do physics!' 'Forget physics! It would be a tragedy for the human race if you gave up French!' And then they all start punching each other.

Yeah, well. That sort of thing really, really doesn't happen to me. I can promise you, I have never ever caused a fight between teachers.

And you don't need to be Sherlock Holmes or whatever to work out that Alicia was a girl who meant something to me. I'm glad there are things you don't know and can't guess, weird things, things that have only ever happened to me in the whole history of the world, as far as I know. If you were able to guess it all from that first little paragraph, I'd start to worry that I wasn't an incredibly complicated and interesting person, ha ha.

This was a couple of years ago – this time when things were ticking along OK – so I was fifteen, nearly sixteen. And I don't want to sound pathetic, and I really don't want you to feel sorry for me, but this feeling that my life was OK was new to me. I'd never had the feeling before, and I haven't really had it since. I don't mean to say that I'd been unhappy. It was more that there had always been something wrong before, somewhere – something to worry about. (And, as you'll see, there's been a fair bit to worry about since, but we'll get to that.) For instance, my parents were getting divorced, and they were fighting. Or they'd finished getting divorced, but they were still fighting anyway, because they carried on fighting long after they got divorced. Or maths wasn't going very well – I hate maths – or I wanted to go out with someone who didn't want to go out with me . . . All of this had just sort of cleared up, suddenly, without me noticing, really, the way the weather does sometimes. And that summer there seemed to be more money around. My mum was working, and my dad wasn't as angry with her, which meant he was giving us what he ought to have been giving us all the time. So, you know. That helped.

If I'm going to tell this story properly, without trying to hide anything, then there's something I should own up to, because it's important. Here's the thing. I know it sounds stupid, and I'm not this sort of person usually, honest. I mean, I don't

3

believe in, you know, ghosts or reincarnation or any weird stuff at all. But this, it was just something that started happening, and . . . Anyway. I'll just say it, and you can think what you want.

I talk to Tony Hawk, and Tony Hawk talks back.

Some of you, probably the same people who thought I spend my time twirling around on ice-skates, won't have heard of Tony Hawk. Well, I'll tell you, but I have to say that you should know already. Not knowing Tony Hawk is like not knowing Robbie Williams, or maybe even Tony Blair. It's worse than that, if you think about it. Because there are loads of politicians, and loads of singers, hundreds of TV programmes. George Bush is probably even more famous than Tony Blair, and Britney Spears or Kylie are as famous as Robbie Williams. But there's only one skater, really, and his name's Tony Hawk. Well, there's not only one. But he's definitely the Big One. He's the J. K. Rowling of skaters, the Big Mac, the iPod, the Xbox. The only excuse I'll accept for not knowing TH is that you're not interested in skating.

When I got into skating, my mum bought me a Tony Hawk poster off the Internet. It's the coolest present I've ever had, and it wasn't even the most expensive. And it went straight up on to my bedroom wall, and I just got into the habit of telling it things. At first, I only told Tony about

4

skating – I'd talk about the problems I was having, or the tricks I'd pulled off. I pretty much ran to my room to tell him about the first rock 'n' roll I managed, because I knew it would mean much more to a picture of Tony Hawk than it would to a real-life Mum. I'm not dissing my mum, but she hasn't got a clue, really. So when I told her about things like that, she'd try to look all enthusiastic, but there was nothing really going on in her eyes. She was all, Oh, that's great. But if I'd asked her what a rock 'n' roll was, she wouldn't have been able to tell me. So what was the point? Tony knew, though. Maybe that was why my mum bought me the poster, so that I'd have somebody else to talk to.

The talking back started soon after I'd read his book, *Hawk – Occupation: Skateboarder*. I sort of knew what he sounded like then, and some of the things he'd say. To be honest, I sort of knew *all* of the things he'd say when he talked to me, because they came out of his book. I'd read it forty or fifty times when we started talking, and I've read it a few more times since. In my opinion it's the best book ever written, and not just if you're a skater. Everyone should read it, because even if you don't like skating there's something in there that could teach you something. Tony Hawk has been up, and down, and gone through things, just like any politician or musician or soap star. Anyway, because I'd read it forty or fifty times, I could remember pretty much all of it off by heart. So for example, when I told him about the rock 'n' rolls, he said, 'They aren't too hard. But they're a foundation for learning balance and control of your board on a ramp. Well done, man!'

The 'Well done, man!' part was actual conversation, if you see what I mean. That was new. I made that up. But the rest, those were words he'd used before, more or less. OK, not more or less. Exactly. I wished in a way that I didn't know the book so well, because then I could have left out the bit where he says 'They aren't too hard'. I didn't need to hear that when I'd spent like six months trying to get them right. I wished he'd just said, you know, 'Hey! They're a foundation for learning balance and control of your board!' But leaving out 'They aren't too hard' wouldn't have been honest. When you think of Tony Hawk talking about rock 'n' rolls, you hear him say, 'They aren't too hard.' I do, anyway. That's just how it is. You can't rewrite history, or leave bits of it out just because it suits you.

After a while, I started talking to Tony Hawk about other things – about school, Mum, Alicia, whatever, and I found that he had something to say about those things too. His words still came from his book, but the book is about his life, not just skating, so not everything he says is about sacktaps and shove-its.

For example, if I told him about how I'd lost

my temper with Mum for no reason, he'd say, 'I was ridiculous. I can't believe my parents didn't duct tape me up, stuff a sock in my mouth and throw me in a corner.' And when I told him about some big fight at school, he said, 'I didn't get into any trouble, because I was happy with Cindy.' Cindy was his girlfriend of the time. Not everything Tony Hawk said was that helpful, to tell you the truth, but it wasn't his fault. If there was nothing in the book that was exactly right, then I had to make some of the sentences fit as best I could. And the amazing thing was that, once you made them fit, then they always made sense if you thought about what he said hard enough.

From now on, by the way, Tony Hawk is TH, which is what I call him. Most people call him The Birdman, what with him being a Hawk and everything, but that sounds a bit American to me. And also, people round my way are like sheep and they think that Thierry Henry is the only sportsman whose initials are TH. Well, he's not, and I like winding them up. The letters TH feel like my personal secret code.

Why I'm mentioning my TH conversations here, though, is because I remember telling him that things were ticking along nicely. It was sunny, and I'd spent most of the day down at Grind City, which as you may or may not know is a skate park a short bus ride from my house. I mean, you probably wouldn't know that it's a short bus ride from my house, because you don't know where I live, but you might have heard of the skate park, if you're cool, or if you know somebody who's cool. Anyway, Alicia and I went to the cinema that evening, and it was maybe the third or fourth time we'd been out, and I was really, really into her. And when I came in, Mum was watching a DVD with her friend Paula, and she seemed happy to me, although maybe that was in my imagination. Maybe I was the happy one, because she was watching a DVD with Paula and not with Steve the rubbish boyfriend.

'How was the film?' Mum asked me.

'Yeah, good,' I said.

'Did you watch any of it?' said Paula, and I just went to my room, because I didn't want that sort of conversation with her. And I sat down on the bed, and I looked at TH, and I said, 'Things really aren't so bad.'

And he said, 'Life is good. We moved into a new, larger house on a lagoon, close to the beach and, more importantly, with a gate.'

Like I said, not everything that TH comes up with is exactly right. It's not his fault. It's just that his book isn't long enough. I wish it were a million pages long, a) because then I probably wouldn't have finished it yet, and b) because then he'd have something to tell me about every-thing.

And I told him about the day at Grind City, and

8

the tricks I'd been working on, and then I told him about stuff I don't normally bother with in my talks with TH. I told him a little bit about Alicia, and about what was going on with Mum, and how Paula was sitting where Steve used to sit. He didn't have so much to say about that, but for some reason I got the impression that he was interested.

Does this sound mad to you? It probably does, but I don't care, really. Who doesn't talk to someone in their heads? Who doesn't talk to God, or a pet, or someone they love who has died, or maybe just to themselves? TH . . . He wasn't me. But he was who I wanted to be, so that makes him the best version of myself, and that can't be a bad thing, to have the best version of yourself standing there on a bedroom wall and watching you. It makes you feel as though you mustn't let yourself down.

Anyway, all I'm saying is that there was this time – maybe it was a day, maybe a few days, I can't remember now – when everything seemed to have come together. And so obviously it was time to go and screw it all up.

2

A couple of other things, before we go on. First of all, my mum was thirty-two years old at the time I'm talking about. She's three years older than David Beckham, a year older than Robbie Williams, four years younger than Jennifer Aniston. She knows all the dates. If you want, she can supply a much longer list. The list hasn't got any really young people on it, though. She never says, 'I'm fourteen years older than Joss Stone,' or anything like that. She only knows about people round about her age who look good.

For a while, it didn't really register that she wasn't old enough to be the mother of a fifteen-year-old boy, but this last year especially, it's started to seem a little bit weird. First of all, I grew about ten centimetres, so more and more people think she's my aunt, or even my sister. And on top of that . . . There isn't a good way of saying this. I'll tell you what I'll do. I'll repeat a conversation I had with Rabbit, who's this guy I know from skating. He's like two years older than me, and he goes to Grind City too, and we meet from time to time at the bus stop with our boards, or at the Bowl, which is the other place we skate at when we can't be bothered to go to Grind City. It's not really a bowl. It's a kind of concrete pond thing that was supposed to cheer up the flats round the corner, but it hasn't got any water in it any more, because they started to worry about kids drowning. They should have worried about kids drinking it, if you ask me, because people used to piss in it on the way back from the pub and all sorts. It's dry now, so if you're looking for somewhere to skate when you've only got half an hour or so, then it's perfect. There are three of us who use it all the time – me, Rabbit and Rubbish, who can't really skate, which is why he's called Rubbish, but who at least talks sense. If you want to learn something about skating, watch Rabbit. If you want a conversation that isn't completely insane, talk to Rubbish. In a perfect world, there'd be somebody who had Rabbit's skills and Rubbish's brain, but, as you know, we don't live in a perfect world.

So this one evening, I was messing around down at the Bowl, and Rabbit was there, and . . . Like I said, Rabbit isn't the most incredible brainbox, but even so. This is what he said.

'Yo, Sam,' he said.

Did I tell you that my name is Sam? Well, now you know.

'All right?'

'How's it going, man?'

'OK.'

'Right. Hey, Sam. I know what I was gonna ask you. You know your mum?'

See what I mean about Rabbit being thick? Yes, I told him. I knew my mum.

'Is she going out with anyone at the moment?'

'My mum?'

'Yeah.'

'Why do you want to know whether my mum's going out with anyone at the moment?' I asked him.

'Mind your own business,' he said. And he was blushing.

I couldn't believe what I was hearing. Rabbit wanted to go out with my mum! I suddenly had this picture of coming into the flat and seeing the two of them curled up on the sofa, watching a DVD, and I couldn't help but smile. My mum wasn't the best judge of boyfriends, but she wasn't that stupid.

'What's funny?' said Rabbit.

'No, no, nothing. But . . . How old do you think my mum is?'

'How old? I don't know.'

'Guess.'

He looked into space, as if he were trying to see her up there.

'Twenty-three? Twenty-four?'

This time I didn't laugh. Rabbit was such a moron that it sort of went beyond laughing.

'Well,' I said. 'I'll give you a hand. How old am I?'

'You?'

He couldn't see the connection.

'Yeah, me.'

'I dunno.'

'OK. I'm fifteen.'

'Right. So what?'

'So. Say she was twenty when she had me.' I wasn't going to say how old she really was. It might not have been old enough to put him off.

'Yeah.' Suddenly he got it. 'Oh, man. She's your mum. I never twigged. I mean, I knew she was your mum, but I never did, like, the sums . . . Shit. Listen, don't tell her I was asking, OK?'

'Why not? She'd be flattered.'

'Yeah, but, you know. Thirty-five. She's probably a bit desperate. And I don't want a thirty-five-year-old girlfriend.'

I shrugged. 'If you're sure.'

And that was it. But you can see what I'm saying, can't you? Rabbit's not the only one. My other friends would never say anything, but I can tell from how they talk to her that they think she's OK. I can't see it, but then you never can if someone's related to you, can you? It doesn't matter what I think, though. The point is that I've got a thirty-two year-old mother that people – *people of my age* – fancy.

Here's the other thing I wanted to say. The story of my family, as far as I can tell, is always the same story, over and over again. Someone – my mum, my dad, my grandad – starts off thinking that they're going to do well in school, and then go to college, maybe, and then make pots of money. But instead they do something stupid, and they spend the rest of their lives trying to make up for the mistake they made. Sometimes it can seem as though kids always do better than their parents. You know – someone's dad was a coal-miner, or whatever, but his son goes on to play for a Premiership team, or wins *Pop Idol*, or invents the Internet. Those stories make you feel as though the whole world is on its way up. But in our family people always slip up on the first step. In fact, most of the time they don't even find the stairs.

There are no prizes for guessing the mistake my thirty-two-year-old mother made, and the same goes for my thirty-three-year-old father. My mum's dad made the mistake of thinking he was going to be a footballer. That was how he was going to make pots of money. He was offered a youth team place at Queen's Park Rangers, back in the days when Rangers were good. So he packed up school and signed on, and he lasted a couple of years. Nowadays they make kids do exams, he says, so that they've got something to fall back on if they don't make it. They didn't make him do anything, and at eighteen he was out, with no skills, and no training. My mum reckons she could have gone to university, but instead she was married just before her seventeenth birthday.

Everyone thought I was going to do something stupid with skating, and I kept trying to tell them there wasn't anything stupid I could do. Tony Hawk turned pro when he was fourteen, but even in California he couldn't make any money out of it for a while. How was I going to turn pro in Islington? Who was going to pay me? And why? So they stopped worrying about that and started worrying about school instead. I knew how much it meant to them. It meant a lot to me too. I wanted to be the first person in the history of our family to get a qualification in something while they were still at school. (My mum got a qualification after she'd left but that's because she messed up school by having me.) I'd be the one to break the pattern. Mrs Gillett asking me whether I'd thought of doing art and design at college . . . That was a big thing. I went straight home and told Mum. I wish I'd kept it to myself now.

Alicia didn't go to my school. I liked that. I've been out with people from school before, and sometimes it seems childish. They write you notes, and even if they're not in your class, you bump into them like fifty times a day. You get sick of them before you've even been anywhere, just about. Alicia went to St Mary and St Michael, and I liked hearing about teachers I didn't know and kids I would never meet. There seemed more to talk about. You get bored, being with someone who knows every zit on Darren Holmes's face.

Alicia's mum knew my mum from the council. My mum works for the council, and Alicia's mum is a councillor, which is like being the prime minister, except you don't rule over the whole country. You just rule over a tiny bit of Islington. Or Hackney, or wherever. It's a bit of a waste of time, to be honest. It's not like you get to drop bombs on Osama Bin Laden or anything like that. You just talk about how to get more teenagers to use the libraries, which is how Mum met Alicia's mum.

Anyway, it was Alicia's mum's birthday, and she was having a party, and she asked my mum. And she also asked my mum to bring me along. According to my mum, Alicia had said she'd like to meet me. I didn't believe it. Who says stuff like that? Not me. And now I know Alicia, not her either. I'd like to meet TH, and Alicia would like to meet, I don't know, Kate Moss or Kate Winslet or any famous girl who has nice clothes. But you don't go round saying you'd like to meet the son of somebody your mum knows from council meetings. Alicia's mum was trying to find some friends for her, if you ask me. Or at least she was trying to find some friends, maybe even a boyfriend, that she approved of. Well, that all went wrong, didn't it?

I don't really know why I went, thinking about it. Actually, that's not quite true. I went because I said to my mum that I didn't want to go, and I didn't want to meet any girl that she liked. And my mum said, 'Believe me, you do.'

And she was dead serious when she said it, which surprised me. I looked at her.

'How do you know?'

'Because I've met her.'

'And you think she's someone I'd like?'

'As far as I can tell, she's someone every boy likes.'

'You mean she's a slag?'

'Sam!'

'Sorry. But that's what it sounds like.'

'That's exactly what I didn't say. I was very careful. I said every boy likes her. I didn't say she likes every boy. Do you see the difference?'

Mum always thinks I'm being sexist, so I try to be careful – not only with her, but with everyone. It seems to make a difference to some girls. If you say something that isn't sexist to the right sort of girl, she likes you more. Say one of your mates is going on about how girls are stupid, and you say, 'Not *all* girls are stupid,' then it can make you look good. There have to be girls listening, though, obviously. Otherwise it's a waste of time.

Mum was right, though. She hadn't said that Alicia was a slag. She'd just said that Alicia was hot, and it is different, isn't it? I hate it when she catches me out like that. Anyway, it got me interested. Mum describing someone as hot . . . It sort of made it official, somehow. I really wanted to see what someone who was officially hot looked like, I suppose. That still didn't mean I wanted to talk to her. But I did want to look.

I wasn't interested in a girlfriend, I didn't think. I hadn't been out with anyone for longer than seven weeks, and about three of those seven didn't count, because we didn't really see each other. I wanted to dump her, and she wanted to dump me, so we avoided each other. That way, we stayed undumped. Otherwise, it's just been a couple of weeks here and three weeks there. I knew that later on I'd have to try harder than that, but I thought I was happier skating with Rabbit than sitting in McDonald's not saying anything to somebody I didn't know very well.

My mum got dressed up for the party, and she looked OK. She was wearing a black dress and a bit of make-up, and you could tell she was making an effort.

'What do you think?' she said.

'Yeah. All right.'

'Is that all right in a good way, or all right in an OK way?'

'A bit better than OK. Not as good as actually good.'

But she could tell I was joking, so she just kind of swiped me round the ear.

'Appropriate?'

I knew what that meant, but I made a face like she's just said something in Japanese, and she sighed.

'It's a fiftieth birthday party,' she said. 'Do you think I'll look right? Or out of place?'

'Fiftieth?'

'Yes.'

'She's fifty?'

'Yes.'

'Bloody hell. So how old's her daughter, then? Like, thirty or something? Why would I want to hang out with a thirty-year-old?'

'Sixteen. I told you. That's normal. You have a baby when you're thirty-four, which is what I should have done, and then when she's sixteen you're fifty.'

'So she was older than you are now when she had this girl.'

'Alicia. Yes. And, like I said, it's not weird. It's normal.'

'I'm glad you're not fifty.'

'Why? What difference does it make to you?'

She was right, really. It didn't make an awful lot of difference to me.

'I'll be thirty-three at your fiftieth.'

'So?'

'I'll be able to get drunk. And you won't be able to say anything.'

'That's the best argument I've ever heard for

having a kid at sixteen. In fact, it's the only argument I've ever heard for having a kid at sixteen.'

I didn't like it when she said things like that. It always felt like it was my fault, somehow. Like I'd persuaded her I wanted to come out eighteen years early. That's the thing about being an unwanted baby, which is what I was, let's face it. You've always got to remind yourself it was their idea, not yours.

They lived in one of those big old houses off of Highbury New Park. I'd never been in one before. Mum knows people who live in places like that, because of work, and her book group, but I don't. We only lived about half a mile from her, but I never used to have any reason to go up Alicia's way until I met her. Everything about her place was different from ours. Hers was big, and we lived in a flat. Hers was old, and ours was new. Hers was untidy and a bit dusty, and ours was tidy and clean. And they had books everywhere. It's not that we didn't have books at home. But it was more like Mum had a hundred and I had thirty. They had about ten thousand each, or that's what it looked like. There was a bookcase in the hallway, and more going up the stairs, and the bookcases all had books shoved on top of them. And ours were all new, and theirs were all old. I liked everything about our place better, apart from I wished we had more than two bedrooms. When I thought about the future, and what it was going to be like, that's what I saw for myself: a house with loads of bedrooms. I didn't know what I was going to do with them, because I wanted to live on my own, like one of the skaters I saw on MTV once. He had this ginormous house with a swimming pool, and a pool table, and a miniature indoor skate park with padded walls and a vert ramp and a half-pipe. And he had no girlfriend living there, no parents, nothing. I wanted some of that. I didn't know how I was going to get it, but that didn't matter. I had a goal.

Mum said hello to Andrea, Alicia's mum, and then Andrea made me walk over to where Alicia was sitting to say hello. Alicia didn't look like she wanted to say hello. She was sprawled out on a sofa looking at a magazine, even though it was a party, and when her mum and I came up to her she acted like the most boring evening of her life just took a turn for the worse.

I don't know about you, but when parents do that pairing off thing to me, I decide on the spot that the person I'm being set up with is the biggest jerk in Britain. It wouldn't matter if she looked like Britney Spears used to look and thought that *Hawk – Occupation*: *Skateboarder* was the best book ever written. If it was my mum's idea, then I wasn't interested. The whole point of friends is that you choose them yourself. It's bad enough being told who your relations are, your aunts and uncles and cousins and all that. If I wasn't allowed to choose my friends either, I'd never speak to another person again, probably. I'd rather live on a desert island on my own, as long as it was made of concrete, and I had a board with me. A desert traffic island, ha ha.

Anyway. It was all right if I didn't want to speak to someone, but who did she think she was, sitting there pouting and looking the other way? She'd probably never even heard of Tony Hawk, or Green Day, or anything cool, so what gave her the right?

I thought about outsulking her. She was sitting on the sofa, sunk down low, her legs stretched out, and looking away from me towards the food table on the wall opposite. I sunk down in the same way, stretched my legs out and stared at the bookshelf by my side. We were so carefully arranged that we must have looked like plastic models, the sort of thing you can get in a Happy Meal.

I was making fun of her, and she knew it, but instead of sulking harder, which would have been one way to go, she decided to laugh instead. And when she laughed, I could feel some part of me flip over. All of a sudden, I was desperate to make this girl like me. And as you can probably tell, my mum was right. She was officially gorgeous. She could have got a certificate for gorgeousness from Islington Council, if she wanted, and she wouldn't even have had to get her mum to pull strings. She had – still has – these enormous grey eyes that have caused me actual physical pain once or twice, somewhere between the throat and the chest. And she's got this amazing straw-coloured hair that always looks messy and cool at the same time, and she's tall, but she's not skinny and flat-chested, like a lot of tall girls, and she's not taller than me, and then there's her skin, which is whatever, like the skin of a peach and all that . . . I'm hopeless at describing people. All I can say is that, when I saw her, I was angry with Mum for not grabbing me by the throat and shouting at me. OK, she gave me a tip-off. But it should have been much more than that. It should have been, like, 'If you don't come, you'll regret it every single minute for the rest of your life, you moron.'

'You're not supposed to be looking,' I said to Alicia.

'Who said I was laughing at what you were doing?'

'Either you were laughing at what I was doing or you're off your head. There's nothing else here to laugh at.'

That wasn't strictly true. She could have been laughing at the sight of her dad dancing, for a start. And there were loads of trousers and shirts that were pretty funny.

'Maybe I was laughing at something I remembered,' she said.

'Like?'

'I dunno. Loads of funny things happen, don't they?'

'So you were laughing at all of them, all at once?'

And we went on like that for a bit, messing around. I was starting to relax. I'd got her talking, and once I've got a girl talking, then she is doomed, and there can be no escape for her. But then she stopped talking.

'What's the matter?'

'You think you're getting somewhere, don't you?'

'How can you tell that?' I was shocked. That was exactly what I thought.

She laughed. 'When you started talking to me there wasn't a single muscle in you that was relaxed. Now you're all . . .' And she threw out her arms and legs, as if she was doing an impression of someone watching TV on the sofa at home. 'Well, it's not like that,' she said. 'Not yet. And it might not ever be.'

'OK,' I said. 'Thanks.' I felt about three years old.

'I didn't mean it like that,' she said. 'I just meant, you know, you've got to keep trying.'

'I might not want to keep trying.'

'I know that's not true.'

I turned to look at her then, to see how serious she was, and I could tell she was half-teasing, so I could just about forgive her for saying it. She seemed older than me, which I decided was because she spent a lot of time dealing with boys who fell in love with her in two seconds flat.

'Where would you rather be right now?' she asked me.

I wasn't sure what to say. I knew the answer. The answer was there wasn't anywhere I'd rather be. But if I told her, I'd be dead.

'I dunno. Skating, probably.'

'You skate?'

'Yeah. Not ice-skating. Skateboarding.' I know I said I'd never use that word again, but sometimes I need it. Not everyone is as cool as me.

'I know what skating is, thank you.'

She was scoring too many points. Soon I'd need a calculator to add them all up. I didn't want to talk about skating, though, until I knew what she thought of it.

'How about you? Where would you rather be?'

She hesitated, as if she was about to say something embarrassing.

'Actually, I'd like to be here, on this sofa.'

For the second time, it was as though she knew what I was thinking, except this time it was even better. She had worked out the answer I had wanted to give, and she was passing it off as her own. Her points score was about to go into the billions.

'Right here. But with nobody else in the room.'

'Oh.' I could feel myself start to blush, and I didn't know what to say. She looked at me and laughed.

'Nobody else,' she said. 'That includes you.'

Deduct the billions. Yes, she could see what I was thinking. But she wanted to use her super-powers for evil, not for good.

'Sorry if that sounded rude. But I hate it when my parents have parties. They make me want to watch TV on my own. I'm boring, aren't I?'

'No. Course you're not.'

Some people would say that she was. She could have gone anywhere in the world for those few seconds, and she chose her own home so that she could watch *Pop Idol* without anyone bothering her. These people, though, wouldn't have under-stood why she said what she said. She said it to wind me up. She knew I'd think, just for a second, that she was going to say something romantic. She knew I'd be hoping she'd say, 'Right here, but with nobody else in the room apart from you.' And she left off the last three words to stamp on me. I thought that was pretty clever, really. Cruel, but clever.

'So you haven't got any brothers and sisters?'

'What's that got to do with anything?'

'Because if your parents weren't having a party, you'd have a chance of being alone in the room.'

'Oh. Yeah, I suppose. I've got a brother. He's nineteen. He's at college.'

'What's he studying?'

'Music.'

'What music do you like?'

'Oh, very smooth.'

For a moment, I thought she meant she liked very smooth music, but then I realized she was taking the piss out of my attempts to make conversation. She was beginning to drive me a bit nuts. Either we were going to talk, or we weren't. And if we were, then asking her what music she liked seemed an OK question. Maybe it wasn't incredibly original, but she made it sound as though I kept asking her to get undressed.

I stood up.

'Where are you going?'

'I think I'm wasting your time, and I'm sorry.'

'You're OK. Sit down again.'

'You can *pretend* there's no one else here, if you want. You can sit on your own and think.'

'And what are you going to do? Who are you going to talk to?'

'My mum.'

'Aaaah. Sweet.'

I snapped.

'Listen. You're gorgeous. But the trouble is, you know it, and you think you can treat people like dirt because of it. Well, I'm sorry, but I'm really not that desperate.'

And I left her there. It was one of my greatest moments: all the words came out right, and I meant everything I said, and I was glad I'd said it. I wasn't doing it for effect, either. I was really, properly sick of her, for about twenty seconds. After twenty seconds I calmed down and started trying to work out a way back into the conversation. And I hoped that the conversation would turn into something else – a kiss, and then marriage, after we'd been out for a couple of weeks. But I was sick of the way she was making me feel. I was too nervous, too keen not to make a mistake, and I was being pathetic. If we were going to talk again, it had to be because she wanted to.

My mum was talking to a bloke, and she wasn't that thrilled to see me. I got the impression that she hadn't got on to the subject of me yet, if you know what I mean. I know she loves me, but every now and again, in exactly this sort of situation, she conveniently forgets to mention that she's got a fifteen-year-old son.

'This is my son, Sam,' my mum said. But I could tell she'd rather have described me as her brother. Or her dad. 'Sam, this is Ollie.'

'Ollie,' I said, and I laughed. And he looked upset, and Mum looked pissed off, so I tried to explain.

'Ollie,' I said again, like they'd get it, but they didn't.

'You know,' I said to my mum.

'No,' she said.

'Like the skate trick.' Because there's a trick called an ollie.

'Is that funny? Really?'

'Yeah,' I said. But I wasn't sure any more. I think I was still all confused after talking to Alicia, and not at my best.

'His name's Oliver,' she said. 'I presume, anyway.' She looked at him, and he nodded. 'Have you ever heard of the name Oliver?'

'Yeah, but . . .'

'So he's Ollie for short.'

'Yeah, I know, but . . .'

'What if he was called Mark?'

'Not funny.'

'No? But, you know . . . Mark! Like a mark on someone's trousers! Ha ha ha!' said Mum.

Never go to a party with your mother.

'Mark on your trousers!' she said again.

And then Alicia came over to us, and I looked at my mum as if to say, 'Say "Mark on your trousers" one more time and Ollie hears some things you don't want him to know.' She understood, I think.

'You're not going, are you?' Alicia said.

'I dunno.'

She took my hand and led me right back to the sofa.

'Sit down. You were right to walk away. I don't know why I was like that.'

'Yes you do.'

'Why, then?'

'Because people let you be like that.'

'Can we start again?'

'If you want,' I said. I wasn't sure whether she could. You know how you're not supposed to make faces because the wind might change and you stay like that? Well, I wondered whether the wind might have changed, and she'd be sulky and cocky for ever.

'OK,' she said. 'I like some hip-hop, but not a lot. The Beastie Boys, and Kanye West. Bit of hip-hop, bit of R&B. Justin Timberlake. Do you know REM? My dad likes them a lot, and I've got into them. And I play the piano, so I listen to classical sometimes. There. That didn't kill me, did it?'

I laughed. And that was that. That was the moment she stopped treating me like an enemy. All of a sudden I was a friend, and all I'd done to change things was walk away.

It was better being a friend than an enemy, of course it was. I still had a party to get through, after all, and having a friend meant I had someone else to talk to. I wasn't going to stand there listening to Mum laughing like a drain at Ollie's bad jokes, so I had to spend it with Alicia. So in the short term, I was glad we were friends. In the long term, though, I wasn't so sure. I don't mean that Alicia wouldn't have been a good friend to have. She'd have been a fantastic friend to have. She was funny, and I didn't know too many people like her. But by that stage, I knew that I didn't want to be her friend, if you know what I mean, and I was worried that her being friendly to me meant that I didn't stand a chance with anything else. I know that's wrong. Mum is always telling me that the friendship has to come first, before anything else. But it seemed to me that when I first arrived at the party, she was looking at me as though I might be a possible boyfriend, which was why she was all sharp and spiky. So what I didn't know was, had she put away the spikes for a reason? Because some girls are like that. Sometimes you know you've got a chance with a girl because she wants to fight with you. If the world wasn't so messed up, it wouldn't be like that. If the world was normal, a girl being nice to you would be a good sign, but in the real world, it isn't.

As things turned out, Alicia being nice to me was a good sign, so maybe the world isn't as messed up as I'd thought. And I understood that it was a good sign pretty much straight away, because she started talking about things we could do. She said she wanted to come to Grind City to watch me skate, and then she asked me whether I wanted to see a film with her.

I was getting butterflies by this time. It sounded to me as though she'd already decided that we were going to start seeing each other, but nothing's ever that easy, is it? And also, how come she didn't have a boyfriend? Alicia could have had anyone she wanted, in my opinion. Actually, that might even be a fact.

So when she mentioned this possible cinema

date, I tried to be as, you know, as blah as possible, just to see how she'd react.

'I'll see what I'm up to,' I said.

'What does that mean?'

'Well, you know. I've got homework some nights. And I usually do quite a lot of skating over the weekends.'

'Suit yourself.'

'Anyway. Do I have to find someone to come with me?'

She looked at me as if I was mad, or stupid.

'What do you mean?'

'I don't want to go to the cinema with you and your boyfriend,' I said. Do you see my clever plan? This was my way of finding out what was going on.

'If I had a boyfriend, I wouldn't be asking you, would I? If I had a boyfriend, you wouldn't be sitting here now, and neither would I, probably.'

'I thought you had a boyfriend.'

'Where did you get that from?'

'I dunno. Why haven't you, anyway?'

'We split up.'

'Oh. When?'

'Tuesday. I'm heartbroken. As you can tell.'

'How long had you been going out?'

'Two months. But he wanted to have sex with me, and I wasn't ready to have sex with him.'

'Right.'

I looked at my shoes. Five minutes ago she didn't

want me to know what music she listened to, and now she was telling me about her sex life.

'So maybe he'll change his mind,' I said. 'About wanting sex, I mean.'

'Or maybe I will,' she said.

'Right.'

Was she saying that she might change her mind about being ready for sex? In other words, was she saying that she might have sex with me? Or was she saying that she might change her mind about having sex with him? And if that was what she meant, where did that leave me? Was it possible that she'd go out with me, but at any moment she might decide that the time had come to go off and sleep with him? This seemed like important information, but I wasn't sure how to go about getting it.

'Hey,' she said. 'Want to go up to my room? Watch some TV? Or listen to some music?'

She stood up and pulled me to my feet. What was this, now? Had she already changed her mind about being ready for sex? Is that what we were going upstairs for? Was I about to lose my virginity? I felt like I was watching some film I didn't understand.

I'd been close to having sex a couple of times, but I'd chickened out. Having sex when you're fifteen is a big deal, if you've got a thirty-one-year-old mum. And this girl Jenny I was seeing kept saying that everything would be all right, but I didn't

33

know what that meant, really, and I didn't know whether she was one of those girls who actually wanted a baby, for reasons that I could never understand. There were a couple of young mums at my school, and they acted like a baby was an iPod or a new mobile or something, some kind of gadget that they wanted to show off. There are many differences between a baby and an iPod. And one of the biggest differences is, no one's going to mug you for your baby. You don't have to keep a baby in your pocket if you're on the bus late at night. And if you think about it, that must tell you something, because people will mug you for anything worth having, which means that a baby can't be worth having. Anyway, I wouldn't sleep with Jenny, and she told a few of her friends, and for a while people shouted things at me in the corridors and that. And the next boy who went out with her . . . Actually, I don't want to tell you what he said. It was stupid and disgusting and it made me look bad, and that's all you need to know. After that I started to take skating a lot more seriously. It meant I could spend more time on my own.

As we were going up the stairs to her bedroom, I had this fantasy that Alicia would close the door, and look at me, and start to get undressed, and to tell you the honest truth, I wasn't sure how I'd feel about that. I mean, there was a plus side, obviously. But on the other hand, she might expect me to know what I was doing, and I didn't. And my mum was downstairs, and who was to say that she wouldn't come looking for me at any moment? And Alicia's mum and dad were downstairs, and also I had a feeling that if she did want to have sex, it was a lot to do with this boy she'd just dumped, and not so much to do with me.

I needn't have worried. We went into her room, and she closed the door, and then she remembered that she was halfway through this film called *The Forty-year-old Virgin*, so we watched the rest of that. I sat in this old armchair she's got in there, and she sat on the floor between my legs. And after a little while, she leaned against me so that her back was pressing into my knees. That was what I remembered later. It felt like a message. And then, when the film had finished, we went downstairs, and my mum was just starting to look for me, and we went home.

But as we were walking up the road, Alicia came running after us in her bare feet, and she gave me this black-and-white postcard of a couple kissing. I stared at the picture, and I must have been looking a bit clueless, because she rolled her eyes and said, 'Turn it over.' And on the back was her mobile number.

'For the cinema tomorrow,' she said.

'Oh,' I said. 'Right.'

And when she'd gone my mum raised her eyebrows up as far as they would go and said, 'So you're going to the cinema tomorrow.'

'Yeah,' I said. 'Looks like it.'

And my mum laughed, and said, 'Was I right? Or was I right?'

And I said, 'You were right.'

Tony Hawk lost his virginity when he was sixteen. He'd just skated in a contest called the King of the Mount at a place called Trashmore in Virginia Beach. He says in his book that he lasted half as long as a run in a vert contest. A run in a vert contest takes forty-five seconds. So he lasted twenty-two and a half seconds. I was glad he'd told me. I never forgot those figures.

The next day was Sunday, and I went down to Grind City with Rabbit. Or rather, I saw Rabbit at the bus stop, so we ended up going together. Rabbit can do tricks I can't – he's been doing gay twists for ages, and he was right on the edge of being able to do a McTwist, which is a 540-degree turn on a ramp.

When I try to talk to Mum about tricks, she always gets muddled up by the numbers. 'Five hundred and forty degrees?' she said when I was trying to describe a McTwist. 'How the hell do you know when you've done five hundred and forty degrees?' As if we spend our time counting the degrees one by one. But a five-forty is just 360 plus 180 – in other words, it's just a turn and a half. Mum seemed disappointed when I put it like that. I think she hoped that skating was turning

36

me into some kind of mathematical genius, and I was doing calculations in my head that other kids could only do on a computer. TH, by the way, has done a 900. Maybe if I tell you that's basically impossible, you'll start to see why he should have a country named after him.

McTwists are really hard, and I haven't even begun thinking about them yet, mostly because you end up eating a lot of concrete while you're practising. You can't do it without slamming every couple of minutes, but that's the thing about Rabbit. He's so thick that he doesn't mind how much concrete he eats. He's lost like three hundred teeth skating. I'm surprised the people who run Grind City don't put his teeth on the tops of walls to stop people getting in at night, the way some people use bits of broken glass.

I didn't have a good day, though. I was distracted. I couldn't stop thinking about the evening at the cinema. I know it sounds stupid, but I didn't want to turn up with a big fat bloody lip, and statistics show that fat lips tend to happen to me more on a Sunday than on any other day of the week.

Anyway, Rabbit noticed that I was just messing around with a few ollies, and he came over.

'What's up? Lost your bottle?'

'Kind of.'

'What's the worst that can happen? That's how I think about it. I've been to casualty like fifteen times because of skating. The worst bit is on the way to the hospital, because that hurts. You're lying there all groaning and moaning, and blood everywhere. And you think, is it worth it? But then they give you something to take the pain away. Unless you're unconscious. Then you don't need it. Not for a while.'

'Sounds good.'

'It's just my philosophy. You know. Pain can't kill you. Unless it's really bad.'

'Yeah. Thanks. Something to think about there.'

'Is there?' He seemed surprised. I don't suppose anyone had ever told Rabbit he'd given them something to think about. It was because I wasn't really listening.

I wasn't going to say anything, because what's the point of talking to Rabbit? But then I realized that it was killing me, not telling anyone about Alicia, and if I didn't talk to him, I'd have to go home and talk to Mum or to TH. Sometimes it doesn't matter who you talk to, as long as you talk. That's why I spend half my life talking to a life-sized poster of a skater. At least Rabbit was a real person.

'I met this girl.'

'Where?'

'Does that matter?' I could see that it was going to be a frustrating conversation.

'I'd like to try and picture the scene,' said Rabbit.

'My mum's friend's party.'

'So is she like really old?'

'No. She's my age.'

'What was she doing at the party?'

'She lives there,' I said. 'She . . .'

'She lives at a party?' Rabbit said. 'How does that work?'

I was wrong. It was much easier explaining things to a poster.

'She doesn't live at a party. She lives in the house where the party was. She's my mum's friend's daughter.'

Rabbit repeated what I'd just said, as if it was the most complicated sentence in the history of the world.

'Hold on . . . Your mum's . . . friend's . . . daughter. OK. I've got it.'

'Good. We're going out tonight. To the cinema. And I'm worried about getting my face all smashed up.'

'Why does she want to smash your face up?'

'No, no. I didn't mean I was worried about *her* smashing my face up. I'm worried about getting my face smashed up here. A bad slam. And then, you know. I'll look terrible.'

'Gotcha,' said Rabbit. 'Is she pretty?'

'Very,' I said. I was sure that was true, but by then I couldn't remember what she looked like. I'd spent so much time thinking about her that I no longer had a clear picture of her in my mind.

'Ah, well,' said Rabbit.

'What does that mean?'

'Let's face it, you're not all that, are you?'

'No, I'm not. I know. But thanks for building up my confidence,' I said.

'Thinking about it, I reckon you might do better if you actually do smash your face up,' said Rabbit.

'How d'you work that out?'

'Well, see, say you go along with, you know, a couple of black eyes, or even a broken nose. You can tell her you look bad because of the skating. But if you go along looking just like that . . . What excuse have you got? None.'

I'd had enough. I'd tried talking to Rabbit, but it was hopeless. And it wasn't just hopeless – it was depressing too. I was really nervous about going to the cinema with Alicia. In fact, I couldn't remember ever feeling as nervous about anything, ever, apart from maybe my first day at primary school. And this fool was telling me that the only way I was going to stand any kind of chance was to make my face all bloody and swollen, so that she couldn't see what I really looked like.

'You know what, Rabbit? You're right. I'm not going to mess about. Acid drops and gay twists, all afternoon.'

'Top man.'

And then, while he was watching me, I picked up my board and walked straight out the gate and into the street. I wanted to talk to TH.

On the way home, I realized that I hadn't even arranged anything with Alicia yet. When the bus came, I went up to the top deck and sat right at the front, on my own. Then I got her postcard out of my pocket and dialled her number.

She didn't recognize my voice when I said hello, and for a moment I felt sick. What if I'd made all this up? I hadn't made up the party. But maybe she hadn't pressed against me the way I remembered it, and maybe she only said something about the cinema because . . .

'Oh, hi,' she said, and I could hear her smiling. 'I was worried that you weren't going to call.' And I stopped feeling sick.

Listen: I know you don't want to hear about every single little moment. You don't want to know about what time we arranged to meet, or any of that stuff. All I'm trying to say is, it was really special, that day, and I can remember just about every second of it. I can remember the weather, I can remember the smell of the bus, I can remember the little scab on my nose I was picking at while I was talking to her on my mobile. I can remember what I said to TH when I got home, and what I wore to go out, and what she was wearing, and how easy it was when I saw her. Maybe some people would think that because of what happened later, it was all just tacky and grubby, typical modern teenager stuff. But it wasn't. It was nothing like that at all.

We didn't even go to a film. We started talking outside the cinema and then we went for a frappuccino in the Borders next door, and then we just sat there. Every now and again one of us said, 'We'd better go, if we're going.' But neither of us made any move to leave. It was her idea to go back to her place. And, when the time came, it was her idea to have sex. But I'm getting ahead of myself.

I think before that night I was a bit scared of her. She was beautiful, and her mum and dad were quite posh, and I was afraid she'd decide that just because I was the only person of her age at her mum's party, it didn't mean we had to go out together. The party was over. She could talk to who she wanted now.

But she wasn't scary, not really. Not in the posh way. She wasn't really what you'd call a brainbox. Or maybe that's not fair, because it wasn't like she was stupid. But seeing as her mum was a councillor and her dad taught at university, you'd think she'd be doing better at school. She spent half the evening talking about the lessons she'd been thrown out of, and the trouble she'd got into, and the number of times she'd been grounded. She'd been grounded the night of the party, which was why she was there. All that stuff about wanting to meet me was bollocks, as I'd suspected.

She didn't want to go to college.

'You do, then?' she said.

'Yeah. Of course.'

'Why "of course"?'

'I dunno.'

I did know. But I didn't want to go into all that stuff about the history of my family. If she found out that none of us – my parents, grandparents, great-grandparents, nobody – had ever been to college, then she might not have wanted to spend any time with me.

'So what are you going to do?' I asked her. 'When you leave school?'

'I don't want to tell you.'

'Why not?'

'Because you'll think it's big-headed.'

'How can it be big-headed? If it's nothing to do with being a big-head?'

'There's more than one way of being a big-head, you know. It doesn't have to involve passing exams and all that.'

I was lost. I couldn't think of a single thing she could say that would make me think she was a big-head, if it didn't involve passing exams, or maybe sport. Suddenly I wasn't even sure what it meant, being a big-head. It meant showing off, right? But didn't it mean showing off about how clever you were? Did anyone ever call TH a big-head because he could do loads of difficult tricks?

'I swear I won't think you're a big-head.'

'I want to be a model.'

Yeah, well, I could see what she meant. She was

showing off. But what was I supposed to say? I can tell you, it was a tricky situation. I was going to tell you to avoid ever going out with anyone who says she wants to be a model, but let's face it, that's sort of what we all want, really, isn't it? Someone who looks like a model, but without the flat chest. In other words, if you're with someone who says she wants to be a model, you probably aren't interested in me telling you she's bad news. (Definitely avoid going out with ugly girls who say they want to be models. Not because they're ugly, but because they're mad.)

I didn't know much about modelling then, and I know even less about it now. Alicia was very pretty, I could see that, but she wasn't as thin as a rake, and she had some spots, so I didn't know whether she stood a chance of being the next Kate Moss. Probably not, I reckoned. I also didn't know whether she was telling me this because it really was her ambition, or because she needed to hear me tell her how much I fancied her.

'That's not big-headed,' I said. 'You could be a model easily, if you wanted to be.'

I knew what I was saying. I knew that I'd just increased my chances with Alicia in all sorts of ways. I didn't know who believed what, but it didn't matter really.

We slept together for the first time that night.

'Have you got anything?' she said, when it was obvious that we might need something.

'No. Of course not.'

'Why "of course not"?'

'Because ... I thought we were going to the cinema.'

'And you don't carry anything around with you? Just in case?'

I just shook my head. I knew blokes at school who did that, but they were just showing off, most of them. They did it to look flash. There was this one kid, Robbie Brady, who must have shown me the same Durex box fifteen times. And I'm like, Yeah, well, anyone can *buy* them. *Buying* them isn't a big deal. But I never said anything. I'd always thought that if I needed anything, I'd know well in advance, because that's the way I am. I never go out thinking, Tonight I'm going to shag someone I don't know, so I'd better take a condom with me. I'd always hoped it would all be a bit more planned than that. I'd always hoped that we might have talked about it beforehand, so that when it happened we were both prepared for it, and it would be relaxed, and special. I never liked the sound of the stories I heard from kids at school. They were always pleased with themselves, but it never sounded like the sort of sex you read about, or saw in porn movies. It was always quick, and sometimes they were outside, and sometimes there were other people nearby. I knew I'd rather not bother than do it like that.

45

'Oh, you're a nice boy,' said Alicia. 'My last boyfriend, he always carried a condom around.'

You see? That was exactly what I meant. He always carried one around, and he never got to use it, because Alicia didn't like the way he was trying to put pressure on her. Sometimes condoms really *really* stop you from making babies. If you're the sort of kid that always has one on you, then no one wants to sleep with you anyway. At least I was with someone who wanted to have sex with me. Did that make me any better off, though? Alicia's ex didn't have sex with her because he always carried a condom around; I wasn't going to have sex with her because I didn't. At least she wanted to have sex with me, though. So on the whole I was glad I was me. Which was probably just as well.

'I'm going to go and steal one,' said Alicia.

'Where from?'

'My parents' bedroom.'

She stood up, and started to walk towards the door. She had a vest on, and her knickers, and if anyone saw her, they wouldn't need to be an incredible genius to work out what had been going on in her room.

'You're going to get me killed,' I said.

'Oh, don't be so soppy,' she said, but she didn't explain why a fear of being killed was soppy. To me, it was just common sense.

So I had probably two minutes on my own in

her bedroom, lying on her bed, and I spent it trying to remember how we'd got from there to here. The truth was, there wasn't much to it. We came in, said hello to her mum and dad, went upstairs, and that was it, pretty much. We never talked about it. We just did what we wanted to do. I was pretty sure, though, that she wanted to go all the way because of her ex. It wasn't much to do with me. I mean, I don't think she'd have wanted to do it if she hated me. But when she'd said to me at the party that she might change her mind, I could see now that she wanted to get him back for something. It was like a joke on him. He kept asking her, and she kept saying no, and then he got pissed off and dumped her, and so she decided to sleep with the next person who came along, as long as he was half-decent. I had a bet with myself that if we did have sex that night, it wouldn't stay a secret between us. She'd have to find some way of letting him know she wasn't a virgin. That was sort of the point of it.

And suddenly I didn't want to do it any more. I know, I know. There was this beautiful girl I really liked, and she had just taken me up to her bedroom, and she'd made it obvious that we were up there for a reason. But when I'd worked out what was going on, it didn't feel right. There were three of us in her bedroom that night, me, her and him, and I decided that because it was my first time, I'd prefer to keep the numbers down. I wanted to wait until he'd gone, just to make sure she was still interested.

Alicia came back in holding a small square silver packet.

'Ta-ra!' she said, and she held it up in the air.

'Are you sure it's, you know, all right? It hasn't gone past its sell-by date?'

I don't know why I said this. I mean, I know I said it because I was looking for excuses. But there were lots of excuses I could have used, and this one wasn't a very good one.

'Why shouldn't it be all right?' she said.

'I dunno.' And I didn't.

'You mean because it's my mum and dad's?'

That was what I meant, I suppose.

'You think that they never have sex? So this has been lying around for years?'

I didn't say anything. But that was what I must have been thinking, which was weird, really. Believe me, I knew that people's parents had sex. But I suppose I didn't really know what it was like for parents who were actually together. I was sort of presuming that parents who were together had sex less often than parents who were apart. I seemed to be very confused by the whole subject of condoms. If anyone had one, then I ended up thinking they weren't having sex, and that can't be true all the time, can it? Some of them had to be bought by people who actually used them.

She looked at the wrapper.

'21/05/09, it says.'

(If you're reading this in the future, then I should tell you that all this was happening long before 21/05/09. We had plenty of time to use that condom, years and years.)

She threw the condom over to me.

'Come on. We haven't got for ever.'

'Why not?' I said.

'Because it's getting late, and my mum and dad know you're up here. They'll start banging on the door soon. That's what they usually do if I've got a boy in here and it's late.'

I must have had some kind of a look on my face, because she knelt down by the side of the bed and kissed me on the cheek.

'I'm sorry. I didn't mean it like that.'

'How did you mean it, then?'

I was just saying anything that came into my head. I wanted it to get even later than it was, so her mum and dad would start banging on the door, and I could go home.

'You don't want to do this, do you?' she said.

'Yeah, course,' I said. And then, 'Not really, no.'

She laughed. 'So you're not confused or anything, then.'

'I don't know why you want to do it,' I said. 'You told me you weren't ready for sex with your ex-boyfriend.'

'I wasn't.'

49

'So how comes you're ready to have sex with me? You don't even know me.'

'I like you.'

'So you didn't like him much, then?'

'No, not really. I mean, I did at first. But then I went off him.'

I didn't want to ask any more questions about all that. None of it made much sense. It was like she was saying that we ought to sleep together quickly, before she stopped liking me – like she knew she wouldn't like me the next day, so we had to do it that night. If you look at it another way, though, everyone is like that. I mean, you sleep with someone because you're not sick of them, and when you're sick of them, you stop.

'If you don't want to do anything, why don't you just go?' she said.

'OK. I will.'

And I stood up, and she started to cry, and I didn't know what to do.

'I wish I'd never said that thing about wanting to be a model. I feel stupid now.'

'Oh, it's nothing to do with that, ' I said. 'If anything, I think you're out of my league.'

'Out of my league?' she said. 'Where did that come from?'

I knew where it came from. It came from having a mum who was sixteen when I was born. If somebody knows about the history of my family, then it's all they can see, and it's all they can hear.

I didn't tell her any of that. I sat down on the bed and held her, and when she'd stopped crying she kissed me, and that was how we ended up having sex even though I'd decided not to. If I broke TH's record of twenty-two and a half seconds, it couldn't have been by more than that half-second.

I told TH when I got home. I had to tell someone, but talking about that stuff is hard, so absolutely the best way is to say anything you've got to say to a poster. I think he was pleased. From what I knew of him, he'd have liked Alicia.

3

I dreamed my way through school for the next
few weeks. I dreamed my way through life, really.
It was all just waiting. I can remember waiting for
a bus in that first week, the 19, which took me
from my house to hers, and suddenly realizing that
waiting for a bus was much easier than anything
else, because it was all just waiting anyway. When
I was waiting for a bus, I didn't have to do anything
else but wait, but all the other waiting was hard.
Eating breakfast was waiting, so I didn't eat much.
Sleep was waiting, so I couldn't sleep much, even
though I wanted to, because sleeping was a good
way of getting through eight hours or whatever.
School was waiting, so I didn't know what anyone
was talking about, during the lessons or at break
times. Watching TV was waiting, so I couldn't
follow the programmes. Even skating was waiting,
seeing as how I only went skating when Alicia was
doing something else.

Usually, though, Alicia wasn't doing anything
else. That was the incredible thing. She wanted to
be with me as much as I wanted to be with her,
as far as I could work out.

We never did much. We watched TV in her

room, or sometimes downstairs, especially if her parents were out. We went for walks in Clissold Park. You know that bit in a film when they show couples laughing and holding hands and kissing in lots of different places while a song plays? We were like that, a bit, except we didn't go to lots of different places. We went to about three, including Alicia's bedroom.

We were in Clissold Park when Alicia told me she loved me. I didn't know what to say, really, so I told her I loved her too. It would have seemed rude not to.

'Really?' she said. 'You really love me?'

'Yeah,' I said.

'I can't believe it. Nobody has ever said that to me before.'

'Have you ever said it to anyone before?'

'No. Course not.'

That explained why nobody had ever said it to her, I thought. Because if someone tells you she loves you, then you're bound to say it back, aren't you? You have to be pretty hard not to.

And anyway, I did love her. Someone like my mum would say, Oh, you're just a kid, you don't know what love is. But I didn't think of anything else apart from being with Alicia, and the only time I felt like I was where I wanted to be was when I was with her. I mean, that might as well be love, mightn't it? The kind of love my mum talks about is full of worry and work and forgiving people and putting up with things and stuff like that. It's not a lot of fun, that's for sure. If that really is love, the kind my mum talks about, then nobody can ever know if they love somebody, can they? It seems like what she's saying is, if you're pretty sure you love somebody, the way I was sure in those few weeks, then you can't love them, because that isn't what love is. Trying to understand what she means by love would do your head in.

My mum didn't want me to be with Alicia all the time. She started to worry about it after a couple of weeks. I never told her about the sex, but she knew I was serious, and Alicia was serious. And she knew about the dreaming, because she could see it with her own eyes.

One night, I came back late, and she was waiting up for me.

'How about we stay in tomorrow night? Watch a DVD?' she said.

I didn't say anything.

'Or we can go out, if you want. I'll take you to Pizza Express.'

I still didn't say anything.

'Pizza Express and the cinema. How about that?'

'No, you're all right,' I said, as if she was being nice to me and offering me something. I mean, she was, in a way. She was offering me a pizza and a film. But in another way, she was just trying to stop me doing what I wanted to do, and she knew it, and I knew it.

'Let me put this another way,' she said. 'We're going to spend the evening together tomorrow. What would you like to do? Your choice.'

Here's the thing about me. I can't be bad. Maybe you think that sleeping with Alicia was bad, but it didn't feel that way, so it doesn't count as badness. I'm talking about things where I know I'm in the wrong. You see kids at school, and they're cussing out the teachers, and picking fights with other kids who are supposed to be gay, or picking fights with the teachers, and cussing out the kids who are supposed to be gay ... I can't do that stuff, and I never could. I'm rubbish at lying, and even worse at stealing. I tried nicking some money out of my mum's bag once, and I felt sick, and put it all back. It's like a disease or something, not wanting to be bad. I mean, I hate Ryan Briggs more than anyone else on earth. He's a horrible, violent, ugly, scary thug. But when I see him punch some kid in the face and take his phone off him, or tell a teacher to fuck off, there's a part of me that envies him, you know? He hasn't got the disease. It's not complicated, being him. Life would be easier if I didn't give a shit, but I do. And I knew that what my mum was asking for wasn't completely out of order. She was asking me to spend one evening away from Alicia, and she was offering me something in return. I tried not to see things this way, her way, but I couldn't, so I was in trouble.

'Can Alicia come?'

'No. That's sort of the point of the evening.'

'Why?'

'Because you're seeing too much of her.'

'Why does it bother you?'

'It's not healthy.'

It's true that I wasn't getting outside very often, but that wasn't what she meant. I didn't know what she did mean, though.

'What does that mean, "Not healthy"?'

'It gets in the way of things.'

'What things?'

'Friends. Schoolwork. Family. Skating . . . Everything. Life.'

The opposite was the truth, because life only happened when I was with Alicia. All the things she was talking about were the waiting things.

'Just one night,' she said. 'It won't kill you.'

Well, it didn't kill me. I woke up the morning after we'd been to Pizza Express and the cinema, and I was still alive. But it was like one of those tortures you read about that are actually supposed to be worse than death, because you would actually prefer to be dead. I'm sorry if that means I'm showing no respect to people who've actually had that sort of torture, but it's the closest I've come so far. (And that's one of the reasons I will never join the army, by the way. I would really, really hate to be tortured. I'm not saying that people who join the army would like to be tortured. But they must have thought about it, right? So they must have decided that it wouldn't be as bad as other things, like being on the dole, or working in an office. For me, working in an office would be better than being tortured. Don't get me wrong. I wouldn't be happy doing a boring job, like photocopying a piece of paper over and over again, every single day, until I died. But on the whole I'd be happier doing that than having cigarettes put out in my eye. What I'm hoping is that those aren't my choices.)

In those few weeks, it was bad enough waking up in the morning and knowing that I wouldn't be seeing her until after school. That was torture. That was pulling out fingernails one by one. But on the Pizza Express day I woke up knowing that I wouldn't see her UNTIL THE END OF THE NEXT DAY, and that was more like the torture that Ryan Briggs, of course, printed off the Internet. I'm not going to go into what it was about. But it involved dogs and balls, and not footballs, either. I still have to sort of squeeze my legs together when I think about it.

OK, not seeing Alicia for about forty-two hours wasn't like having your balls etcetera. But it really was like not breathing. Or not breathing properly, like there wasn't enough oxygen in my tank. In all those hours, I couldn't get a good lungful, and I even started to panic, a bit, like you would if you were at the bottom of the sea and the surface was a long way away and there were sharks coming at you and . . . No, that's overdoing it, again. There were no sharks. There were no dogs, etcetera, and no sharks. Mum would have to be the shark, and she's really nothing like a shark. She was only trying to buy me a pizza. She wasn't really trying to like rip my liver out with her teeth. So I'll stop there, with the surface being a long way away. Alicia = surface.

'Can I make a phone call?' I said to Mum when I got in.

'Do you have to?'

'Yeah.'

I did. I had to. There was no other way of saying it.

'We're going out soon.'

'It's half-past four. Who eats pizza at half-past four?'

'Pizza at half-past five. Film at half-past six.'

'What are we going to see?'

'What about *Brokeback Mountain*?'

'Yeah, right.'

'What does that mean? "Yeah, right"?'

'That's what we say. When someone makes a stupid joke or something,' I said.

'Who's making a stupid joke?' she said.

And then I realized she was serious. She actually

wanted us to go and see *Brokeback Mountain*. We'd already started calling one of the science teachers at school 'Brokeback', because he was all hunched up, and everybody reckoned he was a gay.

'You know what it's about, don't you?' I said.

'Yes. It's about a mountain.'

'Shut up, Mum. I can't go to see that. I'll get slaughtered tomorrow.'

'You'd get slaughtered if you went to see a film about gay cowboys?'

'Yes. Because why am I going? There's only one answer, isn't there?'

'My God,' said my mum. 'Is it really that pathetic at school?'

'Yes,' I said. Because it really was.

We agreed we'd go and see something else, and then I phoned Alicia's mobile, and I just got her answering message. So I left it for a couple of minutes, and then I got her message again, and after that I phoned every thirty seconds or so. Message, message, message. It had never for a moment occurred to me that I wouldn't be able to speak to her, even. And then I started to have, like, dark thoughts. Why didn't she have her phone turned on? She knew I'd be trying to reach her. She knew that today was our bad day. The night before, when I told her about my mum not wanting us to see each other for a night, she'd cried. And now it was like she couldn't be bothered, unless

59

she was seeing somebody else. And I was thinking, you know, Bloody hell. What a bitch. I can't see her for one night and she starts going out with someone else. There are words for girls like that. And actually, if you couldn't go for one night without having sex with someone, then you were a nymphomaniac, weren't you? You had a problem. She was like a crackhead, except instead of crack it was sex.

Really. That was what I was like. And you know what I thought, a little later on, when I'd calmed down a bit? I thought, this isn't healthy. You can't go around calling your girlfriend a bitch and a slag and a nympho just because her charger isn't working. (That was what had happened. She texted me later, when she'd plugged it into her dad's charger. It was a really nice text too.)

Anyway, I was in a bit of state when I went out, so that wasn't the best start. And we went down to the multiplex to see what was on apart from *Brokeback Mountain*, and there wasn't much. Actually, that's not true. There was a lot I wanted to see, like the 50 Cent film, and *King Kong*, and there was a lot my mum wanted to see, for example the one about gardening and the one about Japanese girls who made their feet small. But there wasn't anything we both wanted to see. And we spent so long arguing that we couldn't sit down for our pizza, so we ended up getting a takeaway and eating it out of the box on the way to the cinema. We saw this really bad movie about a bloke who swallowed a piece of his mobile phone by mistake and it turned out he could intercept everyone's text messages with his brain. And at first he got to meet loads of girls who were being dumped by their boyfriends, but then he got this text message about terrorists trying to blow up a bridge in New York, and he and one of the girls stopped them. I didn't mind it too much. It wasn't boring, anyway. But Mum hated it, and we had an argument afterwards. She said the whole thing about swallowing the mobile phone was ridiculous, but I said that we didn't know what would happen if we swallowed parts of our mobiles, so that wasn't the stupid part. She wouldn't even let me tell her what I thought was the stupid part. She just went off on one about how my mind had been turned to mush by video games and TV.

None of this matters now. The important thing about the evening was that Mum met a guy. I know, I know. It was supposed to be about me and Mum spending some quality time together and me and Alicia not seeing each other. And it turned into something else altogether. To be fair to Mum, her meeting a bloke didn't take up a lot of our time. I didn't even know she'd met a bloke until a couple of days later, when he came round. (Or rather, I knew she'd met a bloke. I just didn't know she'd Met A Bloke, if you know what I mean.) When we were waiting for our takeaway pizzas, they told us to sit at a table near the door that they used for takeaway customers. And while we were waiting, I went to the gents, and when I came back, Mum was talking to this guy sitting at the next table with his kid. They were only talking about pizzas, and which pizza places they liked, and so on. But when our takeaway boxes arrived, I said to Mum, 'Oh, you're a fast worker,' and she said, 'No, I don't mess about,' and it was all jokey. Except later it turned out it wasn't. She didn't say anything about it at the time, but she knew him from her work. He'd left a couple of years before, and he remembered her, even though they'd never spoken at the office. They worked in different departments. Mum works in Leisure and Culture, and Mark – yes, Mark, like a mark on your trousers – used to work in Health and Social Care. When he first came round, he said that in Islington he never had time for Health.

We walked home. We had our argument about the film, and then Mum tried to talk to me about Alicia.

'There's nothing to say,' I said. And then, 'That's why I didn't want to come out. Because I didn't want to have A Talk.' I said it like that, so you could hear the capital letters. 'Why couldn't we just go out? And talk about nothing?'

'So when can I talk to you?' she said. 'Because you're never at home.'

'I've got a girlfriend,' I said. 'That's it. That's

all there is to say. Go on. Ask me. Ask me whether I've got a girlfriend.'

'Sammy –'

'Go on.'

'Am I allowed a follow-up question?' she said.

'One.'

'Are you having sex?'

'Are you?' I said.

What I meant was, You can't ask that. It's too personal. But since she'd split up with Useless Steve, she hadn't been seeing anyone, so she didn't mind answering.

'No,' she said.

'Well, were you having sex?'

'What does that mean?' she said. 'Are you asking me if I've ever had sex? Because I would have thought you're the answer.'

'Shut up,' I said, because I was embarrassed. I wished we hadn't started on this.

'Let's forget about me. What about you? Are you having sex?'

'No comment. My business.'

'So that's a yes.'

'No. It's a no comment.'

'You'd tell me if you weren't.'

'No I wouldn't. Anyway. All this was your idea.'

'What was?'

'Alicia. You thought I'd like her, so you made me come to that party. And I did like her.'

'Sam, you know that having you when I did . . .'

'Yeah, yeah. It fucked up your life.'

I never usually use the 'f'-word in front of her, because she gets upset. Not about the 'f'-word itself, especially, but she starts to beat herself up for being a teenage mother who couldn't bring her kid up properly, and I hate that. I think she's done a pretty good job. I mean, I'm not the worst kid in the world, am I? But I swore because I wanted her to think that she'd upset me, even though she hadn't, really.

It's weird, knowing that me being born messed her up. It doesn't bother me, really, for two reasons. First of all, it wasn't my fault, it was hers – hers and Dad's, anyway. And second, she's not messed up any more. She's caught up, more or less, on all the things she missed because of me. You could even argue that she's overtaken herself. She wasn't any great shakes at school, she says, but she was so unhappy about not finishing her education that she pushed herself twice as hard as she would have done. She went to evening classes, got qualifications, got a job at the Council. I'm not saying it was a good idea, her having me when she did, but it only ruined a small part of her life, not her whole life. It's always there, though. And if I want to get out of something – like a conversation about whether

I'd had sex with Alicia – then I can just say, all sad and bitter, that I fucked up her life. And whatever it is I'm trying to get out of is forgotten about. I've never told her that I feel out of everyone's league because of what happened.

'Oh, Sam, I'm sorry.'

'No, it's OK.' But I said it all sort of heroic, so that she'd know it wasn't OK.

'But that isn't what you're worried about anyway, is it?' I said.

'I don't know what I'm worried about. Can I meet her properly?'

'Who?'

'Alicia. Can she come round for something to eat one night?'

'If you want.'

'I'd like that. I wouldn't be so scared of her, then.'

Scared of Alicia! I think I can see it now, although I wouldn't have been able to come out with it properly then. My mum was worried about things changing, her being left on her own, me becoming a part of someone else's life and someone else's family, me growing up and not being her little boy any more, me becoming someone else . . . All of these things or some of them, I don't know. And we couldn't have known it then, but she was right to worry. I wish she'd worried me, really. I wish she'd taken me home that night and locked me in my bedroom and thrown away the key.

So the next night, it was like neither of us had been able to breathe for two days, and so we took deep lungfuls of each other, and we said stupid things to each other, and generally acted like we were Romeo and Juliet and the whole world was against us. I'm talking about me and Alicia, by the way, not me and my mum. We talked as if my mum had taken me away from London for a year, whereas what she'd actually done was take me to Pizza Express and the cinema for an evening.

You know that thing I was saying before? About how telling a story is more difficult than it looks, because you don't know what to put where? Well, there's a part of the story that belongs here, and it's something that no one else knows, not even Alicia. The most important part of this story – the whole point of this story – doesn't happen for a little while. And when it happened in real life, I made out that I was shocked and amazed and upset. And I was definitely shocked and upset, but I couldn't in all honesty say I was amazed. It happened that night, I know it. I never said anything to Alicia, but it was my fault. Well, obviously it was my fault mostly, but she's got to take a tiny part of the blame. We'd been messing about without putting anything on, because she said she wanted to feel me properly, and . . . Oh, I can't talk about this stuff. I'm blushing. But something happened. Half-happened. I mean, it definitely didn't happen properly, because I was still able to pull out and put a condom on and pretend as though everything was normal. But I knew that it wasn't quite normal, because when the thing that's supposed to happen finally happened, it didn't feel right, because it had already half-happened before. And that's the last time I'm ever going, you know, down there.

'Are you OK?' said Alicia. She never normally asked, so something must have been different. Maybe it felt different for her, or maybe I acted different, or maybe I seemed quiet and distracted afterwards, I don't know. And I said I was fine, and we left it at that. I wonder if she ever worked out that it was that night. I don't know. We never mentioned it again.

What's incredible to me is that you can keep out of trouble pretty much every minute of your life apart from maybe five seconds, and that five seconds can get you into the worst trouble of all, just about. It's amazing, when you think about it. I don't smoke weed, don't cuss out teachers, I don't get into fights, I try to do my homework. But I took a risk, for a few seconds, and that turns out to be worse than any of the rest put together. I once read an interview with a skater, I forget who, and he said that the thing he couldn't ever believe about sport was how much concentration it took. You could be doing the best skating of your life, and the moment you started to realize that you were doing the best skating of your life, you were eating concrete. Skating well for nine minutes and fifty-five seconds wasn't good enough, because five seconds was plenty of time to make a complete jerk of yourself. Yeah, well, life's like that too. It doesn't seem right to me, but there you go. And how bad is it, what I did? Not so bad, right? It's a mistake, that's all. You hear about boys who refuse to wear condoms, and you hear about girls who think it's cool to have a baby at fifteen . . . Well, those aren't mistakes. That's just stupidity. I don't want to spend the whole time moaning about life being unfair, but how come their punishment is the same as mine? That can't be right, can it? It seems to me that if you never wear a condom, then you should get triplets, or quintuplets. But it doesn't work like that, does it?

A couple of nights after that, Alicia came round for dinner, and it was OK. More than OK, really. She was nice to my mum, and my mum was nice to her, and they made jokes about how useless I was, and I didn't mind, because I was glad that everyone was happy.

But then Alicia asked my mum about what it was like having a baby at sixteen, and I tried to change the subject.

'You don't want to hear about all that,' I said to Alicia.

'Why don't I?'

'Boring,' I said.

'Oh, it wasn't boring, I can tell you,' said my mum, and Alicia laughed.

'No, but it's boring now,' I said. 'Because it's over.'

It was a stupid thing to say, and I regretted it the moment it came out of my mouth.

'Oh well,' said my mum. 'That's the whole of history, written off, then. Bor-ing.'

'Yeah, well it is,' I said. I didn't mean that, really, because there are lots of bits of history that aren't boring, like World War Two. But I didn't want to back down.

'And also,' said my mum, 'it's not over. You're still here and I'm still here and there are sixteen years between us and it'll be like that for ever. It's not over.'

And I sat there wondering whether it was not over in ways she couldn't even begin to guess.

4

It's not that things started to go wrong between me and Alicia. It just stopped being as good. I can't really explain why, not properly. I just woke up one morning and didn't feel the same way. I didn't like not feeling the same way, because it was a good feeling, and I felt flat without it, but it had gone, and there was nothing I could do to bring it back. I even tried to pretend it was still there, but the trying just seemed to make it worse.

Where did it go? It was like there had been a lot of food on a plate in front of us, and we ate it all really quickly, and then there was nothing left. Maybe that's how couples stay together: they're not greedy. They know that what they have in front of them has to last a long time, so they kind of pick at it. I hope it's not like that, though. I hope that when people are happy together, it feels as though someone keeps piling seconds and thirds on their plates. That night, the night after I hadn't seen her, it felt as though we'd be together for the rest of our lives, and even that wouldn't be long enough. And then two or three weeks later, we were bored with each other. I was bored, anyway. We never did anything but watch TV in her room and have sex, and once we'd had sex, we never had much to say to each other. We'd get dressed, put the TV back on, and then I'd kiss her goodnight and then go through the same routine the next night.

Mum noticed even before I did, I think. I started skating again, and I tried to make out that wanting to skate was just normal and natural, and, thinking about it, it probably was. If we hadn't gone off each other, if we hadn't split up, then somehow we would have found some kind of routine, I suppose. In the end I'd have gone back to skating and playing skating games on the Xbox and all that. It always felt like a holiday, the time with Alicia, and the holiday would come to an end, and we'd still be girlfriend and boyfriend but we'd have a life as well. As it turned out, when the holiday ended, we ended too. It was a holiday romance, ha ha.

Anyway, I came in from skating one afternoon, and Mum said, 'Have you got time for something to eat before you go over to Alicia's?' And I said, 'Yeah, OK.' And then I said, 'Actually, I'm not going over to Alicia's tonight.' And Mum said, 'Oh. Because you didn't go last night, either, did you?' And I said, 'Didn't I? I can't remember.' Which was a bit pathetic, really. For some reason, I didn't want her to know that things with Alicia were different. She'd have been pleased, and I didn't want that.

'Still going strong?' she said.

'Oh yeah. Pretty strong. I mean, not *as* strong, because we wanted to get some schoolwork done and stuff like that. But, yeah. Strong.'

'So, strong, then,' she said. 'Not, you know. Weak.'

'Not weak, no. Not . . .'

'What?'

'Weak.'

'So you were just going to say the same thing twice?'

'How do you mean?'

'You were just going to say, "Not weak. Not weak."'

'I suppose so, yeah. Stupid, really.'

I don't know how my mum puts up with me sometimes. I mean, it must all have been completely obvious to her, but she had to sit and listen to me swear that black was white, or that cold was hot, anyway. It wouldn't have made any difference to anything, telling her the truth. But later, when I needed her help, I remembered all the times I'd been a muppet.

I think I went over to Alicia's the night after that conversation, because if I didn't go three days in a row, then my mum would really have known that something was up. And then I didn't go for a couple of evenings again, and then it was the weekend, and on the Saturday morning she texted me to ask me to lunch. Her brother was around, and they were having this family reunion thing, and Alicia said I was a part of the family.

I'd never met anyone quite like Alicia's mum and dad before I started going out with Alicia, and at first I thought they were dead cool – I can even remember wishing that my mum and dad were like them. Alicia's dad is like fifty or something, and he listens to hip-hop. He doesn't like it much, I don't think, but he feels he should give it a chance, and he doesn't mind the language and the violence. He's got grey hair that he gets Alicia's mum to shave back – I think he has a number 2 – and he wears a stud. He teaches literature at a college, and she teaches drama, when she's not being a councillor. Or she teaches people to teach drama, something like that. She has to go into lots of different schools and talk to teachers. They're all right, I suppose, Robert and Andrea, and they were really friendly at first. It's just that they think I'm stupid. They never say as much, and they try and treat me as if I'm not. But I can tell they do. I wouldn't mind, but I'm smarter than Alicia. I'm not showing off or being cocky; I just know I am. When we went to see films, she didn't understand them, and she never got what anyone was laughing at in *The Simpsons*, and I had to help her with her maths. Her mum and dad helped her with her English. They still thought she was going to go to college to do something or other, and all the model stuff was just her going through a rebellious phase. As far as they were concerned, she was a genius, and I was this nice dim kid she was hanging out with. They acted as if I was Ryan Briggs or someone really scummy like that, but they weren't going to officially disapprove of me because that wouldn't be cool.

At that family lunch, when I was invited because I was part of the family, I was just sitting there minding my own business when her dad asked me what I was going to do after my GCSEs.

'Not everybody is academic, Robert' said Alicia's mum quickly.

You see how it worked? She was trying to protect me, but what she was trying to protect me from was a question about whether I had any future at all. I mean, everyone does something after their GCSEs, don't they? Even if you sit at home watching daytime TV for the rest of your life, it's a future of sorts. But that was their attitude with me – don't mention the future, because I didn't have one. And then we all had to pretend that not having a future was OK. That's what Alicia's mum should have said. 'Not everybody has a future, Robert.'

'I know not everybody is academic. I was just asking him what he wanted to do,' said Robert.

'He's going to do art and design at college,' said Alicia.

'Oh,' said her dad. 'Good. Excellent.'

'You're good at art, are you, Sam?' her mum said.

'I'm all right. I'm just worried about if we have to do essays and stuff at college.'

'You're not so good at English?'

'Not at writing it, no. Or speaking it. I'm fine at all the rest.'

That was supposed to be a joke.

'It's just a matter of confidence,' said her mum. 'You haven't had the same advantages as a lot of people.'

I didn't know what to say to that. I have my own bedroom, a mum who's in work and who likes reading and who gets on my case if I haven't done my homework . . . To be honest, I don't really know how many more advantages I could use. Even my dad not being around was a good thing, because he's not into education at all. I mean, he wouldn't actually stop me trying to study, but . . . Actually, maybe that's not true. It was always a thing between him and Mum. She was desperate to go to college, and he's a plumber, and he's always made decent money, and there was this thing going on between them, because Mum reckoned he felt inferior and tried to cover it up by telling her what a waste of time it was getting qualifications. I don't know. As far as people like Alicia's parents are concerned, you're a bad person if you don't read and study, and as far as people like my dad are concerned, you're a bad person if you do. It's all mad, isn't it? It's not reading and whatever that makes you good or bad. It's whether you rape people, or get addicted to crack and go out mugging. I don't know why they all get themselves into such a stew.

'I think Sam was joking, Mum,' said Alicia. 'He's good at speaking.' I didn't find that very helpful, either. They'd heard me speak. They could make their own minds up. It wasn't like we were talking about my skating skills, something they'd never seen. If they needed to be told that I could talk, then obviously I was in trouble.

'No, he is good, I know,' said her mum. 'But sometimes, if you don't . . . If you haven't . . .'

Alicia started to laugh. 'Go on, Mum. Try and finish the sentence in a way that doesn't piss Sam off.'

'Oh, he knows what I mean,' she said. And I did, but that's not the same as saying I liked it.

I liked Rich, her brother, though. I didn't think I would, because he plays the violin, and any kid who plays the violin is usually King of the Nerds. He doesn't look like a nerd, though. He wears glasses, but they're quite cool, and he likes a laugh. I suppose what I'm saying, if I think about it, is that he likes me. Liked me, anyway. I'm not so sure about now. And that makes a difference, doesn't it? I mean, he wasn't pathetic about it. He didn't like me because he had no other friends in the world. He liked me because I was OK, and I think because he didn't know too many people who weren't from the Nerd Kingdom, what with the violin and music school and everything.

Afterwards, Alicia and Rich and I went to Alicia's room, and she put a CD on, and she and I sat on the bed, and Rich sat on the floor.

'Welcome to the family,' said Rich.

'Don't say it like that,' said Alicia. 'I'll never see him again.'

'They're not that bad,' I said, but they were, really. And to be honest it wasn't just Alicia's parents who were getting on my nerves, either. When I left the house that afternoon, I wondered whether I'd ever go back.

Afterwards, I went down to the Bowl for a little while and messed about on my board. Whoever invented skating is a genius, in my opinion. London gets in the way of every other sport. There are tiny little patches of green where you can play football, or golf, or whatever, and the concrete is trying to eat them away. So you play these games in spite of the city and, really, it would be better if you lived just about anywhere else, out in the countryside, or the suburbs, or some place like Australia. But skating you do *because* of the city. We need as much concrete and as many stairs and ramps and benches and pavements as you've got. And when the world's been completely paved over, we'll be the only athletes left, and there will be statues of Tony Hawk all over the world, and the Olympics will just be a million different skating competitions, and then people might actually watch. I will, anyway. I went to the wheelchair ramp that runs from the back door of the flats round the corner and messed about – nothing too flash, just a few fakie flips and heelflips. And I thought about Alicia, and her family, and started rehearsing what I was going to say to her about us not seeing so much of each other, or maybe not seeing each other at all.

It was weird, really. If you'd have told me at that party that I was going to go out with Alicia, and we were going to start sleeping together, and I'd get sick of her ... Well, I wouldn't have understood. It wouldn't have made any sense to me. Before you have sex for the first time, you can't imagine where it's ever going to come from, and you certainly can't imagine dumping the person who's providing it. Why would you do that? A beautiful girl wants to sleep with you and you're *bored*? How does that work?

All I can say is that, believe it or not, sex is like anything else good: once you have it, you stop being quite so bothered about it. It's there, and it's great and everything, but it doesn't mean you're happy to let everything else go out of the window. If having sex regularly meant listening to Alicia's dad being snobby, and giving up skating, and never seeing mates, then I wasn't sure how much I wanted it. I wanted a girlfriend who'd sleep with me, but I wanted a life as well. I didn't know – still don't know – whether people managed that. Mum and Dad didn't. Alicia was my first serious girlfriend, and it wasn't happening for us, either. What it seemed like was that I'd been so desperate to sleep with someone that I'd swapped too much for it. OK, I'd said to Alicia, if you'll let me have sex, I'll give you skating, mates, schoolwork and my mum (because I was sort of missing her, in a funny sort of way). Oh, and if your mum and dad want to talk to me like I'm some no-hoper crackhead, that's fine by me too. Just . . . get your clothes off. And I was beginning to realize that I'd paid over the odds.

When I got home, Mum was sitting at the kitchen table with the bloke from Pizza Express. I recognized him straight away, but I couldn't work out what he was doing there. I also couldn't work out why he let go of Mum's hand when I walked in.

'Sam, you remember Mark?'

'Oh, yeah,' I said.

'He's come round to . . .' But then she couldn't think of any reason why he'd come round, so she gave up. 'He's come round for a cup of tea.'

'Right,' I said. I think I must have said it in a way that meant, you know, And? Because Mum kept talking.

'Mark and I used to work together,' Mum said.

'And after we bumped into each other at Pizza Express, he called me at the office.'

Right, I thought. Why? I suppose I knew why, really.

'Where have you been, Sam?' said Mark, all friendly. And I was like, Oh, here we go. Uncle Mark.

'Just out skating.'

'Skating? Is there an ice-rink near here?' Mum caught my eye and we both laughed, because she knows I hate it when people get my skating muddled up with the other sort. ('Why don't you just say you're a skateboarder? Or you've been out skateboarding?' she always says. 'What would happen to you? Would you get arrested by the Cool Police?' And I always tell her that 'skateboarding' sounds wrong to me, so she reckons that I deserve what I get.)

'What's funny?' said Mark, like someone who knows it's going to be a great joke if only someone would explain it to him.

'It's not that sort of skating. It's skating with a board.'

'Skateboarding?'

'Yeah.'

'Oh.' He looked disappointed. It wasn't such a great joke after all.

'Has your kid got a skateboard?'

'No, not yet. He's only eight.'

'Eight's old enough,' I said.

'Maybe you could teach him,' said Mark. I made a noise, something like 'Ergh', which was supposed to mean 'Yeah, right', except without sounding rude.

'Where is he today?' I said.

'Tom? He's with his mum. He doesn't live with me, but I see him most days.'

'We were thinking of getting something to eat,' Mum said. 'A takeaway curry or something. Interested?'

'Yeah, OK.'

'No Alicia this evening?'

'Oh-ho,' said Mark. 'Who's Alicia, then?'

He could go either way, this bloke, I thought. That 'oh-ho' didn't sound good to me. It sounded like he wanted to be my mate when he didn't even know me.

'Alicia's The Girlfriend,' said Mum.

'Serious?' Mark asked.

'Not really,' I said. And Mum said, at exactly the same time, 'Extremely.' And we looked at each other again, and this time Mark laughed but we didn't.

'I thought you said things were still going strong?' said Mum.

'Oh, yeah,' I said. 'They're still going strong. They're just not as serious as they were.' And then I got sick of not telling the truth, so I said, 'I think we're breaking up.'

'Oh,' said Mum. 'I'm sorry.'

'Yeah,' I said. 'Well.' What else was there to say? I felt a bit stupid, obviously, because the night Mum met Mark was the night she was trying to tell me to cool it.

'Whose idea is that?' said Mum.

'No one's, really.'

'Have you talked about it?'

'No.'

'So how do you know?'

'That's what it feels like.'

'If you've gone off her, then you should tell her,' said Mum.

She was right, of course, but I didn't. I just never went round, and I left my mobile off, and I didn't reply to her texts. So she probably got the idea, in the end.

One night I got a very sad message from her. It just said . . . Actually, I don't want to tell you what it said. You'll end up feeling sorry for her, which isn't what I want. When I said before that we'd got bored with each other . . . well, that wasn't right. I was bored with her, but she wasn't bored with me, yet, I could see that. Or at least, she didn't *think* she was bored with me. She didn't exactly seem thrilled to be with me on our last few times together. Anyway, I tried talking to TH about it.

'Do you think I'm behaving badly?' I said to him.

'I was an idiot and wanted more freedom,' he said. '(Read: I wanted to spend more time with girls on the road.)' I knew what he was talking about. He was talking about when his girlfriend Sandy moved in with him and then moved out again. That's in his book, which is why he said 'Read' and why there are bits in brackets. Was he telling me that I was an idiot? Was it stupid, wanting more freedom? I couldn't work it out. Maybe he wasn't telling me anything. Maybe I'd just read his book too many times.

5

The funny thing was, going out with Alicia had done me no end of good at school, especially with girls. A few people had seen me with her at the cinema, and they'd told other people that I was with this beautiful girl, and I think it made everyone look at me in a new way. It was as if Alicia gave me a makeover. I think that was how I ended up going to McDonald's with Nicki Niedzwicki, on the night before my sixteenth birthday. (That's how it's spelt. She wrote it down for me when she gave me her mobile number.) She was exactly the sort of girl who wouldn't have looked twice at me before Alicia. She went out with older boys, usually, probably because she looked five years older than any of us. She spent a lot of money on clothes, and you never saw her without make-up on.

When we went to McDonald's, she told me she wanted a baby, and I knew that I wouldn't be having sex with her ever, not even with five condoms on.

'What for?' I said.

'I dunno. I like babies? There isn't anything I really want to study at college? And I can always get a job when my baby's older?' She's one of those people that asks questions all the time. They drive me nuts.

'My mum had a baby when she was sixteen.'

'Yeah, see, that's what I mean,' she said.

'What?'

'Well, you're probably more like mates, aren't you, you and your mum? That's what I want with my kid. I don't want to be like fifty when he's sixteen? You can't go out with them then, can you? To clubs and that? Because you'd be like an embarrassment?'

Oh, yeah, I wanted to say. That's what it's like. Clubbing, clubbing, clubbing. If you can't go clubbing with your mum, then what use is she? I wanted to go home, and for the first time since we'd split up, I missed Alicia. Or at least, I felt nostalgic. I remembered how great it had been, the evening when we hadn't gone to the cinema because we'd had too much to say to each other. Where had all those words gone? They got sucked into Alicia's TV. I wanted them back.

I walked Nikki home, but I didn't kiss her. I was too scared. If she got pregnant some time in the next couple of weeks, I didn't want her to have any saliva or anything that she could use in evidence against me. You can't be too careful, can you?

'Have I done the wrong thing?' I said to TH when I got home. 'Do you think I should still be with Alicia?'

'If something in my life didn't revolve around skating, then I had a hard time figuring it out,' said TH. He was talking about Sandy again, his first real girlfriend, but it might have been his way of saying, 'How the hell do I know? I'm only a skater.' Or even, 'I'm only a poster.' I decided he was telling me that I should stick to skating for the time being, and leave girls alone. After my evening with Nikki, that seemed like pretty good advice.

I never had the chance to put it into action, though. The next day, my sixteenth birthday, my life started to change.

The day began with cards and presents and doughnuts – Mum had already been to the baker's by the time I woke up. My dad was supposed to be coming over for tea and cake in the afternoon, and in the evening, believe it or not, Mum and I were going to go to Pizza Express and the cinema. I got the first text from Alicia straight after break-fast – it just said, 'I NEED 2 C U URGENT Axx'.

'Who was that?' said Mum.

'Oh, no one.'

'Is that a Miss No One?' said Mum. She was probably thinking of Nikki, because she knew we'd been out the previous evening.

'Not really,' I said. I knew it didn't make any sense, because either someone was a girl or they weren't, unless you're talking about men who dress up as girls, but I didn't care. Part of me was panicking. It wasn't my head so much as my guts – I think my guts knew what it was about, even if my head didn't. Or pretended it didn't. I'd never forgotten that time when something half-happened when I hadn't put anything on. The part of me that was panicking because of the text had never really stopped panicking since the half-happening day.

I went and locked myself in the bathroom and texted her back. I said, 'NOT 2DAY MY BIRTHDAY Sxx'. If I got something back from that, then I knew I was in trouble. I flushed the loo and washed my hands, just to make Mum think I'd actually been doing something, and even before I'd opened the door my phone beeped again. The text just said, 'URGENT, OUR STARBUCKS 11am'. And then all of me knew – guts, head, heart, fingernails.

I texted back 'OK'. I didn't see how I could do anything else, even though I wanted to do anything else.

When I went back into the kitchen, I wanted to sit on my mum's lap. I know that sounds stupid and babyish, but I couldn't help it. On my sixteenth birthday, I didn't want to be sixteen, or fifteen, or anyteen. I wanted to be three or four, and too young to make any kind of mess, apart from the mess you make when you scribble on walls or tip your food bowl upside down.

'I love you, Mum,' I said when I sat down at the table.

She looked at me as if I'd gone mad. I mean, she was pleased, but she was pretty surprised.

'I love you too, sweetheart,' she said. I tried not to get choked up. If Alicia was going to tell me what I thought she was going to tell me, I reckoned it would be a long time before Mum said that again. It might be a long time before she even felt it.

All the way there, I was doing all kinds of deals, or trying to. You know the sort of thing: 'If it's OK, I'll never skate again.' As if it had anything to do with skating. I offered never to watch TV again, and never to go out again, and never to eat McDonald's again. Sex never came up, because I already knew I was never going to have sex again, so that didn't seem like a deal God would be interested in. I might as well have promised Him that I wouldn't fly to the moon, or run down Essex Road naked. Sex was over for me, for ever, no doubt.

Alicia was sitting at the long counter in the window with her back to everyone. I saw her face as I was walking in, without her seeing me, and she looked pale and frightened. I tried to think of some other things that could make her that way. Maybe her brother was in trouble. Maybe her ex-boyfriend had threatened her, or threatened me. I wouldn't mind taking a beating, I thought. Even if it was a serious beating, I'd be better in a few months, probably. Say he broke both my arms and both my legs . . . I'd be walking around again by Christmas.

I didn't go over and say hello straight away. I got in the queue to buy myself a drink. If my life was about to change, then I wanted the old life to last for as long as possible. There were two people in front of me, and I hoped they had the longest and most complicated orders Starbucks had ever heard of. I wanted someone to order a cappuccino with all the bubbles taken out by hand, one by one. I felt sick, of course, but it was better to feel sick without knowing for sure. In the queue I could still imagine that it was only going to be a beating, but once I'd spoken to her, that would be that.

The woman in front of me wanted a cloth to wipe up some orange juice her kid had spilled on the table. It took no time at all. And I couldn't think of a difficult drink. I asked for a frappuccino. At least the ice takes a long time. And then when I'd got my drink there was nothing else to do except go and sit next to Alicia at the counter.

'Hello,' I said.

'Happy birthday,' she said. And then, 'I'm late.'

I understood straight away what she meant.

'You were here before me, even,' I said. I couldn't resist it. I wasn't trying to be funny, and I wasn't being thick. I was just putting off the moment, hanging on to the old Sam. I didn't want the future to come, and what Alicia was about to say was the future.

'I'm late with my period,' she said, straightaway, and that was it. The future had arrived.

'Right,' I said. 'I thought you were going to say that.'

'Why?'

I didn't want to tell her I'd always been worried about that one time.

'It's the only thing I could think of that could be this serious,' I said. She seemed to accept that.

'Have you been to the doctor's?' I said.

'What for?'

'I dunno. Isn't that what you do?' I was trying to speak in a normal voice, but nothing would come out right. I sounded all quivery and croaky. I couldn't remember the last time I'd cried, but I was pretty close to crying now.

'No, I don't think so. I think you buy a pregnancy test,' she said.

'Well, have you done that?'

'No. I wanted you to come with me.'

'Have you told anyone?'

'Oh, yeah. Course. I've told everyone. Fucking hell. I'm not stupid.'

'How late are you?'

'Three weeks.'

Three weeks sounded very late to me, but what did I know?

'Have you ever been three weeks late before?' I said.

'No. Nowhere near.'

And then I'd run out of questions. I'd run out of questions that I could actually ask, anyway. I wanted to ask things like, 'Am I going to be OK?' 'Are your parents going to kill me?' 'Do you mind if I go to college anyway?' 'Can I go home now?' Stuff like that. But these were all questions about me, and I was pretty sure that I was supposed to ask questions about her. Her and it.

'Can you just buy pregnancy tests in a chemist's?' There. That was another good question. I didn't care whether you could or couldn't, but it was something to say.

'Yeah.'

'Are they expensive?'

'I don't know.'

'Let's go and have a look.'

We slurped the last bits of our drinks through the straws and slammed the cups down on the counter both at the same time. I still think about that, sometimes. I'm not sure why. Partly it's because the slurping noise sounded childish, and yet we were making it because we were in a hurry to find out whether we were going to be parents. And partly it's because when we put the cups down at exactly the same moment, it seemed like a good sign. It wasn't, though. Maybe that's why it's stuck in my memory.

There was a little chemist's next door to the Star-bucks, so we went in there, but we got out quick when Alicia saw a friend of her mum's in there. She saw us too, this woman, and you could tell she thought we'd gone in to buy condoms. Ha! Condoms! We were way beyond condoms, missus! Anyway, we realized that we could never go into a chemist's that size – not just because we might have been spotted, but because neither of us would be able to ask for what we wanted. Condoms were bad enough, but pregnancy tests were in a different class of trouble and embarrassment altogether. We walked on to the Superdrug round the corner, because it seemed like we wouldn't stick out there.

The cheapest one was £9.95.

'How much have you got?' Alicia said.

'Me?'

'Yes. You.'

I fished about in my pockets.

'Three quid. You?'

'A fiver and . . . sixty pence in change. One of us is going to have to go home for more money.'

'If you'd told me as soon as I came in,' I said, 'I wouldn't have bought that drink.' I knew she couldn't have told me as soon as I came in, because she didn't know I was there, and I didn't want her to know I was there.

'Doesn't matter now, does it? Who's going home?'

'I can't,' I said. 'I've already disappeared once.

I can't disappear again. I'm supposed to be spending the day with my mum and dad.'

She sighed. 'OK. Wait here.'

'I'm not standing here for half an hour.' Alicia lived ten minutes' walk away. Ten minutes there, ten minutes back, ten minutes to persuade whoever was there to cough up.

'Go back to Starbucks, then. But don't buy a drink. We can't afford it.'

'Can't you just get a fiver? So I don't have to stay here without a drink?'

She sighed again, and swore to herself, but she didn't say no.

I went back to Starbucks, spent my three quid, waited twenty-five minutes, and then went home. And I turned my mobile off, and left it turned off.

My birthday is one of the only days of the year when you'll catch my mum and dad in the same room together. They pretend they're all friends together now, and the past is the past, and all that, but they never see each other unless it's a special occasion involving me. If I'd been the star of the football team, or, I don't know, the violinist in the school orchestra or something, they'd probably have turned out to see me. But luckily for them, I don't do anything apart from have birthdays. I've entered a couple of skating competitions, but I never tell Mum and Dad about them. Tournaments are hard enough, without worrying about whether those two are arguing about who said what to who fifteen years ago.

I was in a right state for my birthday tea, as you can imagine. All they seemed to talk about was what it was like when I was a baby, and even though they try not to go on about how hard it was, there's always a story about my mum sitting her exams at school while my gran jiggled me up and down in the corridors. (She failed her maths because she needed to feed me in the middle, and even then I wouldn't settle.) When they come out with these stories, one of them always says something like, 'Well I'm glad we can laugh about it now . . .' If you think about it, that means there wasn't much laughing back then. That particular birthday was the first time I'd been able to see just how unfunny it must have been. And when they weren't talking about how hard it was when I was little, they were talking about how I'd grown up, and they couldn't believe how quickly the time had gone, and blah blah. And that didn't help, either. I didn't feel grown up – I still wanted to crawl on to my mum's lap – and the time hadn't gone quickly. They were talking about my whole life, which seemed to me to have lasted for ever. And if Alicia was pregnant, that meant . . . I didn't want to think about that. I didn't want to think about tomorrow, or the day after, let alone the next sixteen years.

I couldn't eat any cake, of course. I told them

my stomach wasn't good, and Mum remembered
me rushing off to the toilet after breakfast, when
I had to send Alicia a text. So I sat there, and
picked at my food, and listened to them tell stories,
and fiddled around with the mobile in my pocket.
I wasn't ever tempted to put it on, though. I just
wanted one more day of my old life.

I blew the candles out.

'Speech!' said my dad.

'No.'

'Shall I make one, then?'

'No.'

'Sixteen years ago today,' said my dad, 'your
mum was in the Whittington Hospital, making a
lot of noise.'

'Thanks,' said my mum.

'I got there late, because I was on a job with
Frank, God rest his soul, and I didn't have a mobile
then, and it took ages for anyone to track me
down.'

'Is Frank dead?' said Mum.

'No, but I don't see him any more, do I? Anyway,
I got a bus going up Holloway Road, and you know
what that's like. We just sat there. So I had to jump
off and leg it, and by the time I got there I was
cream crackered. Seventeen years old and I was
wheezing like an old man. I was still smoking roll-
ups then. Anyway. I sat down on one of the old
flower bed things outside the hospital to get my
breath back, and . . .'

'I love this story,' said Mum. 'We hear it every year. And every year there's no place either for Sam or his mother. There was only one hero that day. There was only one person who suffered for his first-born. And it was the man who ran all the way up the Holloway Road.'

'Last time I looked, women hadn't completely taken over the world,' said my dad. 'Men are still allowed to speak. Probably when your next birthday comes around, son, we'll all be in prison with gags on. But let's enjoy our freedom while it lasts.'

You look at my mum and dad now, and you can't believe they ever lived in the same borough in the same century, let alone got married. Let alone . . . Well, we don't need to think about that. She went one way and he went another way, and . . . Actually, that's not true. My mum stayed here, and my dad went to Barnet. But my mum has come a long way, and my dad has gone nowhere.

They've only got one thing in common, and that one thing is talking to you now. They wouldn't even be speaking if it wasn't for me, and I can't say that makes me feel proud, really. Some people shouldn't speak to each other.

You could tell what I spent the afternoon thinking about. It was like it wasn't my birthday any more. It was somebody else's, someone who hadn't even been born yet. There were three of us that afternoon. How many would be there for my seventeenth?

We didn't go out in the evening in the end. I told Mum I was still sick. We watched a DVD and she ate scrambled eggs on toast, and then I went up to my room to talk to Tony.

'Alicia might be pregnant,' I said to him. And then, 'I'm shitting myself.'

'She called to tell me she'd taken the test and that I was going to be a dad,' said Tony.

'How did you feel?' I asked him. I knew the answer, but I wanted to keep the conversation going.

'It was not exactly what you'd call expected, but I was happy just the same.'

'You were twenty-four when you had Riley, though,' I said. 'And you were earning decent money. You could afford to be happy.'

And now we come to the part that I was talking about before, the part where I don't know whether what happened really happened.

'Tricks are strange,' said TH. 'I'm extremely proud of some of the ones I've invented, and some of them are hilarious to look back on and wonder what I was thinking at the time.'

I looked at him. I knew what he was talking about: skate tricks. He says that right at the end of the book, before going through all the tricks from back in the day. But why bring that up? I didn't want to know about skate tricks.

'Yeah, well, thanks a lot, man,' I said. I was cross with him. You couldn't talk to him about serious stuff, even though he was a dad himself. I was trying to tell him that the whole world was about to end, and he wanted to tell me about kickflip McTwists and half-cab frontside blunt reverts. I decided to take the poster down whether Alicia was pregnant or not. It was time to move on. If he was so great, how come he couldn't help me? I'd been treating him like a god, but he wasn't a god. He was nothing. Just a skater.

'How the park locals stopped themselves from beating me up I'll never know,' said TH. 'I could be a real idiot sometimes.'

'You said it,' I told him.

And then TH played a strange trick on me, so he probably is a god after all.

6

I know this sounds stupid, but normally you know when things have happened to you, don't you? Well, I don't. Not any more. Most of the story I'm telling you happened to me for sure, but there are a couple of little parts, weird parts, I'm not absolutely positive about. I'm pretty sure I didn't dream them up, but I couldn't swear that on Tony Hawk's book, which is my bible. So we're about to come to one of these parts now, and all I can do is tell it straight. You'll have to make your own minds up. Suppose you were abducted by aliens during the night, and dumped back in your bed before breakfast. If that happened to you, you'd be sitting there eating your cereal the next morning and thinking, did that really happen? And you'd be looking around for evidence. That's how I feel. I didn't find any evidence, and I'm still looking.

Here's what I think happened. I can't remember going to bed, or falling asleep; all I remember is waking up. I woke up in the middle of the night. I wasn't in my own bed, and there was someone in the bed with me, and there was a baby crying.

'Oh, shit.' The person in bed with me was Alicia.

'Your turn,' she said.

I didn't say anything. I didn't know where I was or even when I was, and I didn't know what 'Your turn' meant.

'Sam,' she said. 'Wake up. He's awake. Your turn.'

'Right,' I said. And then, 'My turn for what?'

'He can't need feeding again,' she said. 'So he either needs winding or he has a dirty nappy. He hasn't been changed since we went to bed.'

So this baby had to be mine, and he was a boy. I had a son. This is what I got for not turning my mobile on. I felt sick with shock, and I couldn't speak for a little while.

'I can't,' I said.

'What do you mean, you can't?'

'I don't know how.'

I could see that from her point of view that must have sounded weird. I hadn't had much time to work all this out, but Alicia must have gone to bed with a different Sam, right? She must have gone to bed with someone who at least knew he was a father. And if he knew he was a father, then presumably he'd winded a baby, and changed a nappy. The trouble was, I wasn't that Sam. I was the old Sam. I was the Sam who'd turned his mobile off so that he wouldn't find out if his ex-girlfriend was pregnant or not.

'Are you awake?'

'Not really.'

She whacked me with her elbow. She got me right in the ribs.

'Ow.'

'You awake now?'

'Not really.'

I knew I was going to get another whack, but the alternative was that I got up and did something terrible to this baby.

'Ow. Ow. That really hurt.'

'You awake now?'

'Not really.'

She put the bedside light on and stared at me. She looked terrible, to be honest. She'd put weight on, so her face was much fatter, and her eyes were puffy from sleep, and her hair was greasy. I could see that we were in her bedroom, but it was different. We were sleeping in a double bed, for example, and she used to have a single. And she'd taken down her Donnie Darko poster, and put up kiddy stuff in its place. I could see this horrible pink and blue animal alphabet.

'What's wrong with you?' she said.

'I don't know,' I said. 'I just seem to stay asleep no matter how hard you hit me. I'm asleep now. I'm sleep-talking.' That was a lie, really.

The baby carried on crying.

'Just pick the bloody baby up.'

I was pretty confused, obviously, but I was

beginning to work some things out. I knew, for example, that I couldn't ask how old the baby was, or what he was called. That would make her suspicious. And there wasn't much point in trying to explain that I wasn't the Sam she thought I was, that somebody, maybe Tony Hawk the skater, had put me in some sort of time machine, for reasons best known to himself.

I got out of bed. I was wearing a T-shirt of Alicia's and the pair of boxer shorts I put on that morning, or whatever morning it was. The baby was sleeping in a little cot at the end of the bed. He was all red in the face from crying.

'Smell his bottom,' Alicia said.

'What?'

'Smell his bottom. See if he needs changing.'

I bent down and put my face near him. I was breathing through my mouth to stop myself from smelling anything.

'He's all right, I think.'

'Just jig him about a bit, then.'

I'd seen people do this with babies. It didn't look too hard. I picked him up just under his armpits, and his head went flying backwards, as if he had no neck. He was crying even harder now.

'What are you doing?' said Alicia.

'I don't know,' I said. And I really didn't know. I didn't have a clue.

'Have you gone mad?'

'A bit.'

'Hold him properly.'

I didn't know what that meant, obviously, but I had a guess. I put one hand behind his head, and the other hand against his back, and I put him against my chest, and jiggled him up and down. After a little while he stopped crying.

'About bloody time,' said Alicia.

'What shall I do now?' I said.

'Sam!'

'What?'

'It's like you've got Alzheimer's or something.'

'Just pretend I have.'

'Is he asleep?'

I looked down at his head. How were you supposed to tell?

'I don't know.'

'Have a look.'

I carefully moved the hand that was holding his head, and it flopped over to one side. He started crying again.

'He was, I think. He's not now.'

I got him back against my chest and jiggled, and he went quiet again. I didn't dare stop, this time, and I kept jiggling, and Alicia went back to sleep, and I was alone in the dark with my son on my chest. I didn't mind. I had a lot to think about. Like: did I live here now? What sort of a dad was I? How did Alicia and I get on? Have Mum and Dad forgiven me? What did I do all day? Would

I ever go back to my own time? I couldn't answer any of these questions, of course. But if I really had been projected into the future, then I'd find out the next morning. After a little while I put the baby back in its cot and got back into bed. Alicia put her arms around me, and eventually I went back to sleep.

As I was waking up, I was convinced that I'd had this really weird dream. I moved my legs forward under the bedclothes, just to see if I kicked Alicia, but there was nothing there, so I opened my eyes. The first thing I saw was the animal alphabet poster on the wall, and then I looked down the bed and saw the empty cot. I was still in Alicia's bedroom.

I got out of bed and put on the pair of trousers I saw draped over Alicia's armchair. They were mine, I recognized them, but the shirt underneath them was new. It looked like a Christmas present from somebody, because I couldn't imagine I'd have bought it. I never wear proper shirts with buttons, because buttons are boring.

I went to the kitchen, just to see if anybody else was around, and they were all in there – Alicia, her mum and dad, Rich. The baby was in there too, of course. He was sprawled out in Alicia's lap, holding a small plastic spoon in his fist and looking at the lights in the ceiling.

'Oh, good morning, Sleeping Beauty,' said Alicia's mum.

'Hello,' I said. I was going to say, 'Hello, Mrs Burns,' but I didn't know whether I called her that any more, and I didn't want to start the day with that whole Alzheimer's thing.

'You were so weird in the night I let you sleep in,' said Alicia. 'You feeling better?'

'I don't know,' I said. 'What time is it?'

'Nearly *eight*,' she said, as if eight o'clock in the morning was like lunchtime. 'Roof did well, though.'

I had no idea what this meant.

'Yeah?' 'Yeah' seemed like a safe thing to say.

'Yeah. Seven-fifteen. You're a good boy, Roof, aren't you? Yes you are.' And she lifted the baby up and blew a raspberry on his tummy.

This baby – my baby, Alicia's baby, *our* baby – was called Roof. Whose idea was that? What did it mean? Maybe I hadn't heard right. Maybe it was a boy called Ruth. I think on balance I'd rather he was called Ruth than Roof. At least Ruth was a name.

'What's happening today?' said Alicia's dad.

'I'm going to college this afternoon, and Sam's looking after Ruth,' said Alicia. To be honest, she said Roof again, but I was going to stick with Ruth for the time being. Being called Ruth wouldn't cause him any trouble until he started school, and then he'd get the shit kicked out of him.

'Have you got college this morning, Sam?'

'I think so,' I said. I wasn't sure, though, because

I didn't even know I went to college, or where that college might be, or what I studied there.

'Your mum's helping you this afternoon, isn't she?'

'Is she?'

'Yeah. You told me she's taken the afternoon off.'

'Oh. Right. Is she coming round here or am I going round there?'

'You made the arrangement. You'd better call her.'

'Yeah. I'll do that.'

Alicia's mum handed me a cup of tea.

'You'd better get your breakfast if you're going to get to college on time,' she said.

There were bowls and milk and cereal on the table, so I helped myself, and no one said anything. At least I'd done something normal. It felt like I was playing some sort of game that everyone else knew the rules for except me. I could do or say anything at any moment, and it would be wrong, and I'd be out. I tried to think. College probably started at nine, and it probably took me half an hour to get there. Most places take you half an hour to get to in London. I decided to walk out of the door at half past eight. Until then, I'd just try and keep out of the way.

Even though I didn't need to go, I went to the downstairs toilet, locked myself in and stayed there for longer than anyone usually stays in a toilet.

'Are you OK?' she said when I finally came out.

'Bit of a weird stomach.'

'You OK to go to college?'

'Yeah, yeah.'

'You can't go out like that. Go and put your coat on.'

My parka was hanging up with all the other coats in the hall. I did as I was told and put it on. Then I went back to the kitchen, hoping that someone would say something like, 'Hurry up, Sam, you've got to catch the number 4 to So-and-So College and then walk to room 19 to study art and design.' But no one said anything like that, so I said goodbye to everyone and walked out the door.

I didn't know what to do or where to go, so I walked home. No one was in, and I didn't have any keys, so that was a complete waste of time, but wasting time was sort of the point, so I didn't mind. I wandered around for a bit. Nothing had changed. No one was zooming around on flying scooters or anything like that. It was just the future, not, you know, The Future.

I was thinking a lot while I was mooching around. Most of it was just the same little thought, over and over again: I've got a baby, I've got a baby, I've got a baby. Or: I'm going to have a baby, I'm going to have a baby, I'm going to have a baby. (See, I didn't know whether

I already had one or whether I was going to have one – whether that was it, now, whether my old life was over, or whether TH was going to project me back into it at some stage.) And I thought about how come I was living at Alicia's house, and sharing a bed with her, and I thought about whether I could find out the results of some horse races or the next *Big Brother* or something, so I could bet on them if I ever got sent back to my own time.

And also, I thought about why TH had done this, if it was him. The way I saw it was this: if he'd done it a while back, before I'd had sex with Alicia, then there'd be a point to it. He could have been trying to teach me a lesson. If I'd been projected magically into the future then, I'd have thought, you know, Aaaagh! I don't want a baby yet! We'd better not have sex! But it was too late for a lesson. Back in my own time, there was probably a text message on my mobile phone telling me that my ex-girlfriend was pregnant, so what was I supposed to learn from this? It was like TH was saying, Yo, sucker! You shouldn't have had sex! That just seemed mean to me, and not like him. He wasn't mean.

I was about to go home when I saw Rabbit sitting on the steps that lead up to his flats. He had his board at his feet, and he was smoking, and it didn't look like a cigarette.

'Yo, Sammy! Where you been?'

108

At first I didn't want to talk to him, because it seemed as though I couldn't talk to anyone without making myself look like an idiot. But then I realized that Rabbit was actually a pretty good person to talk to. You couldn't look like an idiot when you were talking to Rabbit, unless there was someone else apart from Rabbit there to witness it. Rabbit wouldn't notice. I could tell him anything and a) he wouldn't understand it, and b) he'd forget it anyway.

– For example:

'Sam,' he said when I'd walked over to him. 'I been meaning to ask you. How old is your mum?'

'We've been through this, Rabbit,' I said.

'Have we?'

'Yeah.'

He shrugged. He still couldn't remember, but he was prepared to take my word for it.

'When was the last time you saw me?' I said to him.

'I don't know. I got like this feeling that it's been ages.'

'Have I got a kid?'

'Oh, Sammy, Sammy,' he said. 'That sort of stuff you should remember. Even I wouldn't forget that.'

I wasn't so sure, but I didn't say anything.

'It's not that I've forgotten,' I said. 'But I couldn't remember if I'd told you or not.'

'You didn't have to tell me,' he said. 'I've seen you with him loads of times. You bring him over to see your mum, don't you? Little . . . What's his name again?'

'Ruth,' I said.

'Nah. Ruth? That's not right.'

'Roof?'

'That's it. Roof. Funny name. What was that about, then?'

'I don't know. Alicia's idea.'

'I was wondering about whether it was, you know, where . . . What's the word?'

'I don't know.'

'You know Brooklyn Beckham?'

'Yeah.'

'They say that's where he was, you know . . .'

'You're losing me, Rabbit.'

'David Beckham and Posh Spice have sex in Brooklyn. And nine months later they have a baby. What's the word? Brooklyn was somethinged in Brooklyn.'

'Conceived.'

'Exactly. I was wondering whether yours was conceived on the roof.'

'Oh. No.'

'Just an idea,' said Rabbit.

'So you've seen me a fair bit over here?' I asked him.

'Yeah.'

'But I don't live here any more.'

'No. You moved over to your girlfriend's place when she had the baby, I heard.'

'How did you hear that?'

'I think you told me. What's all this about? Why don't you know nothing about your own life?'

'I'll be honest with you, Rabbit. What's happened is, I've been like whizzed forward a year in time.'

'Wow.'

'Yeah. Just today. So in my head, it's still a year ago. And I don't know what's happened to me. I didn't even know I had a kid, so I'm kind of freaking out. I need help. Any information you can give me.'

'Right. Well. Information.'

'Yeah. Anything you think might help.'

'Who'd just won *Celebrity Big Brother* before you got whizzed?'

'It's not that sort of stuff I'm looking for, to be honest, Rabbit. I'm trying to find out what's happened to me. Not to, you know, the world.'

'That's all I know. You had a baby and you moved into your girlfriend's house. And then you disappeared.' And he made a disappearing noise, like, Pfffft.

I felt a little shiver then, as if I really had ceased to exist.

'So it's good to see you haven't,' said Rabbit. 'Because you wouldn't be the first person I knew who'd dematerialized. There was this kid called

Matthew, and I was watching him one day, and he just . . .'

'Thanks, Rabbit. I'll see you later.' I wasn't in the mood.

'Oh. Yeah. Right.'

On the way back to Alicia's, I found two two-pound coins in my pocket, so I stopped in McDonald's to get something to eat. I couldn't remember how much a cheeseburger and fries cost last time I was in there, but it didn't seem to have gone up by much. It wasn't a thousand pounds, or anything like that. I could afford a Coke as well, and I still had some money left over. I sat down at a table on my own and started to unwrap my burger, but before I could take a bite, this girl started waving at me.

'Oi! Sam! Sam!'

I waved back. I'd never seen her in my life before. She was a black girl, about seventeen or so, and she had a baby with her. She'd taken the baby out of the pram and sat it on her knee while she ate.

'Come and sit here,' she said. I didn't want to, but what could I do? She might have been my best friend.

I put my food and drink back on the tray and walked across the restaurant to join her.

'How's it going?' I said.

'Yeah, not so bad. This one was up half the night, though.'

'They're terrible, aren't they?' I said. This seemed safe enough. Parents were always saying things like that.

'How's Roof?' she said. It was definitely Roof. Everyone said so.

'Yeah, all right, thanks.'

'You seen anyone?' she said.

'No,' I said. And then, 'Like who?' I was hoping I might recognize a name, and then I'd understand who this girl was, and how I knew her.

'You know, like Holly? Or Nicola?'

'No.' I knew a lot of girls, all of a sudden. 'Haven't seen them for ages.'

She suddenly lifted up her baby and sniffed at its bottom. You had to spend half your life doing that if you had a baby, apparently. 'Phwooar. Off we go, young lady.'

She got a bag out from the base of the pram and stood up.

'Can I come with you?' I said.

'To change her nappy? Why?'

'I want to watch you do it.'

'Why? You're good at it.'

How did she know? Why would I change Roof's nappy in front of her?

'Yeah, but . . . I'm sick of the way I do it. I want to try something different.'

'There isn't much you can do with a nappy,' she said. I just kept my mouth shut and followed her downstairs.

'You'll have to come in the Ladies, you know that?' she said.

'That's OK,' I said. It wasn't OK, really, but the nappy-changing thing was really worrying me. From what I'd seen overnight and this morning, there wasn't a lot I couldn't work out for myself. Mostly it just seemed like you had to pick the baby up and take it somewhere, and I could do that. I didn't even know how to take a baby's clothes off, though. I was worried about breaking its arms and legs.

There was nobody in the Ladies anyway, thank God. She pulled out this table thing out of the wall and put the baby down on it.

'I just do it like this,' she said.

She sort of ripped off the all-in-one tracksuit thing that babies wear (after she'd done the ripping I could see there were lots of poppers down the legs and round the bottom bit), then she pulled its legs out and undid the tags on the side of the nappy. Then with one hand she held the legs up, and with the other she wiped its arse with a wet paper hankie thing. The actual crap part wasn't too terrible. There wasn't much of it, and it smelled more like milk than dog shit. That was why I hadn't wanted to do it during the night. I thought it would smell of dog shit, or human shit, anyway, and I'd throw up. My new friend folded the dirty nappy up and put it in this little blue carrier bag with the dirty wet hankies, and then put a new nappy on in about ten seconds flat.

'What do you reckon?' she said.

'Awesome,' I said.

'What?'

'You're brilliant,' I said, and I meant it.

It was the most incredible thing I'd ever seen. It was the most incredible thing I'd ever seen in a ladies' toilet, anyway.

'You can do that, though,' she said.

'Can I?' I couldn't believe it. If I'd learned to do that in a few weeks, then I was a lot cleverer than I thought I was.

There was a bunch of keys in my parka pocket too, so I was able to let myself back into Alicia's house, after about twenty minutes of putting the wrong keys in the wrong locks. My mum was already there, sitting at the kitchen table with Roof on her lap. She looked older, my mum, older than a year older, if you see what I mean, and I hoped that the worry lines that had suddenly appeared on her forehead were nothing to do with me. I was so pleased to see her, though. I nearly ran for her, but I might have seen her the day before, so she might have thought it was a bit weird.

'Here's Dadda,' she said, and of course I looked around to see who she was talking about, and then I laughed as if I'd been joking.

'Alicia let me in, but she's gone for a walk,' my

mum said. 'I made her go out. I thought she was looking a bit peaky. And there's no one else here.'

'Just the three of us, then,' I said. 'That's nice.' That seemed safe enough. Me, my mum and a baby – that had to be nice, didn't it? But I was still nervous, because I didn't really know what I was talking about. Maybe I hated Mum, or she hated me, or Roof and Mum hated each other . . . How was I supposed to know? But she just smiled.

'How was college?'

'Yeah, good,' I said.

'Alicia told me about your bit of trouble.'

It was like a computer game, getting whizzed into the future. You had to think on your feet, really quickly. You were driving fast down a straight road and then suddenly something was coming straight at you and you had to swerve. Why would I be in trouble? I decided I wouldn't.

'Oh,' I said. 'That. It was nothing.'

She looked at me. 'Sure?'

'Yeah. Honest.'

And I was being honest, every way you looked at it.

'How are things?' she said.

'Not bad,' I said. 'How about yours?' I didn't want to talk about me, mostly because I didn't really know about me.

'Yeah, OK,' she said. 'Very tired.'

'Oh,' I said. 'Oh, well.'

'What a pair, eh?' And she laughed. Or she made a noise that was supposed to be something like laughing, anyway. Why were we a pair? What did she mean? I'd heard people like my mum say 'What a pair!' one zillion times, and I'd never thought about what it meant before. So now I had to try and remember when and why people said it. Suddenly I could hear it. Last year, or the year before last, depending on what year we were in now, we both got food poisoning from a dodgy takeaway. And I was sick and she was sick and I was sick and she was sick, and we were taking it in turns to lock ourselves in the bathroom to throw up. 'What a pair,' she said. And another time . . . Rabbit and I, coming back from Grind City, and we'd both slammed, and Rabbit had a bloody nose, and I had a graze down the side of my cheek. 'What a pair,' she said when she saw us. So people usually said it when something had gone wrong, when two people were sick or injured, when there was some sign that they'd messed up.

'Are we going to take him out for a walk?' my mum said.

'Yeah, that'd be good,' I said.

'So I'd better go to the loo. For the one hundredth time today.'

She lifted Roof up and passed him across the table to me. She was sitting in the window, behind the kitchen table, and so I hadn't been able to look at her properly. But when she pushed the table out and stood up, I could see she had a football up her jumper. I laughed.

'Mum!' I said. 'What are you doing . . .' I stopped. That wasn't a football. My mum wouldn't have put a football up her jumper. My mum was pregnant.

I made a noise, like 'Eeek!'

'I know,' said my mum. 'I look massive today.'

I don't know how I got through the rest of the day, really. I probably seemed weird and spaced out, but the football up my mum's jumper was just about the last straw for me. I'd had it up to here with the future. I mean, it was fine if you just let it happen, day by day. But missing out chunks of time like this . . . It was no good. It was doing my head in.

We put Roof in this sort of backpack thing that goes on your front, not your back. I carried him, because Mum couldn't, and also, I suppose, because he was my kid and not hers, and he made my chest all sweaty, but he stayed asleep. We went to the park, and walked around the little lake, and I tried not to say anything, so most of the time we were quiet, but every now and again Mum asked me a question. Like, 'How are you getting on with Alicia?' Or, 'It's not too difficult, is it, living in someone else's house?' Or, 'Have you thought about what to do when this course finishes?' And I just said, you know, 'It's OK,' or, 'It's not so bad,' or, 'I dunno.' I could imagine it was the sort of thing I might have said anyway, whether I knew the answers or not. We went for a cup of tea, and then I – we, I suppose, if Roof counts as a person – walked Mum home. I didn't go in. I would have wanted to stay.

On the way back we went for a walk down by the New River, and this guy was there, sitting on a bench, smoking a cigarette with one hand and pushing a pram with the other.

'Hello,' he said as we walked past.

'Hello.'

'I'm Giles,' he said. 'Remember? From the class?'

I'd never met him before in my life. He was quite posh, much older than me.

'You didn't come back, did you?' he said.

'I don't think so,' I said. Not a good answer, I realized as soon as I'd come out with it. I should probably have known whether I went back somewhere or not, even if I hadn't been for the first time yet.

'What did you have?' he said, nodding at Roof.

'A boy.'

'Called?'

'Oh,' I said. 'It's complicated.' I wasn't very

happy with that as an answer, but I didn't want to get into the whole Roof nightmare.

He looked at me, but he left it at that.

'You?' I said.

'Yeah, a boy. Joshua. How's it going?'

'You know,' I said.

'Yeah,' he said. 'Can I ask you something? Is your, you know, your partner . . . Is she happy?'

'Well,' I said. 'She seems OK.'

'You're lucky,' he said.

'Yeah.'

'Mine's in a terrible state,' he said.

'Oh.'

'Cries all the time. Won't let me touch her.'

'Oh.'

'I don't mean sex,' he said. 'I'm not, you know. After anything.'

'No.'

'It's just that she won't let me hold her. She freezes up. And I don't even think she wants to hold the baby, particularly.'

'Right,' I said.

'I'm at my wits' end, to be honest. I don't know what to do.'

'Oh,' I said. I didn't think that I'd have any advice for him even if I hadn't been whizzed. I'd need to be about fifty, I thought, before I could deal with this guy and his problems.

'Write to a magazine,' I said.

'Sorry?'

'Like, you know, a woman's magazine.'

I sometimes looked at the problem pages in my mum's magazines, because you could read about sex without it looking as though you were reading about sex.

He didn't look impressed.

'It seems a bit more urgent than that,' he said.

'They come out once a month,' I said. 'And it's the middle of the month, so if you wrote to them quickly, you might get in the next issue.'

'Yes. Well. Thanks.'

'That's OK. We'd better be going,' I said. 'See you later.'

I think he wanted to talk some more. But I just walked away.

Nothing much happened in the afternoon or evening. We all ate together, Alicia and her mum and dad and me, and then we all watched TV while Roof slept. I pretended I was interested in the programmes, but actually I had no idea what I was looking at. I just sat there feeling homesick and sad and sorry for myself. I missed my old life. And even if I got whizzed back to my own time, my old life wouldn't be there for much longer. I'd turn on my mobile, and there'd be a text telling me that in a year's time I'd have a kid, and I'd be living with people I didn't really know and didn't like much. I wanted to be whizzed back further than that, to a time when I hadn't met Alicia and when I wasn't interested in having sex. If Tony Hawk let me be eleven again, I wouldn't mess it up a second time. I'd become a Christian or something, one of those people who never do anything. I used to think they were mad, but they're not, are they? They know what they're doing. They don't want to watch TV with someone else's mum and dad. They want to watch TV on their own, in their bedroom.

We went to bed at ten o'clock, but we didn't turn the light out then because Alicia had to feed Roof. When she'd finished, she asked me to change him.

'Change him? Me? Now?'

'Have you gone funny again?'

'No,' I said. 'Sorry. I was, you know. Just checking I heard you right.'

Just as I was getting out of bed Roof made a noise like yoghurt going down a plughole.

'Bloody hell,' I said. 'What was that?'

Alicia laughed, but I meant it.

'Good timing, young man,' she said.

After a while I realized what Alicia meant. She meant that the noise of yoghurt going down the plughole was actually the sound Roof made when he was crapping. And now I was supposed to do something about it.

I picked him up and started to walk to the bathroom.

'Where are you going?'

I didn't know where I was going. Obviously.

'Just . . .' But I couldn't think of a good answer, so I left it at that.

'Are you sure you're all right?'

'Sure.'

But being sure I was all right didn't help me with where I was going. I stood there.

'Have we run out of nappies?'

Suddenly I noticed Alicia's old toy box at the end of the bed. When I was last in this room it was still a toy box, full of old stuff she used to play with when she was a kid. Now it had like this plastic mattress on it, and on the floor beside it there was a bag full of nappies and a box full of those wet tissue things that my friend the black girl had been using in McDonald's.

Roof was half asleep. His eyes were rolling around in his head like he was drunk. I undid the poppers on his all-in-one tracksuit, pulled up the legs and undid the Sellotape on the sides of the nappies, like I'd seen the girl do at lunchtime. And then . . . You probably don't want to know how to change a nappy. And even if you do, I'm probably not the person to teach you. The point is, I did it, without messing it up too much. I couldn't remember the last time I was so pleased with myself. Probably when I slept with Alicia for the first time. Which was funny, if you thought about it. First I was proud of myself for sleeping with her. And then I was proud of myself for doing something that happened all because I slept with her.

Maybe that was what TH was trying to do when he whizzed me into the future. Maybe he was trying to teach me how to change nappies. It seemed like the hard way of doing things to me. He could have just sent me to classes.

'You do love me, Sam, don't you?' Alicia said when Roof was back in his cot and I'd gone back to bed. I just lay there with my back to her, pretending to be asleep. I didn't know whether I loved her or not. How could I?

It took me a long, long time to get to sleep after that, but when I woke up in the morning, I was in my own bed. It didn't feel like my own bed any more, though. Your own bed is usually somewhere you feel safe, but I didn't feel safe there any more. I knew everything that was going to happen to me, and it felt like my life was over, however many years I managed to keep breathing. I was a hundred per cent sure that Alicia was pregnant. And if it was my life that I'd seen, well, I didn't want to live it. I wanted my old life back, I wanted someone else's life. But I didn't want that one.

7

The summer before all this happened, Mum and I went on holiday to Spain, and we spent a lot of time hanging out with this English family we met in a bar. They were called the Parrs, and they lived in Hastings, and they were all right. There was a kid called Jamie, who was six months older than me, and Jamie had a sister called Scarlett, who was twelve. And Mum liked Tina and Chris, the parents. They used to sit in this English bar, night after night, taking the piss out of English people who only went to English bars. I didn't get it, but they thought they were funny. A few weeks after we'd come back from holiday, Mum and I went down to Hastings on the train to see them. We played miniature golf on the seafront, and ate fish and chips, and skimmed stones. I liked Hastings. It had the funfairs and the arcades and all that, but it wasn't too tacky, and it had a little railway that went to the top of the cliffs. We never saw the Parrs again, though. We got a Christmas card from them, but Mum never got round to sending Christmas cards last year, so they sort of gave up on us after that.

And Hastings was the first place I thought of

when I woke up that morning, the morning after I'd been whizzed into the future. I was positive that Alicia was pregnant, and I knew I didn't want to be a father. So I had to move out of London and never come back, and Hastings was the only other place in the whole of England that I knew. We never go anywhere, apart from Spain, and I couldn't go abroad on my own, with no money and no credit card. So I had breakfast with my mum, and when she'd gone to work, I packed a bag and picked up my skateboard and went to live in Hastings.

I knew I was being a coward, but sometimes you have to be a coward, don't you? There's no point in being brave if you're just going to get destroyed. Say you walked round the corner and there are fifty Al Qaida there. Not even fifty. Five. Not even five. One, with like a machine gun, would be enough. You might not feel good about running for your life, but what are your choices? Well, I had walked round the corner, and there was an Al Qaida with a machine gun, except he was just a baby, and he didn't actually have a machine gun. But in my world a baby, even without a machine gun, is like a terrorist with a machine gun, if you think about it, because Roof was every bit as deadly to my chances of going to college to do art and design etcetera as an Al Qaida operative. And actually, Alicia was another Al Qaida, plus also her mum and dad, plus also my mum, because when she found out she would literally kill me dead. So that was five Al Qaida waiting round the corner. One would have been enough to send you running off to Hastings or wherever.

I had forty pounds that I'd been saving for a pair of Kalis Royals, but all skate stuff was going to have to wait until I was set up in Hastings with a job and a flat and all that. Forty pounds would get me to Hastings, and I reckoned I could find a bed and breakfast place to stay in, and then I wanted to get a job on the seafront doing something cool. There was this giant outdoor ten-pin bowling thing that I'd played on with Jamie Parr, and the guy who ran it was OK. He might give me a job, I thought. Or I could look after the boats on the boating lake. Or I could work in the arcade, giving people change, although that wouldn't be my top choice. There were loads of things I could do, anyway, and all of them were better than changing Roof's nappy and living with Alicia's mum and dad.

I went to Charing Cross on my Oyster card, so that was free, and then it cost me twelve quid from Charing Cross to Hastings, which left me with twenty-eight pounds plus a few coins I had in my pocket, including maybe three pound coins. This was the beauty of emigrating to Hastings rather than say Australia. I'd already dealt with all my travel expenses and I still had thirty-one pounds left. Also, I left home at about nine thirty and I was there by lunchtime the same day.

I walked through the town to the seafront, which took about ten minutes, and bought some chips from one of the fish and chip shops near the miniature golf course. I suppose it made me a bit sad, watching the families playing golf, because that's what I'd been doing a year ago. I watched a kid of about my age playing with his mum and his younger brother, and you could tell he had no troubles. He was trying to get the ball up the slope at the eighth hole, and it kept rolling back to him, and his mum and his brother were laughing at him, and he threw his club down and sat on the wall, so in a way he did have troubles; in fact, there was a moment when he looked over to me, sitting on the bench eating my bag of chips, and you could see he was thinking, I wish I was him. Because I must have looked like I had no troubles. I wasn't in a sulk like him, and nobody from my family was laughing at me, and the sun was on my face. And then I didn't feel quite as sad, because all those things were true, and I had come to Hastings to escape my troubles, which meant that they were all back in London, and not here by the seaside. And as long as I didn't turn on my mobile, which would be full of bad messages, bad news, my troubles would stay in London.

'Oi!' I shouted at the kid. 'Will you watch my stuff?'

I pointed at the skateboard and my bag, and he nodded. And then I got up, walked across the pebbles down to the sea, and threw my mobile phone as far into the water as I could. Easy. Everything gone. I went back to the bench and spent a happy thirty minutes on my deck.

There was nobody playing on the giant ten-pin bowling game, and the bloke who ran it was sitting in his little booth, smoking and reading the paper.

'Hello,' I said.

He raised his eyebrows, or at least I think he did. That was his way of saying hello back. He didn't look up from the paper.

'Do you remember me?'

'No.'

Of course he wouldn't remember me. Stupid. I was nervous, so I wasn't being very sharp.

'Do you need any help?'

'What does it look like?'

'Yeah, but it gets busy, though, doesn't it? I played here last year and there was a queue.'

'And then what would you do? If there was a queue? People just stand there. It's no skin off of my nose. I don't need no riot police.'

'No, no, I wasn't thinking of the queue. I was thinking, you know, you might have been looking for someone to put the skittles back up and all that.'

'Listen. There isn't really a job for me here, let alone anyone else. If you want to put skittles back up, you're welcome, but I wouldn't be paying you for it.'

'Oh. No. I'm looking for work. A job. Money.'

'Then you've come to the wrong place.'

'Do you know anyone else?'

'No, I meant, the wrong town. Look.'

He waved his hand down the seafront, still without looking up from his paper. There was the miserable kid playing miniature golf, nobody on the boating lake, nobody on the trampolines, four or five families waiting for the miniature railway, a couple of old ladies sipping tea at the cafe.

'And the weather's good today. When it rains it all calms down a bit.' And he laughed. Not a big laugh, just a 'Ha!'.

I stood there for a moment. I knew I wasn't going to get a job in Hastings doing graphic design or whatever. I wasn't aiming too high. But I did think I'd be able to get some work for the summer from one of those places. Nothing fancy, just forty quid in cash at the end of the day, sort of thing. I thought back to last year, to the day we spent with the Parrs eating ice creams and playing on the giant ten-pin bowling game. There was nobody on the seafront then, either. I'd somehow managed to forget about that. Or maybe I had remembered, but I didn't see what it had to do with anything.

I just thought that it would be a boring job, waiting for people to come. It didn't really occur to me that there wouldn't be a job at all.

I asked at a couple of the other places. I went to the fairground, and a couple of chip shops, and even at the little railway that went up the cliff, but there was nothing at any of them, and most of the people there made the same sort of joke.

'I was wondering how I was going to cope today,' said the man at the cliff railway. He was leaning on the counter, looking at a fishing-rod catalogue. He had no customers.

'I've got a good job for you,' said the guy on the trampolines. 'Go and round up some children. You might have to go to Brighton. Or London.' He was playing some card game on his mobile phone. He had no customers either.

'Fuck off,' said the man who ran the fruit machines in the arcade. That wasn't really a joke, though.

I had chips for tea, and then I started looking for somewhere to stay. What I was really looking for was a place to live, seeing as I couldn't go home ever again, but I tried not to look at it that way. There were loads of little bed and breakfast places if you walked far enough out of the city centre, and I chose the grottiest-looking one, because I was pretty sure that was all I'd be able to afford.

It smelled of fish inside. There are lots of parts

of Hastings that smell of fish, and most of the time you don't mind. Even the smell of rotting fish down by the tall black fishermen's huts is OK, I think, because you understand that it has to be that way. If there are fishing boats, there are going to be rotting fish, and fishing boats are all right, so you can put up with anything that comes with them. But the smell of fish inside the Sunnyview B&B was different. It was the sort of fish smell you get inside some old people's houses, where it seems as though fish have got into the carpets and the curtains and their clothes. The rotting fish smell out by the fishermen's huts is a sort of healthy smell, even though the fish aren't very healthy, obviously, otherwise they wouldn't be rotting. But when it's soaked into curtains, it doesn't seem healthy at all. You feel like putting the neck of your T-shirt over your mouth, like you do when someone breaks out a killer fart, and breathing that way.

There was a bell on the reception desk, so I pinged it, but nobody came for a while. I watched one of the ancient guests walk down the hallway towards the door on one of those frame things.

'Don't just stand there, young lady. Open the door for me.'

I looked around, but there was no one else behind me. He was talking to me, and even if he'd called me 'young man' he'd have been rude. How was I to know he wanted the door opened? But he hadn't called me 'young man', he'd called me 'young lady' – because of my hair, I suppose, seeing as I don't wear a skirt or spend my whole life texting people.

I opened the door for him and he just kind of grunted and walked past me. He couldn't go much further, though, because there were like twenty steps down from the front door to the street.

'How am I going to get down there?' he said angrily. He looked at me as if I'd built the steps myself, in the last two hours, just to keep him away from the public library or the chemist or the betting shop or wherever it was he wanted to go.

I shrugged. He was pissing me off.

'How did you get in?'

'My daughter!' he shouted, like if there was one fact in the world everyone knew, even more than they knew that David Beckham is the capital of France or whatever, it was that this old geezer's daughter shoved him up some steps on his frame into a bed and breakfast.

'Shall I go and get her?'

'She's not here, is she? Good God. What do they teach you in schools now? Not common sense, that's for sure.'

I wasn't going to offer to help him. First of all it looked like it would take about two hours. And second of all he was a miserable old bastard, and I didn't see why I should put myself out.

'Aren't you going to help me, then?'

'OK.'

'Yes. I should think so. It says something about young people today that I even had to ask.'

I know what some of you would say. You'd say, Sam's too nice! This old bloke was rude to him and he still agreed to get him down the steps! But I know what the rest of you would say too. The rest of you would say, If he was halfway decent, he wouldn't even be in Hastings! He'd be back in London, looking after his pregnant girl-friend! Or ex-girlfriend! So the rude old guy was sort of God's punishment! And to tell you the truth, I'd agree with this last lot. I didn't want to be messing around with pensioners. But it was still better than dealing with everything that would be going on back home. I suddenly thought of the mobile at the bottom of the sea, bleeping away with its messages, and the fish all freaking out.

It didn't take two hours to get him down on to the street, but it did take about fifteen minutes, and fifteen minutes can seem like two hours if you've got your hands buried deep in some old guy's armpits. He moved the frame down step by step while I stopped him from falling forwards or backwards. The forwards bit was the hardest to stop, and the scariest to think about. Falling back-wards, he'd have only hurt his bum, if anything, although more likely he would have just squashed me. It was a long way down, though, and there were a lot of steps, and if he'd gone down that way, I reckon things would have just fallen off him, legs and arms and ears, because they didn't seem very firmly connected to his body.

Every time he lurched forwards he shouted, 'That's it! I'm going! You've killed me! Thanks for nothing!' You'd think he'd have realized that if he could spit all that out then he wasn't going anywhere. Anyway, we got to the bottom, and he started to shuffle himself down the hill towards town, but then he stopped and turned.

'I'll be about half an hour,' he said. That was obviously a lie, because in half an hour he'd have moved about seven paving stones, but that wasn't the point. The point was that he was expecting me to wait for him.

'I won't be here in half an hour,' I said.

'You do as you're told.'

'Nah,' I said. 'You're too rude.'

I don't normally talk back, but you have to make an exception for people like that. And I wasn't at school any more, or even at home, and if I was going to make a life for myself in Hastings then I had to talk back, otherwise I'd just be standing outside bed and breakfasts for the rest of my life waiting for old people.

'And also, I'm not a girl.'

'Oh, I worked that out ages ago,' he said. 'But I didn't say anything because I thought it might make you get a haircut.'

'Well, see you later,' I said.

'When?'

'Just . . . you know. Whenever I see you.'

'You'll see me in half an hour.'

'I won't be here.'

'I'll pay you, you fool. I don't expect anybody to do anything for nothing. Not these days. Three pounds for an up and down.' He waved at the steps. 'Twenty pounds a day if you'll do as you're told. I've got money. Money's not the problem. Getting out of that bloody place to spend it is the problem.'

I'd found a job. My first day in Hastings, and I was in work. I was pretty sure then that I'd be able to get by on my own.

'Half an hour?' I said.

'Oh, I thought money would interest you,' he said. 'Heaven forbid that anyone would do anything out of the kindness of their hearts.'

And he shuffled . . . Well, I was going to say he shuffled off, or he shuffled away, but that wouldn't be right, because he was going so slowly that he never actually went anywhere. I could have watched him for fifteen minutes and I'd still have been able to spit chewing gum on to his head. So we'll just leave it like that. We'll just say that he shuffled.

I hadn't even got myself a room yet. I went in, dinged the bell again and prayed that no other old geezer would appear from nowhere asking for help. Although what if he did? I thought to myself. Maybe I could do better than earn enough money for food and a room. Maybe I could make a fortune out of old people. But nobody appeared apart from the lady who ran the place, and she could move under her own steam.

'How can I help you?' she said. I got why the whole place smelled of fish. Fish don't smell of fish as much as she did. It was like she's been boiling cod or whatever for a thousand years.

'I need a room,' I said.

'For yourself?'

'Yes.'

'Where is she?'

'Who?'

'How old would you say I was?'

I looked at her. I'd played this game before, with one of my mum's friends from work. For some reason mum's friend asked me to guess how old she was and I said fifty-six and she was thirty-one and she started crying. It never ends well. And this woman – she definitely wasn't, I don't know, under forty. I don't think. But she could have been sixty-five. How was I supposed to know? So I stood there, probably with my mouth open.

'I'll help you out,' said the woman. 'Would you say I'm more than one day old?'

'Yes,' I said. 'Course. You're *much* older than a day.' And even then she sort of frowned a bit at the way I said it, as if I was telling her she was a horrible ancient old witch, whereas all I actually meant was that she wasn't a new-born baby. I mean, what are you supposed to say to these people? 'Oh you look so young you could even be a new-born baby not even a day old?' Is that what they want?

'Right,' she said. 'So I wasn't born yesterday.'

'No.' Ah. I got it now.

'And that's how I know you have a girl waiting outside.'

A girl! That was too funny. She thought I wanted a room so that I could sleep with a girl in her hotel, when the truth was that I was never going to sleep with anyone for the rest of my life, in case I made her pregnant.

'Come out and look.'

'Oh, I know she won't be standing out on the street. You may be naive, but I'm sure you're not actually daft.'

'I don't know anyone in Hastings,' I said. I didn't think I should go into the whole thing with the Parrs. She wouldn't care about them. 'I don't know anyone in Hastings and I don't like girls.'

That was a mistake, obviously.

'Or boys. I don't like girls or boys.'

And that didn't sound right.

'I like them as friends. But I'm not interested in sharing a room in a B&B with anyone.'

'So what are you doing here?' she said.

'It's a long story.'

138

'I'll bet it is.'

'You can bet,' I said. She was annoying me. 'You can bet any money.'

'I will.'

'Go on, then.'

This was turning into a stupid conversation. Nobody was going to bet anything on how long my story was, and yet we'd ended up talking about that instead of what I wanted to talk about, which was where I was going to spend the night.

'So you're not going to give me a room.'

'No.'

'So what am I supposed to do, then?'

'Oh, there are plenty of other places that will take your money. But we're not like that here.'

'I'm working for one of your guests,' I said. I don't really know why I stuck at it. There were plenty of other places – places that might smell of cabbage, or old bacon fat, or anything other than fish.

'Is that right?' She was finished with me, and she wasn't interested. She started tidying up the desk, checking her phone for messages, that sort of thing.

'Yeah, and I promised him I'd be here to help him up the steps in a few minutes. He's got one of those frame things.'

'Mr Brady?'

She looked at me. She was scared of him, you could see it.

'I don't know his name. He's just a rude old guy with a frame. I just met him and he asked me to be his assistant.'

'His assistant. What are you going to do? Help him with his tax and VAT?'

'No. Help him up and down the steps. Get him stuff, maybe.'

Obviously I was making up that last bit, because we hadn't yet had a chance to talk about the job in any detail.

'Anyway. He warned me about you.'

'What did he say?'

'He said not to let you throw me out, or he'd cause trouble.'

'He causes trouble anyway.'

'So it's just a question of whether you want any more.'

She turned her back on me, which I think was her way of saying, Sit down! Make yourself at home!

So I sat down on the bench in the reception. There was a local paper there, so I flicked through it and tried to learn something about my new home, and after a little while I heard Mr Brady shouting for me.

'Oi. Stupid boy. Where are you?'

'That's me,' I said to the woman.

'You'd better go and help him, then,' she said. 'And I'm not giving you a double room.'

A single room was twenty quid a night, and

Mr Brady was going to give me twenty quid a day. So I had made it. I could live. And that's the story of how I got a job and somewhere to sleep in Hastings.

8

I was OK checking into the room and putting my stuff away and all that. It felt weird, of course, being in a strange room in a strange town and breathing fish, but not weird in a bad way. I had a shower, put a T-shirt and boxers on, then lay down on the bed and fell asleep. It was in the middle of the night that everything started to feel bad.

I'm sure I would have slept straight through if Mr Brady hadn't started banging on my door at four o'clock in the morning.

'Stupid!' he was shouting. 'Stupid! Are you in there?'

I didn't say anything for a while, because I was hoping he'd just go back to his room if I ignored him. But he kept knocking, and a couple of other guests opened their doors and started threatening him, and he started threatening them back, so I had to get up just to calm everybody down.

'Come in here,' I said to Mr Brady.

'You're naked,' he said. 'I'm not going to employ naked people.'

I told him that someone with a T-shirt and boxer shorts on wasn't naked. I didn't tell him that you couldn't ask someone never to get undressed just because they worked for you. He wouldn't come into the room, and he wouldn't whisper.

'I've lost my remote control,' he said. 'Not lost it. I dropped it down the side of the bed and I can't reach it.'

'It's four o'clock in the morning,' I said.

'This is what you're being paid for,' he said. 'You think I'm paying you twenty pounds a day to push me up and down the stairs a couple of times? I don't sleep, so you don't sleep. You don't sleep when I haven't got the remote, anyway.'

I went back into my room, put my jeans on and walked down the corridor with him. His room was huge, and it didn't smell of fish; it smelled of some chemical that must have been used to kill Germans in the war or something. He had his own bathroom, and he had a TV and a double bed and a sofa. I didn't have anything like that.

'Down there,' he said, pointing to the side of the bed next to the wall. 'Anything else you feel down there, just leave it. And if you do touch anything, I've got a lot of carbolic soap. I bought a job lot.'

This was one of the most disgusting things anyone has ever said to me, and as I was reaching down, I was actually scared. What did he think might be down there? His dead pet dog? His dead wife? A lot of old pieces of fish that he hadn't wanted to eat and had been scraping off the plate and down the side of the bed for the last twenty years?

And that's when I decided to go home. It was four o'clock in the morning and I was maybe about to feel the rotting remains of a dead dog and I was being paid twenty pounds for a whole day's work, and that whole day's work was actually a whole day and half the night, and possibly involved dead dogs. And twenty pounds was exactly what it was costing me to stay in this terrible smelly B&B. Was it possible that rotting dog actually smelled of fish, if it rotted for long enough? I was going to be working all day and half the night for a profit of nought pounds and nought pence.

So the question I asked myself, as I was groping down the side of a strange old man's bed, was, Could having a baby be any worse than this? And the answer I gave myself was, No it could not.

As it turned out, there wasn't much down there apart from the remote control. I might have felt a sock, and it gave me a fright for a second, but the sock was definitely made out of cotton or wool and not fur or flesh, so it was OK. And I came back up with the remote and gave it to Mr Brady, and he didn't say thank you, and I went back to bed. But I couldn't sleep. I was homesick. And I felt . . . well, stupid too. Mr Brady was right. My mum should have called me Stupid. What had I been thinking?

– I had a pregnant girlfriend, or ex-girlfriend, and I'd run out on her.

– I hadn't told my mum where I'd gone, and she'd be worried sick, because I'd been away for a night.

– I had really believed that I was going to live in Hastings and become either a putter-upper of giant bowling pins or a lifter-upper of old people who needed to climb a lot of stairs. I had told myself that I could make a living doing these things, and I had also told myself that this was a life that I would enjoy, despite having no friends or family or money.

It was all stupid, stupid, stupid. Of course, I felt bad about everything, but it wasn't the guilt that stopped me from sleeping, it was the embarrassment. Can you imagine that? Embarrassment stopping you from sleeping? I was blushing. There was literally too much blood in my face for me to close my eyes. Well, maybe not literally, but that was absolutely what it felt like.

At six o'clock I got up, got dressed and walked back to the railway station. I hadn't paid for the room, but then, Mr Brady hadn't paid me. He could sort it out. I was going back home to marry Alicia and look after Roof, and I was never going to think about running away again.

It's not enough, though, just to decide not to be stupid. Otherwise, why don't we *decide* to be really clever – clever enough to invent something like the iPod and make a lot of money? Or, why don't we just *decide* to be David Beckham? Or Tony Hawk? If you are actually stupid, then you can make as many clever decisions as you like and it won't help you. You're just stuck with the brain you were born with, and mine must be the size of a small pea.

Listen to this.

First of all, I was pleased that I got home at nine o'clock in the morning, because Mum goes to work at 8.30. So I thought I could make myself a cup of tea and some breakfast, watch daytime TV and say sorry and all that to Mum when she came back. Stupid? Stupid. It turned out that Mum hadn't gone to work the morning after I'd run away from home without telling her where I'd gone. It turned out that she'd been worrying about me since yesterday afternoon and hadn't even gone to bed. Who would have guessed that? You, maybe. And everyone else in the world over the age of two. But not me. Oh no.

It gets worse, though. When I turned the corner into our street, there was a police car outside our flat. So I walked down the road wondering who was in trouble, or hoping that nothing bad had happened to Mum, or praying that no burglars had come into the house overnight and taken our DVD player. Stupid? Stupid. Because it turned out that when it got to three o'clock in the morning and Alicia hadn't heard from me and Mum hadn't heard from me and nobody could phone me on my mobile because it was at the bottom of the sea, they'd all panicked and brought the law in! Isn't that amazing?

Even when I put my key in the lock I thought I was going to see a flat with no DVD player in it. In fact, the DVD player was the first thing I saw. The second thing I saw was my mum wiping her eyes with a Kleenex, and two policemen. One of the policemen was a woman. And even when I saw Mum wiping her eyes, I thought, Oh, no! What's happened to Mum?

She looked at me, and then looked around for something to throw at me, and she found the remote control. She didn't hit me with it, but if she had, it might have made me go back to Hastings, and I could have spent the whole day going to Hastings and back because of things involving TV remotes, and that would have been funny. Or, at least, funnier than anything else that was happening to me.

'You stupid, stupid boy,' she said. People were really beginning to notice this stupid thing. 'Where have you been?'

And I just made a sort of sorry face, and said, 'Hastings.'

'Hastings? Hastings?' She was really screaming now. The policewoman who was sitting on the floor by her feet touched her on her leg.

'Yeah.'

'Why?'

'Well. Do you remember we went there to play mini-golf with the Parrs?'

'I DON'T MEAN WHY HASTINGS! I MEAN WHY DID YOU GO ANYWHERE?'

'Have you spoken to Alicia?'

'Yes. Of course I have. I've spoken to Alicia, I've spoken to Rabbit, I've spoken to your father, I've spoken to everyone I could think of.'

I got distracted for a moment by the idea of my mum talking to Rabbit. I wouldn't have known how to get hold of him, so I don't know how she managed it. Also, I wondered whether he'd been tempted to ask her out.

'What did Alicia say?'

'She said she didn't know where you were.'

'Nothing else?'

'I didn't stop to chat with her about the state of your relationship, if that's what you mean. She was upset, though. What have you done to her?'

I couldn't believe it. The only good thing about the last twenty-four hours, as far as I was concerned, was that Alicia would have told Mum she was pregnant, which meant that I didn't have to. And now it sounded like nothing had happened.

'Oh.'

'Where's your mobile?'

'Lost it.'

'Where did you stay?'

'Just . . . in a hotel. A B&B sort of thing.'

'How did you pay for it?'

The policewoman stood up. We'd gone from talking about whether I was dead or alive to talking about how I paid for the B&B, so I suppose she thought she wasn't needed any more. To me, that wasn't professional. I could have just been waiting until she'd gone out the door to tell Mum that I'd sold crack or mugged some pensioners. And then she would have missed the chance of an arrest. Maybe she wasn't bothered because it all happened in Hastings, and not on her patch.

'We'll be getting on,' the policewoman said. 'I'll give you a call later.'

'Thanks for all your help,' said Mum.

'Not at all. We're just happy he's back safe and sound.'

She looked at me, and I'm pretty sure the look had a meaning, but I have no idea what it was. It could have been: *Be nice to your mum*, or: *I know how you paid for that room*, or: *Now we know you are bad we'll be watching you FOR EVER*. It wasn't just goodbye, that's for sure.

I was sorry to see them go, because once they'd gone there was nothing to stop Mum committing illegal acts on me, and I could tell she was in the mood to. She waited until she heard the front door close behind them, and then she said, 'Right. What's all this about?'

And I didn't know what to say. Why hadn't

Alicia told Mum she was pregnant? There were lots of different answers to this question, of course, but the answer I chose – because I'm an idiot – was this one: Alicia hadn't told Mum she was pregnant because she wasn't pregnant after all. What was my evidence? Especially if you take away the whole whizzing forward into the future thing, which you couldn't really rely on. My evidence was that Alicia wanted to buy a pregnancy tester. I never got to hear the results of the test, because I switched my phone off and then threw it in the sea. Well, loads of people must buy testers and find out they're not pregnant, right? Otherwise, there'd be no point to them, would there? So if Alicia wasn't pregnant, there was no need to tell Mum anything about anything. That was the good news. The bad news was that if Alicia wasn't pregnant, I didn't have a very good reason for running away from home for a night.

We sat there.

'Well?' said Mum.

'Can I have some breakfast?' I said. 'And a cup of tea?'

I was clever, or as clever as it was possible for a stupid boy to be. I said it in a way that meant, It's a long story. And it would be a long story, when I'd made it up.

My mum walked over to me and hugged me, and we went into the kitchen.

She made me scrambled eggs, bacon, mushrooms, beans and potato waffles, and then she made me exactly the same thing again. And I was starving, because in Hastings I'd had two bags of chips, but one breakfast would have been fine. It was more that, while she was cooking and I was eating, I didn't have to tell her anything. Every now and again, she'd ask me something, like, How did you get to Hastings, or, Did you speak to anyone? So I did end up talking about Mr Brady, and the job I'd got, and the remote control story, and she was laughing, and everything was OK. But I knew I was just putting things off. I wondered for a moment whether I could manage a third breakfast and a fourth cup of tea, just so that we could stay cosy, but I would have thrown it up again.

'So?'

I frowned at my plate, like someone would do if they were about to get something off their chest.

'I just . . . I don't know. I just freaked out.'

'But about what, sweetheart?'

'I don't know. A lot of stuff. Splitting up with Alicia. School. You and Dad.'

I knew that she'd focus on the last thing first.

'Me and your dad? But we divorced years ago.'

'Yeah. I dunno. It was like it suddenly sunk in.'

Any normal person would just laugh at this. But

in my experience, parents want to feel guilty. Or rather, if you make out that you've been scarred for life by something that they've done, they don't notice how stupid it sounds. They take it really, really seriously.

'I knew we should have done things differently.'

'Like what?'

'I wanted to see a family counsellor, but of course your dad thought that was bollocks.'

'Yeah. Well. Too late now,' I said.

'Ah, but that's the thing,' said Mum. 'It's not. I read this book about a guy who was tortured by the Japanese fifty years ago, and he couldn't come to terms with it, so he went to talk to someone. It's never too late.'

I wanted to laugh, for the first time in days, but I couldn't.

'Yeah. I know. But what you and Dad did . . . It messed me up, I suppose, but it wasn't like being tortured by the Japanese. Not really.'

'No, and it's not fifty years ago that we got divorced, either. So, you know.'

I didn't, but I just nodded.

'Oh, God,' she said. 'You hold this baby in your arms, and you look at him, and you think, I don't want to mess you up. And then what do you do? You mess him up. I can't believe what a – what a pig's ear I've made of everything.'

'Oh, it's OK,' I said. But not very, you know,

strongly. I wanted to show that I'd be able to forgive her one day, but not for another ten years or so.

'Will you come with me to talk to someone?'

'I don't know.'

'Why don't you know?'

'I don't know, you know . . . what I've got to say about it all now.'

'Of course you don't know. That's why we've got to go to family counselling. All sorts of things will come up that you might not know about. I'll make your father come too. He's not as narrow-minded as he was. Carol made him go and talk to someone when they couldn't have a baby. I'm going to do some research at work. The sooner the better.'

And she hugged me. I had been forgiven for running away from home because I couldn't handle my parents splitting up. So that was good. On the bad side, though: I was going to have to sit in a room talking to a stranger about feelings I didn't have, and I'm not very good at making things up. And also: my mum still had no idea why I'd gone to Hastings for a night, and I couldn't think of a way to tell her.

Mum wanted to go to work, and she made me promise that I wouldn't go anywhere. I didn't want to go anywhere. I wanted to sit at home watching *Judge Judy* and *Deal or No Deal* all day. But I knew I couldn't. I knew I had to go to Alicia's house and see what was up. I could have called her from our home phone, but something stopped me. I suppose it was the thought of her going off on one on the phone, and me just standing there with my mouth opening and closing. If I was standing in front of her, at least I'd feel like I was a person. On the phone I'd just be an opening and closing mouth.

My plan was to get the bus to Alicia's house, and hide in the bushes until I could see something that let me know one way or the other what was going on. There were two flaws in the plan, I discovered:

– no bushes;
– what actually was there to look at?

In my mind, I'd been away for a few months, so I thought that what I'd see would be Alicia walking along slowly with a swollen belly, or Alicia stopping somewhere to be sick. But the truth was that I'd only been away for a day and a half, and so when I did see her, she looked pretty much exactly like she did when we met in Starbucks to buy a home testing kit. I was confused by a lot of things. I was confused because I'd spent so much time thinking about Alicia being pregnant. But also, being whizzed into the future hadn't helped, either. I was living in three different time zones at once.

As there were no bushes, I had to make do with a lamp-post opposite her house. This wasn't much use as a lookout, because the only way I could properly hide was to put my back and head against it and keep still. So of course I couldn't see anything apart from the house in front of me, which was the house on the other side of the road from Alicia's house. What was I doing? It was eleven o'clock in the morning, and Alicia was probably at school. And if she wasn't at school she was inside a house I wasn't looking at. And if she came out of the house I wasn't looking at, then I couldn't see her anyway. And then Rabbit walked past with his board under his arm. I tried to hide from him, but he saw me, so that just made the hiding seem even more stupid.

'Who we hiding from?' he said.

'Oh. Hi, Rabbit.'

He dropped his board down beside the tree with a clatter.

'Do you want a hand?'

'A hand?'

'I've got nothing to do. I might as well help out. Shall I hide with you? Or find somewhere else?'

'Maybe somewhere else,' I said. 'There isn't really room for two behind a lamp-post.'

'Good point. Why are we hiding, anyway?'

'We don't want the people in that house there to see us.'

'Right. Cool. Why don't we just go home? They'll never see us there.'

'Why don't you go home, Rabbit?'

'You don't have to be like that. I know when I'm not wanted.'

If Rabbit knew when he wasn't wanted, he'd be living in Australia by now. But it wasn't his fault that I'd run away from my pregnant girlfriend and I didn't have the guts to knock on her door.

'I'm sorry, Rabbit. I just think I should do this on my own.'

'Yeah. You're right. I never really understood what we were up to anyway.'

And he went.

After Rabbit had gone, I changed my tactics. I moved round to the other side of the lamp-post and leaned against it that way. So I was pretty much staring through the window of her sitting room, and if anyone was in there and wanted to come out and talk to me, then they could. Nobody did. Phase Two of my mission was over, and I couldn't see how there could be a Phase Three, so I walked back to the bus stop. I spent the rest of the day watching *Judge Judy* and *Deal or No Deal*, and eating rubbish food which I paid for out of the money that was supposed to support me in my new life in Hastings. That was just one of the great things about coming home. I could spend the rest of my forty pounds in one day on crisps if I wanted to.

Just before Mum got home from work, I realized that I could have done something apart from lean on one side of the lamp-post and then the other side of the lamp-post. I could have knocked on Alicia's door, and asked whether she was pregnant, and how she was, and how her parents were. And then I could have got on with the next part of my life.

But I didn't want to do that yet. I had seen what the next part of my life looked like, when I was whizzed into the future, and I didn't like the look of it one bit. If I sat at home and watched TV, then the next part of my life would never come.

9

And for maybe two days, it worked, and I felt powerful. I could stop time! At first, I was careful: I didn't go out, didn't answer the phone, not that it ever rang much anyway. I told Mum I had picked up a bug from the crappy hotel and coughed a lot and she let me stay off school. I ate toast and messed around on YouTube and designed a new T-shirt for Tony Hawk. I hadn't spoken to him since I got back. I was a little scared of him now. I didn't want to go back to the place that he'd sent me the last time we talked.

On the third day, there was a knock at the door, and I answered it. Mum buys stuff off Amazon sometimes, and because there's nobody in, we had to go to the sorting office to collect it on Saturdays, so I thought I'd save us a trip.

But it wasn't the postman. It was Alicia.

'Hello,' she said. And then she started crying. I didn't do anything. I didn't say hello back, didn't ask her in, didn't touch her. I thought of the phone at the bottom of the sea, and how this was like all the phone messages and texts coming at once.

I woke up, finally. I pulled her indoors, made her sit down at the kitchen table, asked her if she wanted a cup of tea. She nodded, but she kept crying.

'I'm sorry,' I said.

'Do you hate me?'

'No,' I said. 'No. No way. Why should I hate you?'

'Where did you go?'

'Hastings.'

'Why wouldn't you call me?'

'Threw my phone in the sea.'

'Do you want to know the results of the pregnancy test?'

'I think I can guess.'

And even then, when I said it, with her crying and coming round to my house during the day and all the millions of other things that told me there was bad news, my heart started to beat faster. Because there was still a one in a trillion chance that she was going to say, 'I'll bet you can't,' or 'No, that's not it at all.' It wasn't all over yet. How was I to know that she wasn't upset about us splitting up, or her parents splitting up, or some new boyfriend being horrible to her? It could have been anything.

But she just nodded.

'Do your mum and dad want to kill me?'

'God, I haven't told them,' she said. 'I was hoping you'd do that with me.'

I didn't say anything. OK, so I'd only been in Hastings for one night, but nothing had happened while I was there at all, and that had been half the point of me going: so that things would happen. So that my mum could find out from Alicia's parents, and get upset. But then she'd get worried about me disappearing and forgive me. I wanted to go back to Hastings. I was wrong about the job with Mr Brady being just as bad as or even worse than having a baby. It wasn't. Having a baby was going to kill my mum and Alicia's mum and dad and probably me and Alicia, and there wasn't anything you could feel down the side of Mr Brady's bed that was going to do that much damage.

'What are you going to do?' I said.

She was quiet for a while.

'Can you do me a favour?' she said. 'When we talk about this, can you say "we"?'

I didn't understand, and I made a face to show her I didn't.

'You said, What are *you* going to do? And it should be, What are *we* going to do?'

'Oh. Yeah. Sorry.'

'Because . . . Well, I've been thinking about this. The splitting up doesn't matter, because it's your baby too, right?

'I suppose. If you say so.'

In just about every film or TV programme I've ever seen, the bloke says that at some point in these situations. I didn't even mean anything by it, really. I was just saying the lines you say.

'I knew you'd be like that,' she said.

'Like what?'

'I knew you'd try to wriggle out of it. Boys always do.'

'Boys always do? How many times have you been in this situation, then?'

'Fucking go and fuck yourself.'

'Fucking go and fuck yourself,' I said back, in a silly voice.

The kettle boiled. I took a long time getting mugs out and dunking teabags and pouring milk and throwing teabags away.

Before I go on with this conversation, I have to stop and say this: I'm eighteen years old now. I was just sixteen when this conversation happened. So it was only two years ago, but it feels more like ten years ago. It feels like that not just because a lot has happened since then, but also because the boy who was talking to Alicia that afternoon . . . he wasn't sixteen. He wasn't just two years younger than the person who's talking to you now. It feels now, and it even felt then, as though that boy was eight or nine years old. He felt sick, and he wanted to cry. His voice wobbled just about every time he tried to say anything. He wanted his mum, and he didn't want his mum to know.

'I'm sorry,' I said. Alicia had stopped crying for a bit, but now she was at it again, so I had to say something.

'Not a very good start, is it?'

I shook my head, but the word 'start' made me feel even worse. She was right, of course. This was a start. But I didn't want it to be a start. I wanted this to be the worst of it, and the end, and it wasn't going to be.

'I'm going to keep the baby,' she said.

I sort of knew that, because of the night and day I'd spent in the future, so it was funny to think this was news. To tell you the truth, I'd forgotten there was any choice.

'Oh,' I said. 'What happened to "we"?'

'How d'you mean?'

'You just told me I should be talking about what *we're* going to do. And now you're telling me what *you're* going to do.'

'It's different, isn't it?'

'Why?'

'Because while the baby's in here, it's my body. When it comes out, it's our baby.'

There was something that felt not quite right about what she was saying, but I couldn't put my finger on what it was.

'But what are we going to do with a baby?'

'What are we going to do with it? Look after it. What else can you do with it?'

'But . . .'

Later, cleverer people than me would come up with some arguments. But right then, I couldn't think of anything. It was her body, and she wanted the baby. And then, when we had the baby, we would look after it. There didn't seem like there was much else to say.

'When you going to tell your mum and dad?'

'We. When are we going to tell my mum and dad.'

We. I was going to sit there while Alicia told her mum and dad something that would make them want to kill me. Or maybe she was going to sit there while I told them something that would make them want to kill me. When I ran away to Hastings, I'd sort of worked out that things were going to be bad. I just hadn't worked out how bad.

'OK. We.'

'Some girls don't tell their parents for ages. Not until they have to,' she said. 'I've been reading stuff on the Net.'

'Sounds sensible,' I said. Wrong.

'You reckon?' And she made a snorting noise. 'Sounds sensible to you, because you just want to put it off.'

'No I don't.'

'What are you doing tonight?' she said.

'Tonight's no good,' I said, not too quickly, but not too slowly either.

'Why?'

'I said . . .' (What did I say? What did I say?) '. . . I'd go with . . .' (Who? Who? Who?) '. . . my mum to . . .' (Where? Where? Shit!) '. . . this work thing she's got on. Everyone always goes with someone, and she always goes on her own, so I told her ages ago . . .'

'Fine. Tomorrow night?'

'Tomorrow night?'

'You don't want to put it off, remember?'

Oh, but I did. I really did. I wanted to put it off for ever. I just knew I wasn't allowed to say so.

'Tomorrow night,' I said, and even the sound of the words coming out of my mouth made me want to go to the toilet. I couldn't imagine what my guts would feel like in twenty-four hours' time.

'Promise? You'll come round after school?'

'After school. Promise.'

Tomorrow night was hundreds of years away. Something would have changed by then.

'Are you going out with anyone?' Alicia said.

'No. God. No.'

'Me neither. That sort of makes things easier, doesn't it?'

'I suppose.'

'Listen,' said Alicia. 'I know you got sick of me . . .'

'No, no. It wasn't that,' I said. 'It was . . .' But I couldn't think of anything, so I stopped.

'Whatever,' she said. 'But I know you're OK. So if this had to happen with someone, I'm glad it was you.'

'Even though I ran away?'

'I didn't know you'd run away. I just knew you weren't at school.'

'I couldn't handle it,' I said.

'Yeah, well. Neither could I. Still can't.'

We drank our tea and tried to talk about other

things, and then she went home. When she'd gone, I puked into the kitchen sink. Too many breakfasts, I suppose. And even though I wasn't talking to TH, I suddenly heard his voice. 'I sat on the toilet while shakily holding a trash can in front of my face as my stomach contents blew out my nose and mouth with equally impressive force,' he said. Funny what you think of at times like that, isn't it?

I missed talking to TH, but what was happening in the present was bad enough, so I really didn't want to know anything that might happen to me in the future. Instead of chatting with him, I read his book again. Even though I'd read it a thousand times, there were still things in there that I'd forgotten. I'd forgotten how he asked Erin to marry him, for example, that thing with the coyotes and the flashlight. Maybe it wasn't so much that I'd forgotten it. Maybe it was more that I'd never found it that interesting before. It had never meant that much to me. His first marriage was just about bearable when I was fourteen or fifteen, because every now and again you meet someone you think about marrying. I was pretty sure I was going to marry Alicia for the first couple of weeks, for example. But you're not really thinking about second marriages when you're that age, in my opinion. Now, though, it was like my first marriage, which hadn't actually yet started, was over, and we had a kid, and it was all a mess. So reading about

TH and Erin was helpful, because TH had married Cindy and had Riley and they'd got over it. TH and Erin were the future. If I ever survived this mess, I'd never get married again, I was absolutely positive about that. But maybe there'd be something on the other side. Something to look forward to. Something like Erin, except not Erin, or any other woman or girl.

And this is why *Hawk – Occupation: Skate-boarder* is such a brilliant book. Whenever you pick it up, there's something in it that helps you with your life.

When Mum came back from work, she told me we were going straight out again, because someone at the council had put her in touch with a family counsellor, and because this counsellor was a friend of a friend we could jump the queue, and we had an appointment at 6.30.

'What about tea?' I said. It was the only thing I could think of, but even I could see it wouldn't be enough to get me out of going.

'Curry afterwards. The three of us can go out and talk.'

'The three of us? How do we even know we'll get on with this counsellor?'

'Not the counsellor, you muppet. Your dad. I persuaded him to drive down. Even he could see it was serious, you running away.'

Well, it couldn't really have been any more of a

disaster, could it? My whole family was going to see someone to talk about problems we didn't have. The problems we did have, though, they didn't know about, and they weren't going to find out about. It would be funny, if anything was ever going to be funny again.

The lady's name was Consuela, which was enough to put my dad into a bad mood from the very first minute. I don't know if you could call Dad a racist, because I've never heard him say anything bad about black people or Muslims or Asians. But he hates pretty much anyone from Europe. He hates the French, the Spanish, the Portuguese and the Italians . . . For some reason, he hates anyone who comes from somewhere you might want to go on holiday. He has been to all these places on holiday. He always says that he didn't start it, and that they hated him first, but I went on one or two of those holidays with him, and that's not true. Each time he got off the plane and started sulking. We've all tried talking to him about it, but we never get anywhere. It's his loss, anyway. Last year he went to Bulgaria, but that wasn't any better, he said. The truth is that he hates going abroad, so it's a good thing that Africa and other places where black people live are so far away, otherwise he'd be a proper racist, and we'd all have to stop talking to him.

We couldn't even pretend that Consuela wasn't Spanish, because she had a Spanish accent. Every time she said 'yust' instead of 'just' or something like that, you could almost see the steam coming out of Dad's ears.

'So,' she said. 'Sam. You ran from home, is that right?'

'Ran away,' my dad said.

'Thank you,' said Consuela. 'I occasionally makes mistakes with my English. I'm from Madrid.'

'I'd never have guessed,' said Dad, all sarcastic.

'Thank you,' said Consuela.

'So,' she said. 'Sam. Can you explain why you ran?'

'Yeah, well,' I said. 'I was telling Mum. School was getting on top of me, and then I, I dunno. I just started to feel bad about Mum and Dad splitting up.'

'And when did they split up?'

'Only about ten years ago,' said Dad. 'So it's early days yet.'

'Yes, go on,' said Mum. 'A little bit of gentle piss-taking will help.'

'He doesn't give a monkey's about us splitting up any more,' said Dad. 'It wasn't because of us he buggered off to Hastings. Something's going on that he's not telling us about. He's pinched something. He's been taking drugs. Something.'

He was right, of course. But he was being right in a really, really annoying way. He was presuming that I was telling lies about something because he's

168

a bad-tempered bastard who always thinks the worst of everyone.

'So what do you think that is, Dave?' said Consuela.

'I dunno. Ask him.'

'I'm asking you.'

'What's the point of asking me? I don't know what he's been up to.'

'We're asking you because these sessions give everyone a chance for saying their minds,' said Consuela.

'Oh, I get it,' said Dad. 'We've all decided it's all my fault already.'

'When did she say that?' said Mum. 'You see? This is what he's like. You can't talk to him. No wonder Sam ran off.'

'So it is my fault,' said Dad.

'Can I say something?' I said. 'Is that allowed?'

Everyone shut up and looked guilty. All this was supposed to be about me, and nobody was paying me any attention. The only problem was I didn't really have anything useful to say. The only thing worth saying was that Alicia was pregnant, and this wasn't the time or the place.

'Oh, never mind,' I said. 'What's the point?' And then I folded my arms and looked at my shoes, like I was never going to speak again.

'Is that your feeling?' said Consuela. 'That there's no point in saying anything?'

'Yes,' I said.

'He doesn't feel like that at home,' said Mum. 'Just here.'

'Except that his feelings about your divorce and so on are a bit surprising to you. So maybe he doesn't talk so much at home than you think.'

'How does someone Spanish end up working for the council anyway?' said my dad. If he'd been listening to what she'd actually been saying, instead of the mistakes in her English, he could have had a go at Mum back. Consuela had just pointed out that Mum didn't seem to know much about me. But that's Dad all over. Sometimes I wonder what life would have been like if I'd gone off to Barnet to live with Dad instead of Mum. Would I have ended up hating Spanish people like him? I probably wouldn't have been a skater, because there isn't as much concrete where he lives. And he wouldn't have been interested in me drawing all the time. So I probably would have been worse off. On the other hand, I'd never have met Alicia. Not meeting Alicia would have been good. Not meeting Alicia beat everything.

'Is a problem for you that I'm Spanish?'

'No, no,' said my dad. 'I was just wondering.'

'I marry-ed an Englishman a long time ago. I have been living here since many, many years.'

Dad made a face at me without her noticing, and I nearly laughed. It was a brilliant face, really, because it was a face that said, Well, why is her

English so bloody useless, then? And that's a hard face to make.

'But please. Sam has many problems, it sounds. We need to talk about them in the time we have.'

Many, many problems.

'Sam, also you said school is a problem.'

'Yeah.'

'Can you explain?'

'Not really.' And I stared at my shoes again. It was going to be much easier than I thought, wasting this hour.

Afterwards, the three of us had to go out and eat and talk some more. We went for a curry, and when they'd brought the popadums my mum started up again.

'Did you find that helpful?'

'Yeah,' I said. And that was true, sort of. If there had been any problems with school or Mum and Dad splitting up, that would have been exactly the right sort of place to talk about it all. The trouble was, I didn't have any problems like that, but I couldn't blame Consuela for that, and neither could anyone else.

'What about Alicia?' said my mum.

'Who's Alicia?' said my dad.

'This girl Sam was seeing. She was pretty much your first serious girlfriend, I'd say. Isn't that right?'

'S'pose.'

'But you're not with her now?' Dad asked.

'Nah.'

'Why not?'

'Dunno. Just . . .'

'So there's nothing in the timing?' said Mum.

'What timing?'

'First you split up with Alicia and then you take off to Hastings.'

'Nah.'

'Really?'

'Well, you know.'

'Ah! Finally!' said my dad. And then he had a go at my mum again. 'See, why didn't you bring that up in there?'

'He hasn't said it was anything to do with anything.'

'He did! He just said, "Well, you know"! That's as close as he ever comes to saying anything! In Sam language, what he just said was, That girl really screwed me up and I couldn't handle it and I cleared off.'

'Is that what you just said?' my mum asked. 'Is that what "Well, you know" means in Sam language?'

'Yeah, I suppose.'

I didn't feel like I was lying. At least we were talking about the person who mattered, as opposed to things that didn't matter, like school and their divorce. So I felt a kind of relief. And she had screwed me up, Alicia, sort of, in a way. And I definitely couldn't handle it.

'What good was running off going to do you?' said my dad. Which was a fair question, really.

'I didn't want to live in London any more.'

'So you went to Hastings for good?' said my mum.

'Well. Not really. Cos I came back. But, yeah, I thought I was going for good.'

'You can't leave town every time someone dumps you,' said my dad. 'You've got a lifetime of this stuff. You'd be living in a lot of different towns.'

'I feel bad because I introduced them,' said Mum. 'I didn't think it would cause all this trouble.'

'But how did you think it was going to help?' said Dad. 'Moving to Hastings?'

'I knew I wouldn't see her down there.'

'Is she local, then?'

'Where do you think she's from? New York? When do kids ever go out with someone who isn't local?' said Mum.

'I can't make head or tail of this,' said my dad. 'I'd understand if you'd knocked her up or something. But . . .'

'Oh, that's lovely,' said Mum. 'That teaches him responsibility, doesn't it?'

'I didn't say it would be the right thing, did I? I just said I'd understand. Like, that would be some kind of explanation.'

He was right again. It would be some kind of explanation. Maybe the best explanation.

'People do strange things when they've had their hearts broken. But you wouldn't know about that.'

'Oh, here we go again.'

'You weren't dying of a broken heart when we split up, were you? You didn't disappear off anywhere. Apart from to your girlfriend's.'

And they were off again.

Sometimes, listening to my mum and dad talking was like being a spectator in a stadium when people are running the 10,000 metres in the Olympics. They go round and round and round and round, and there's one bit each lap where they pass right in front of you, and you're really close to them. But then they disappear off round the bend and they're gone. When Dad started talking about me knocking Alicia up, it was like he'd jumped the perimeter fence and was coming straight for me. But then he got distracted and rejoined the race.

I went back to school the next day, but I didn't speak to anyone, didn't listen to anything, didn't pick up a pen the whole day. I just sat there, with things churning over and over in my head and in my stomach. Some things I thought were:

– I'm going back to Hastings.
– It didn't make any difference that I'd been to

Hastings before. I could go anywhere. Any seaside town.

– What is a good name for a baby? (And then a lot of baby names, like Bucky, Sandro, Rune, Pierre-Luc. I just basically went through a list of cool skaters in my head.) One thing I knew, and one thing I'd learned from the future: Roof was a rubbish name. Nothing would ever change my mind about that. You know how in *The Terminator* they're trying to protect the unborn baby who will one day go on to save the world? Well, my mission was to prevent my unborn baby from being called Roof.

– Will Alicia's mum and dad actually attempt to attack me? Physically? It wasn't only my fault.

– My mum. I didn't really have any thoughts or questions, so much. I just kept thinking of what she'd look like when I told her. When she said that thing about her heart breaking the night before, it made me sad, because I knew that I was going to break her heart too. That meant the whole of our family would have broken her heart.

– Did I have to go and watch the baby being born, because I was the dad? I didn't want to. I'd seen a baby being born on TV and it was terrible. Would Alicia make those noises? Could I ask her not to?

– What was I going to do to make some money? Would all our parents pay for everything?

– And when I got whizzed into the future, was

that really the future? Was I going to live with Alicia at her mum and dad's house? Was I going to share a bed with her?

None of it went anywhere, but I couldn't get rid of it either. It just stayed in there. I was like one of those guys who work at the funfairs – I hopped off one teacup, jumped on to the next one, spun that round and made people (in other words me) frightened, and moved on. At lunchtime I went up to the chip shop with some people from my class, but I didn't eat anything. I couldn't. It felt like I'd never eat anything again. Or not until Pierre-Luc was born, and Alicia had stopped making that noise.

As I walked out of school at the end of the day, I could see Alicia waiting for me on the other side of the road. I started to feel annoyed that she didn't trust me, but seeing as I'd disappeared on her once, you could hardly blame her. And anyway, she was pleased to see me, and she smiled, and I remembered why we'd gone out in the first place. All that seemed like a long time ago now, though. She looked older, for a start. Older and paler. She was pretty white.

'Hello,' she said.

'Hello. Are you OK?'

'Not really,' she said. 'I spent the morning throwing up, and I'm scared stiff.'

'Do you want to go and get something to drink first? Starbucks or somewhere?'

'I'd probably throw up again. I could drink some water. Water might be OK.'

You had to say that it was worse for her than it was for me. I was feeling scared sick, and so was she. I couldn't really pretend I was more scared than she was. In fact, seeing as I was even more afraid of telling my mum than of telling her mum and dad, then she was probably feeling the worst about what we were about to do. And on top of all that, she had baby sickness too. I could have gone to Starbucks and managed a caramel frappuccino, with cream on top, but I could see that if she tried to drink one of those it would come up again pretty quickly. When I thought about that, I didn't want one either.

We took the bus to hers and went straight up to her room, because nobody else was around yet. She sat in the armchair, and I ended up sitting between her feet. I hadn't been in her room since the future, and in the future it was different. (That sounds weird, doesn't it? It should be, 'In the future things *will be* different', shouldn't it? But if I say that, it means what I saw was definitely the future, and I'm not a hundred per cent about that. So I'm going to stick with talking about the future like it was the past.) Anyway, the Donnie Darko poster that wasn't there in the future was back, not that it had ever been away yet. I was pleased to see it.

'How do you know they're coming straight home?' I said.

'I asked them to. They know I haven't been happy, and I said I wanted to talk to them.'

She put on some sad, slow music that made my watch seem to stop. It was a woman singing about somebody who had left her, and she was remembering all these things about him like his smell and his shoes and what he had in his jacket pockets if you put your hand in there. There wasn't anything she didn't remember, it sounded like, and the song lasted for ever.

'Do you like this?' she said. 'I've been playing it a lot.'

'It's all right,' I said. 'Bit slow.'

'It's supposed to be slow. It's a slow song.'

And we went quiet again, and I started to think about living in this room with her and a baby, listening to slow, sad music. It wouldn't be so bad. There were worse things. I wouldn't be in here all the time, would I?

We heard the door slam underneath us, and I stood up.

'We'll stay up here until they're both home,' said Alicia. 'Otherwise I know what will happen. My mum will make us talk before my dad's home, and then we'll have to go through it all twice.'

My heart was banging away so hard that if I'd lifted up my T-shirt and had a look down the front I'd probably have been able to see my chest moving, like there was a little man trapped in there.

'What are you doing?' said Alicia.

What I was doing was, I was looking down my T-shirt to see if there was a little man trapped down there. I didn't really know what I was doing any more.

'Nothing,' I said.

'This is going to be hard,' she said, as if me looking down my T-shirt was going to make it harder.

'I won't look down there when we're telling them,' I said, and she laughed. It was nice to hear.

'Alicia?' her mum shouted.

'Ignore it,' Alicia whispered, as if I was going to come out of her bedroom and say something.

'Alicia? Are you up there?'

'She came in with someone about half an hour ago,' her dad shouted. He'd been in all the time, having a bath or reading in his bedroom or some thing.

She walked out of her room and I followed her.

'We're here,' she said.

'Who's we?' said her mum, all cheerful. And then, not so cheerful, as she saw us coming down the stairs, 'Oh. Sam. Hello.'

We sat round the kitchen table. There was a lot of messing around with tea and milk and sugar and biscuits, and I was beginning to wonder whether they'd guessed, and all the business with the kettle and so on was just a way of hanging on to their old life just a little bit longer. It was like me throwing my mobile into the sea. The longer someone's not telling you what you don't want to hear, the better. It wouldn't have been hard to guess, really. What could the two of us have wanted to say? We split up a while ago, so we weren't going to tell them we wanted to get married. And Alicia hadn't been anywhere, so we weren't going to tell them that we'd already run off somewhere and got married. What was there left?

'What's on your mind?' said Alicia's dad.

Alicia looked at me. I cleared my throat. Nobody said anything.

'I'm going to have a baby,' I said.

I don't think I need to tell you that I wasn't trying to be funny. It just came out wrong. I think it was because Alicia had given me that little lecture about how everything had to be 'we' from now on. I'd taken it too seriously. I knew the baby wasn't just hers, but now I'd overdone it, and made it so that the baby was just mine.

Whatever the reason, we couldn't have had a worse start. Because Alicia made a kind of snorting sound, which was her trying not to laugh. I'd said something stupid because I was nervous, and Alicia had wanted to laugh because she was nervous, but her dad didn't take any notice of our nerves. He just went nuts.

'You think this is FUNNY?' he shouted, and I realized that they had guessed. In films, and I think probably in life too, people go quiet when they hear bad news. Or they repeat the last word. You know, 'A *baby*?' But he didn't do that. He just started shouting. Alicia's mum wasn't shouting, though. She started crying and sort of slumped on the kitchen table with her arms over her head.

'And we're keeping it,' said Alicia. 'I'm not getting rid of it.'

'Don't be so ridiculous,' said her dad. 'You can't care for a baby at your age. Either of you.'

'Plenty of girls my age do,' said Alicia.

'Not girls like you,' said her dad. 'Usually they've got more sense.'

'Do you hate us?' said her mum suddenly. 'Is that what this is about?'

'Mum, you know I don't hate you,' said Alicia.

'I'm talking to him,' said her mother. And then, when I looked at her, all confused, she said, 'Yes. You.'

I just shook my head. I didn't know what else to do.

'Because this stops her getting away, doesn't it?'

I didn't know what she was talking about, really.

'How do you mean?' I said.

'How do you mean?' she said, in a stupid voice that I think was supposed to show I was thick.

'He's got nothing to do with it,' said Alicia. And

then, before her parents could say anything, she said, 'Well, something to do with it. But it was my decision to keep the baby. He didn't want to, I don't think. And also, I'd already got away. He didn't want to be with me.'

'How did this happen?' said her mum. 'I presumed you were having sex. I didn't think you were too stupid to use contraception.'

'We did use contraception,' said Alicia.

'So how did this happen?'

'We don't know.'

I knew, but I didn't really want to go into all that stuff about things half happening just at the wrong time. It didn't really matter now.

'And what makes you think you want a baby? You couldn't look after a goldfish.'

'That was years ago.'

'Yes. Three years ago. You were a kid then, and you're a kid now. God. I don't believe we're having this conversation.'

'What happened to the goldfish?' I said. But everyone ignored me. It was a stupid question. What happened to her goldfish was probably the same thing that happened to my goldfish, and everybody else's goldfish. You don't sell them, or have them adopted, do you? They all get flushed down the toilet in the end.

'What about your mother, Sam? What does she think?'

'She doesn't know yet.'

'Right. Let's go and talk to her. Now. All of us.'

'That's not fair, Mum,' said Alicia.

I didn't think it was fair either, but I couldn't think of a reason why it wasn't.

'Why is it "snot fair"?' said her mum. She put on another silly voice, this time one that was supposed to show that Alicia was a whiny little girl.

'Because we should have the chance to tell her without you being there. She's not here now, is she? When we told you?'

'Can I ask you something, Sam?' said Alicia's dad. He hadn't spoken for a while.

'Yeah. Course.'

'I remember your mother at the party where you met Alicia. She's very pretty, isn't she?'

'I dunno. S'pose, yeah.'

'Young and pretty.'

'Yeah.'

'How old is she?'

'She's . . . Well, yeah, she's thirty-two.'

'Thirty-two. So she was sixteen when you were born.'

I didn't say anything.

'Jesus Christ,' he said. 'Don't you people ever learn anything?'

They did come with us in the end. They calmed down, and Alicia's mum told her dad off for what he'd said, and he apologized. I knew I wasn't going to forget it, though. 'You people'. Which people? The people who have babies when they're sixteen? What kind of people are they? It was my idea that we all went together. I was afraid. It wasn't as if I thought my mum would do anything to me. I was just afraid of how miserable she was going to be. Of all the things she was afraid of, this was probably number one. It would be better, I thought, if she'd always been afraid of me getting hooked on drugs, and I turned up with a syringe sticking out of me. At least she could pull it out. It would be better if she'd always been afraid of me being decapitated, and I turned up with my head tucked under my arm. At least I'd be dead. So I was hoping that if the four of us turned up on the doorstep, she'd have to put a lid on it, at least until they'd gone. Oh, everything was in the short term. That was the only way I could think. If I went to Hastings, I could put things off for a day. If Alicia's mum and dad came with me to my house to tell my mum I'd made their daughter pregnant, it wouldn't be quite so terrible for an hour or so. I couldn't bear to think about the proper future, so I just tried to make things better for the next twenty minutes or so, over and over again.

I'd told Mum I was going out after school, so I had no idea whether she was going to be in or not. I'd told her I was going round to a friend's for tea, and I'd be back around eight. If she knew I wasn't coming back straight after school, she sometimes went out for a drink with someone from work, or went round someone's house for a cup of tea. I'd warned them, but Alicia's mum and dad said that seeing as it was a serious situation, they'd just come in and wait for her if she wasn't there.

Something made me ring on the doorbell, rather than just get out my key and let everybody in. I suppose I didn't think it was right to let Alicia's mum and dad in without warning Mum first. Anyway, there was no answer at first, but just as I'd got my keys out, Mum came to the door in her dressing gown.

She knew something had happened straight away. I think she probably knew what that something was, as well. Alicia, her mum, her dad, four unhappy faces . . . Put it this way, she probably wouldn't have needed three guesses. It had to be sex or drugs, didn't it?

'Oh. Hi. I was just in the middle of . . .'

But she couldn't think what she was in the middle of, which I took to be a bad sign. I suddenly got worried about the dressing gown. Why couldn't she tell us she was having a bath? If that was what she was doing? Having a bath is nothing to be ashamed of, is it?

'Anyway. Come in. Sit down. I'll just go and put something on. Put the kettle on, Sam. Unless you'd like something stronger? We've got some wine open,

I think. We don't usually, but . . . And there might be some beer. Have we got beer, Sam?'

She was babbling. She wanted to put it off too.

'I think we're fine, thanks, Annie,' said Alicia's mum. 'Please, can we say something before you get dressed?'

'I'd rather . . .'

'Alicia's pregnant. It's Sam's, of course. And she wants to keep it.'

My mum didn't say anything. She just looked at me for a long time, and then it was like her face was a piece of paper that someone was screwing up. There were these folds and lines and creases everywhere, in places where there was never usually anything. You know how you can always tell when a piece of paper has been screwed up, no matter how hard you try to smooth it out? Well, even as she was making that face, you could tell those creases would never go away, however happy she got. And then this terrible noise. I'd never see her if she ever found out I was dead, but I can't imagine the noise would be any different.

She stood there crying for a little while, and then Mark, her new boyfriend, came into the living room to see what was going on. So Mark explained the dressing gown. You didn't have to have any special powers to read the minds of Alicia's mum and dad. Their minds were easy to read, because they were written all over their faces and eyes. You people, I could hear her dad saying to me, even though he wasn't saying anything now, just looking. You people. Do you ever do anything else? Apart from have sex? And I wanted to kill Mum, which was a coincidence, because she wanted to kill me.

'Of all the things, Sam,' Mum said after what seemed like ages and ages. 'Of all the things you could do. All the ways you could hurt me.'

'I wasn't trying to hurt you,' I said. 'Really. I didn't want to get Alicia pregnant. It was the last thing I wanted to do.'

'Here's a good way of not getting someone pregnant,' said Mum. 'Don't have sex with them.'

I didn't say anything. I mean, you couldn't argue with that, could you? But her argument did mean that I could only have sex two or three times in my life, and not even that many times if I decided I didn't want kids. That decision wasn't mine to make any more, though. I was having kids whether I liked it or not. One kid, anyway, unless Alicia was having twins.

'I'm going to be a grandmother,' said Mum. 'I'm four years younger than Jennifer Aniston and I'm going to be a grandmother. I'm the same age as Cameron Diaz and I'm going to be a grandmother.'

Cameron Diaz was a new one. I hadn't heard her mention Cameron Diaz before.

'Yes,' said Alicia's father. 'Well. There is a great

deal about this whole thing that is unfortunate. But at the moment we're more worried about Alicia's future.'

'Not Sam's?' said my mum. 'Because he had a future too.'

I looked at her. Had? I *had* a future? Where was it now? I wanted her to tell me that everything was going to be all right. I wanted her to say that she'd survived, so I could too. But she wasn't telling me that. She was telling me that I didn't have a future any more.

'Of course. But we're more worried about Alicia because she's our daughter.'

That sounded fair enough to me. When Mum started howling, it wasn't because she was upset about Alicia.

'Alicia, love,' said my mum. 'You've only just found out, right?'

Alicia nodded.

'So you don't know what you think, yet, do you? You can't possibly know whether you want to keep it or not.'

'Oh, I know that,' said Alicia. 'I'm not killing my baby.'

'You're not killing a baby. You're . . .'

'I've been reading about it on the Internet. It's a baby.'

Alicia's mum sighed.

'I wondered where you'd been getting this stuff

from,' she said. 'Listen. The people who post things on the Internet about abortions, they're all evangelical Christians, and . . .'

'Doesn't matter what they are, does it? Facts are facts,' said Alicia.

The whole conversation was a mess. It was all over the place. Cameron Diaz, evangelical Christians . . . I didn't want to be listening to any of this stuff. I didn't know what I did want to listen to, though. What would have been better?

'I'd better be off,' Mark said. We'd all forgotten he was there, and we all looked at him as if we still weren't quite sure whether he was.

'Home,' said Mark.

'Yes,' said my mum. 'Course.' She waved at him half-heartedly, but he didn't have his shoes on, so he had to go back into Mum's bedroom.

'So where does all this leave us?' said Alicia's dad.

Nobody spoke for a while, apart from when Mark walked back through and said goodbye again. I didn't really understand how anyone could expect talking to leave us anywhere at all, apart from in the place we already were. Alicia was pregnant, and she wanted the baby. If things stayed like that, then you could talk until you were blue in the face and it wouldn't make any difference.

'I need to talk to my son in private,' said Mum.

'There isn't any private any more,' said Alicia's dad. 'Anything you have to say to him involves us. We're all family now.'

I could have told him that was a stupid thing to say. Mum went nuts.

'I'm sorry, but I'll be talking to my son in private for the rest of my life if that's what he and I want to do. And we're not family. Not now, and maybe not ever. Sam will always do what's right, and so will I, but if you think that allows you to come into my house and demand the right to hear my private conversations then you've got another think coming.'

Alicia's dad was about to have a go back, but Alicia stepped in.

'You're not going to believe this,' she said. 'But Dad's actually quite clever most of the time. He wasn't very clever just then, though. Dad, do you think you'll ever want to talk to me in private without Sam and his mum being around? Yes? Well, shut up, then. God. Honestly.'

And her dad looked at her, and then he smiled, sort of, and so did my mum, and it was all over.

The first thing Mum said when they'd all gone was, 'Do you think it's just bad luck? Or are we stupid?'

I was conceived because my mum and dad didn't use contraception. So what I wanted to say was, You were stupid, and I was unlucky. But I thought it was probably best not to. And anyway, I couldn't really tell whether I'd been stupid or not. Probably I had. One thing it doesn't say on the side of a condom packet is, WARNING! YOU MUST HAVE AN IQ OF A BILLION TO PUT THIS ON PROPERLY!

'Bit of both, I expect,' I said.

'It doesn't have to ruin your life,' she said.

'I ruined yours.'

'Temporarily.'

'Yeah. When I'm your age, everything will be OK.'

'Ish.'

'And then my baby will have a baby.'

'And I'll be a great-grandmother, age forty-eight.'

We were sort of being jokey with each other, but we weren't happy-jokey. We were both staring at the ceiling trying not to cry.

'Do you think she'll change her mind about having it?'

'I dunno,' I said. 'I don't think so.'

'You're not leaving school,' she said.

'I don't want to. Anyway, she's not having the baby until November or something. I can do my GCSEs at least.'

'Then what?'

'I don't know.'

I hadn't spent an awful lot of time thinking about what I was going to do with my life. I'd thought about college, and that was about it. And Alicia hadn't ever thought about her future, as far as I knew. Maybe that was the secret. Maybe people who had it all worked out . . . maybe they never got pregnant, or made anyone pregnant. Perhaps none of us, Mum and Dad and Alicia and I, had ever wanted the future badly enough. If Tony Blair knew that he wanted to be Prime Minister when he was my age, then I'll bet he was careful with his condoms.

'Your dad was right, wasn't he?'

'Yeah,' I said. I knew what she was talking about. She was talking about what had happened at Consuela's.

'That's why you went to Hastings?'

'Yeah. I was going to move there and never come back.'

'You did the right thing in the end, anyway.'

'I suppose.'

'Do you want me to tell him?'

'My dad? Would you?'

'Yeah. You owe me, though.'

'OK.'

I didn't mind owing her for that. There was no chance I'd ever be able to pay her back for everything else, so that was just a bit extra on top that she wouldn't even remember.

10

Here are some things that happened in the next few weeks.

– My mum told my dad, and he laughed. Really. OK, that wasn't the first thing he did. He called me a few names first, but you could tell he was doing it because he knew he was supposed to. And then he laughed, and then he said, 'Bloody hell, my grandchild's going to be able to watch me playing Sunday League. Had you thought of that?' And I was going to say, 'Yeah, that was the first thing me and Alicia said to each other,' but seeing as this was my dad, he'd probably have thought we were being serious. 'I'm really going to look after myself now,' he said. 'Forget about seeing me play. He can play with me. Two of our players are fifty. And we've got this really good fifteen-year-old keeper. So if your kid's any good, he could be playing alongside me. I'll only be forty-nine when he's fifteen. He might have to move to Barnet, though. And drink in the Queen's Head.' It was all stupid, but it was better than a bollocking. And then he said that he'd help us out if we needed help.

– They found out at school. I was in the toilets,

and this kid came up and asked me whether it was true, and I just made this stupid face while I tried to work out what to say, and then I said, 'I dunno.' And he said, 'Well, you should find out, man, because that's what she's telling people. My mate goes out with someone from her school, and everyone knows there.' And when I asked her about telling people, she said she'd told one person, and that person was dead as of that minute. Anyway, once this kid knew, everyone knew. So I went home and told Mum, and she called up the school, and we went in to talk to them. If I was asked to write down one word that described the reactions I got from the head and the teachers, that word would be 'interested'. Or maybe 'excited'. Nobody had a go at me. Maybe they thought that wasn't their job. Anyway, it turned out that the school had just introduced a strategy for teen pregnancies, but they had never had a chance to use it before, so they were pleased really. Their strategy was to tell me that I could still come to school if I wanted, and to ask me whether we had enough money. And then to ask me to fill out a form to tell them whether I was happy with their strategy.

– Alicia and I went to hospital for a scan, which is where you look at the baby on an X-ray machine and they tell you everything is normal, if you're lucky. They told us everything was normal. And also they asked whether we wanted to know the sex of the baby, and I said no and she said yes, and then I said I didn't care either way, really, and they told us it was a boy. And I wasn't really surprised.

– Alicia and I kissed, on the way back from the scan.

I suppose this last bit is headline news, really. I mean, you could say that everything was headline news, in a way. A year ago, if you'd told me that the teachers at school weren't too bothered about me making someone pregnant, I'd have said that there were about ten pieces of headline news in that one sentence. I'd have said it's one of those days when they have to make the news longer, and the programme on afterwards is late, and they say, 'And now, a little later than advertised . . .' But none of it seemed such a big deal now. Alicia and I kissing, though, that was something new. Or rather, it was new again, because there had been a time when it was old. (And before that, a time when it was new for the first time.) You know what I mean, anyway. It was a new development. And a good one too. If you were going to have a baby with someone, then it was better to be on kissing terms with them, on the whole.

It was different with Alicia now. It changed when she stuck up for me and my mum at our house. I could see that she wasn't just an evil girl who wanted to destroy my life. I hadn't even realized that I'd been thinking of her that way until she told her dad to back off, but a part of me must have been, because it was like she came out of a shadow, and I was like, She's not terrible! It was my fault just as much as it was hers! Probably more my fault! (A long time later, someone told me about something called a morning-after pill, which you can get from your doctor if you're worried that for example your condom might have come off. So if I'd owned up that night, the night that something half-happened and then half-happened again, none of this would have happened. So if you look at it that way, it was 150 per cent my fault and maybe 20 per cent hers.) And also, she was still very pretty. And also, her looking so ill made me want to look after her better. And also, everything was a bit of a drama, and I couldn't imagine spending any time with people who weren't on the stage with me.

And then when we came out of the hospital after the scan, she just put her hand in mine, and I was glad. It wasn't that I was in love with her or anything. But it's a weird thing, seeing your kid inside someone, and it needed some kind of, I don't know, celebration or something. And there aren't many ways you can celebrate when you're walking down a street near a hospital, so a bit of hand-holding was about as close as we could get to making sure the moment was something special.

'You OK?' she said.

'Yeah. You?'

'Yeah.'

'Good.'

'Is it all right if I do this?'

'What?'

And she squeezed my hand, to let me know what the what was.

'Oh. Yeah.'

And I squeezed her hand back. I'd never got back together with anyone before. Whenever I'd split up with anyone, I'd stayed split up, and I'd never really wanted to see them again. There was one couple at school who were always splitting up and getting back together, and I'd never understood it, but I could see it now. It was like coming back to your house when you'd been on holiday. Not that anything had been much of a holiday since we were last together. I'd been to a seaside town, but I hadn't had a lot of fun there.

'You got sick of me, didn't you?' she said.

'Didn't you get sick of me too?'

'Yeah. I suppose. A bit. We saw each other too much. Didn't see anyone else. I don't mean, you know, boys. Or girls. Just friends.'

'Yeah. Well, I know what. Let's have a baby. That's a good way of, you know, seeing less of each other,' I said.

She laughed.

'That's what my mum and dad said. I mean, not exactly that. But when they were trying to talk me into having an abortion, they said, You'll have to see Sam for the rest of your life. If he wants to stay in touch with his kid. I hadn't thought of that. If you are a proper father, I'll know you for ever.'

'Yeah.'

'How do you feel about that?'

'I dunno.' And after I'd said it, I did know. 'Actually, I like it. I like the idea of it.'

'Why?'

'I dunno.' And after I'd said it, I did know. Maybe I should never say anything, I thought. I should just listen to the questions and answer them on text or email when I got home. 'Well. It's because I've never thought of the future that much before. And I like knowing something about it. I don't know if I like the reason I'll know you for ever. The baby and all that. But even if we're only friends . . .'

'Do you think you might want to be more than friends?' And that's when I stopped and kissed her, and she kissed me back, and she cried a bit.

So on that day, two things happened that made what I'd seen that night when I got whizzed into the future more likely. We found out she was having a boy. And we got back together.

I wasn't stupid. The chances of staying together weren't that good, really. We were a long way from being grown-ups. My mum split from Dad when she was twenty-five, which means they were together for ten years or so, and I'd never managed ten months. Maybe not even ten weeks. What it felt like was, there was this big hump in the road coming up, e.g. the baby. And we needed a bit of a push to get us over that hump. And maybe getting back together would do it. The thing about humps in the road, though, is that you go up and then you come down again, and you can coast down the other side. Did I say I wasn't stupid? Ha! What I didn't know then was that there wasn't another side. You just have to keep pushing for ever. Or until you run out of steam.

We saw each other a lot, after the scan. We did homework round each other's houses, or watched TV with my mum or her mum and dad. But we never disappeared off upstairs to have any sex. When we went out before we had sex a lot. Alicia didn't feel like it. I felt like it sometimes, but I was serious about never having sex again, so even though some parts of me were interested, my head wasn't. Sex was bad news. Alicia said that you couldn't get pregnant while you were pregnant, which is why people are never three or four months older than their brothers or sisters, which I suppose I knew, really, if I'd thought about it. But she wasn't telling me that because she was trying to persuade me. She just read it to me out of a book. She was reading a lot of books about it all.

She wanted to find out more about . . . well, about everything, more or less. There wasn't much we knew about anything. So Alicia's mum arranged for us to go to classes called NCT classes, which stands for Something Childbirth Something. Alicia's mum said she'd found it very useful when she was pregnant. They were supposed to teach you how to breathe and what to take to the hospital and how to tell when you're actually having a baby and all that.

We met outside the place, which was one of those big old houses in Highbury New Park. I got there early because Alicia said I had to be there before her, because she didn't want to stand there on her own, but I didn't know when she was going to be there, so I got there forty-five minutes early to be on the safe side. I played the Tetris game that was on my new mobile phone until people started arriving, and then I watched them.

They were different from us. They all came in cars, and every single person was older than my mum. Or at least, they looked older, anyway. They didn't do themselves any favours with the way they dressed. Some of the men had suits on, I suppose because they had come after work, but the ones that didn't wore old combat trousers with cord jackets. The women all wore big hairy jumpers and puffa jackets. Lots of them had grey hair. They looked at me as if they thought I was going to sell them crack, or mug them. I was the one with the mobile phone. They didn't look worth mugging to me.

'I'm not going in there,' I said to Alicia when she turned up. You could see she was pregnant now, and she moved much more slowly than she used to. She'd still have beaten any of the other women in a race, though.

'Why not?'

'It's like a school staff room in there,' I said.

And then the moment I said that, one of the teachers from school turned up with her husband. She'd never taught me for anything, and I wasn't even sure what subject she was. I hadn't seen her around for ages. Languages, I thought. But I recognized her, and she recognized me, and I think she must have heard about me, because she looked surprised and then not surprised, like she suddenly remembered.

'Hello. Is it Dean?' she said.

'No,' I said. And I didn't say anything else.

'Oh,' she said, and walked through the gate.

'Who was that?' said Alicia.

'Teacher from school,' I said.

'Oh, Christ,' said Alicia. 'We don't have to go in. We could try somewhere else.'

'No, you're all right,' I said. 'Let's see how it goes.'

We walked through the front door and up the stairs, and then into this big room with a carpet and loads of beanbags. Nobody was talking much, but when we turned up they all went dead quiet.

We didn't say anything, either. We sat down on the floor and looked at the walls.

After a while a woman walked in. She was small and a bit fat and she had loads and loads of hair, so she looked like one of those little dogs that people put coats on. She noticed us straight away.

'Hello,' she said. 'Who are you with?'

'Her,' I said, and pointed at Alicia.

'Oh,' she said. 'Oh. Sorry. I thought you'd come . . . Anyway. That's great. Nice to see you.'

I blushed and didn't say anything. I wanted to die.

'We might as well all introduce ourselves,' she said. 'I'm Theresa. Terry.' And then she pointed at me, and I nearly but not quite said, 'Sam.' It probably sounded like 'Er'. Or maybe 'Um'. Alicia was next to get the pointed finger, and she took the piss, and talked like she was on *Balamory* or something.

'Hello, everyone. I'm Alicia,' she said, in a sing-song voice. Nobody laughed. It seemed to me that we needed a lot of classes about other things before we needed pregnancy classes. We need a class about how to behave when you went to a pregnancy class, for a start. Neither of us had ever sat in a room full of a load of adults we didn't know. Even walking into the room and sitting down felt weird. What were you supposed to do when everyone went quiet and stared at you?

When everyone had said their names, Terry divided us up into groups: boys and girls. Men and women, whatever. We were given a big piece of cardboard, and we were told to talk about what we expected from fatherhood, and someone was supposed to write the things we said down with a marker pen.

'OK,' said one of the men in a suit. And then he held the marker pen out to me. 'Do you want to do the honours?'

He was probably only trying to be nice, but I wasn't having that. I'm not the best speller in the world, I wasn't having them all laughing at me.

I shook my head and looked at the wall again. There was a poster of a naked pregnant woman in the place I was staring at, so then I had to look at another bit of wall, otherwise they would all have thought that I was staring at her boobs, and I wasn't.

'So. What do we expect from fatherhood? I'm Giles, by the way,' said the man in the suit. I recognized him then. It was the man I met when I was out on my walk with Roof, when I got whizzed into the future. He looked different with a suit on. I felt a bit sad for him. Here, he was all excited and happy. Judging from the state of him when I met him, it was all going to go wrong. I looked over at the women and tried to guess which one was his wife. There was one who seemed nervous and neurotic. She was talking a lot and chewing her hair. I decided it was her.

After a little while all these words started flying out of the men.

'Satisfaction.'

'No sleep!' ('Ha ha.' 'Too right.')

'Love.'

'A challenge.'

'Anxiety.'

'Poverty!' ('Ha ha.' 'Too right.')

'Focus.'

And loads of other words. I didn't understand a single thing anyone said. When we'd finished, Giles handed the big piece of cardboard back to Terry, and she started reading the words out, and they all started talking about them. I got distracted by the marker pen. I know I shouldn't have done it, and I don't know why I did, but it was just lying there on the carpet, and everyone was distracted by the conversation, so I put it in my pocket. Afterwards, I found out that Alicia had swiped hers too.

'We're never going back there,' I said to Alicia afterwards.

'You don't have to persuade me,' she said. 'They were all so old. I mean, I know we're young. But some of them had grey hair.'

'Why did she send us there?'

'She said we'd meet nice people. She said she'd met lots of friends there, and they used to go to Starbucks together with their babies. Except I don't think they had Starbucks then. Coffee, anyway.'

'I'm not going to Starbucks with teachers. Or any of those people.'

'We'll have to go to classes where there are people like us. Teenagers,' said Alicia.

I thought about that girl I'd gone out with once, who said she wanted a baby soon, and wondered whether she'd be in a class like that.

'The trouble is,' I said, 'the people in that sort of class . . . They'd be stupid, wouldn't they?'

Alicia looked at me and laughed, except it was the sort of laugh you do when something's not funny.

'And how clever are we, do you think?'

When I got back home after that class, Mum was sitting watching TV with Mark. He spent a lot of time at ours now, so I wasn't surprised to see him or anything, but when I came in, Mum got up and switched off the TV and said that she had something she wanted to talk about with me. I knew what it was, of course. I'd been doing some sums. If I really had seen the future that night, then I reckoned TH had whizzed me forward a year. So there could only be five or six months between Alicia's baby and Mum's baby. Roof had been four months old in the future, and Mum had looked big to me, so perhaps she'd been eight months pregnant. Which meant that her baby would be born when Roof was five months old. And Alicia was five months pregnant now, so . . .

'Do you want to talk in private?' said Mark.

'No, no,' said Mum. 'We'll have plenty of time on our own to talk things through. Sam, you know Mark and I have been seeing a lot of each other.'

'You're pregnant too,' I said.

Mum looked shocked, and then she burst out laughing.

'Where did that come from?'

I didn't think there was any point in trying to explain, so I just shook my head.

'Is that what you're worried about?'

'No. Not worried. Just . . . At the moment, when people have news, that seems to be what it is.'

'I've just thought,' said Mum, 'if I had another baby, then he or she would be younger than yours. My child would be younger than my grandchild.' And she and Mark laughed.

'Anyway. No,' she said. 'That's not the news. The news is, how would you feel if Mark moved in. Well, that was a question, not news. We're not telling you he's moving in. We're asking. How would you feel if Mark moved in? Question mark?'

'And if it's a problem for you we'll forget about it,' said Mark.

'But he's been spending a lot of time here, and . . .'

I didn't know what to say. I didn't know Mark, and I didn't particularly want to share a house with him, but I wasn't sure I was going to be living there for much longer anyway. Not if the future was right.

'Fine,' I said.

'You must think more than that,' said Mum. And of course she was right, I did. I thought a lot of things. For example:

– Why would I want to live with someone I don't know?

– And so on.

In other words, I had one big question and a lot of smaller questions involving televisions, bathrooms and dressing gowns, if you understand what I mean by dressing gowns. And his kid. I didn't want to get stuck with him.

'I don't want to get stuck with his kid,' I said.

'Sam!'

'You asked me what I was thinking. That was what I was thinking.'

'Fair enough,' said Mark.

'It sounded rude, though,' said my mum.

'I just meant that I'm going to have enough babysitting on my plate,' I said.

'It's not babysitting if it's your baby,' she said. 'That's just called "being a parent".'

'He lives with his mum,' said Mark. 'You won't have to look after him.'

'OK, then. Fine.'

'So you're saying it's all right as long as you don't have to put yourself out,' said Mum.

'Yeah. More or less.'

I didn't see why I should have to put myself out. It wasn't my idea, him coming to live with us. The truth was, he was going to move in whatever I said, I could tell. And anyway, if it wasn't him there'd be somebody else, one day. And that might be worse, because we could end up going to live with him and, I don't know, his three kids and his Rottweiler.

Listen. I've got no problem with people getting divorced. If you can't stand someone, then you shouldn't have to be married to them. It's obvious. And I wouldn't have wanted to grow up with my mum and dad arguing all the time. To be honest, I wouldn't have wanted to grow up with my dad full stop. But the trouble is that divorce leaves you open to stuff like this. It's like going out in the rain with only a T-shirt on, isn't it? You increase the chances of catching something. The moment your dad's out of the house, then there's a possibility of someone else's dad moving in. And then things can start getting weird. There was this kid at school who didn't hardly know anyone he lived with. His dad moved out, some other bloke with two daughters moved in, his mum didn't get on with the two daughters. She met someone else, moved out, didn't take her son with her, and this kid found himself stuck with three people he hadn't

even met a year before. He didn't seem that bothered, but I wouldn't have liked it much. Home is
supposed to be home, isn't it? A place where you
know people.

And then I remembered that, according to the
future, I was going to end up living with a lot of
people I didn't know.

11

I didn't call Alicia's dad Mr Burns any more. I called him Robert, which was better, because every time I said Mr Burns I thought of an ancient bald bloke who owned the Springfield nuclear reactor. And I didn't call Alicia's mum Mrs Burns, either. I called her Andrea. We were on first-name terms.

They had obviously decided that they were going to Make An Effort with me. Making An Effort meant asking me how I was feeling about every-thing every couple of days, and what was worrying me. Making An Effort meant laughing for an hour if I said something that wasn't absolutely deadly serious. And Making An Effort meant Talking About The Future.

They started Making An Effort around the time they stopped trying to talk Alicia into having an abortion. They tried talking to both of us, and they tried talking to me, and they tried talking to her. All of it was a waste of time. She wanted the baby. She said it was the only thing she'd ever wanted, which made no sense to me, but at least it made her sound serious. And every time Robert and Andrea tried talking to me, I said, 'I see what you mean. But she won't do it.' And then it got to the stage where you could see the bump, which was close to when you weren't allowed to have an abortion any more, and they gave up.

I knew what they thought of me. They thought I was some hoodie chav who'd messed up their daughter's future, and they sort of hated me for it. I know it sounds funny, but I could understand that. I mean, I certainly hadn't helped, had I? And the hoodie chav bit, that was just their ignorance. The important bit was that their plans for Alicia had gone up in smoke. I don't really think they had any actual plans, to be honest, but whatever plans they had didn't involve a baby. People like them didn't have a pregnant daughter, and they couldn't get their heads around it, you could see that. But they were trying, and part of the trying was trying to treat me like part of the family. That was why they asked me to live with them.

I was round there for supper, and Alicia was going on about this book she was reading about how a baby could learn ten languages if you taught it early enough. And Andrea wasn't really listening, and then she said, 'Where are you going to live when the baby's born?'

And we looked at each other. We'd already decided. We just hadn't told them.

'Here,' said Alicia.

'Here.'

'Yeah.'

'Both of you?' said Robert.

'Which both?' said Alicia. 'Me and Sam? Or me and the baby?'

'All three of you, then.'

'Yeah.'

'Wow,' said Andrea. 'Right. OK.'

'What did you think was going to happen?' said Alicia.

'I thought you'd be living here with us, and Sam would come and visit,' said Andrea.

'We're together,' said Alicia. 'So if we don't live here, we'll have to live somewhere else.'

'No, no, darling, of course Sam's welcome here.'

'Sounds like it.'

'He is. Really. But you're very young to be living as man and wife under your parents' roof.'

When she put it like that, Alicia's idea sounded completely insane. Man and wife? Man? Wife? I was going to be a man? And Alicia was going to be my wife? I don't know if you ever play word association games, like where someone says 'fish' and you say 'chips', or 'sea', or 'finger'. But if someone said to me 'man', I would have said things like 'beer', or 'suit', or 'shave'. I didn't wear a suit or shave, although I had drunk beer. And now I was going to have a wife.

'Don't be melodramatic, Andrea,' said Robert. 'She means that she'll be sharing a room with Sam and the baby. At least for the time being.'

That didn't sound much better, really. I had never shared a room with anyone since I was nine, when I used to go on sleepovers. I stopped because I could never get to sleep with someone else fidgeting in the next bed. This was all beginning to sound real. Real and terrible.

'Maybe you should see how it goes with Sam living up the road,' said Andrea.

'If you want me to be unhappy we could do that,' said Alicia.

'Oh, for God's sake,' said Robert. 'Not everything we say or do is calculated to destroy your life, you know. Sometimes, just very occasionally, we try and think about what's best for you.'

'Very occasionally,' said Alicia. 'Very, very occasionally.'

'I was being sarcastic.'

'And I wasn't.'

'Do you know, Sam, how terrible it is sharing a bedroom with somebody?'

Robert looked at her.

'Sorry, but it's the truth,' said Andrea. 'The lack of sleep. The farting and snoring.'

'I don't fart or snore,' said Alicia.

'You don't know what you do,' said Andrea. 'Because you've never shared a bed with anybody. And you don't know what a baby will do to you.'

'No one's stopping you from moving out,' said Robert.

'You think I haven't thought of it?' said Andrea.

'Well, this is a good example, I must say,' said Andrea. 'Welcome. Sam. Come and join our happy family.'

If I had been Robert or Andrea, I would have said, Don't you see? This is what it's like? Man and wife? Let Sam stay with his mum! He can see the baby all day every day! But they didn't say that. They must have thought it, but they didn't say it, however much I wanted them to.

I needed my skateboard.

When I got home that night, I went straight to my room to pick up my board. I hadn't used it since my trip to Hastings. It was leaning on the wall underneath my poster of TH, and I could tell that he was disappointed in me.

'I've had a lot on my plate,' I said.

'I didn't want the responsibility of including someone so closely in my life and have her involved on all different levels,' said Tony. I didn't want to get involved in a conversation, so I just picked up the board and ran.

Rubbish was down at the Bowl, on his own, doing a few tricks. I hadn't seen him since I'd found out about Alicia, but he didn't ask where I'd been, because he knew. He knew about the baby, anyway. Nobody had ever talked about me before, as far as I knew, because what was there to talk about? I'd never done anything. People found out stuff about me because I told them, not because they were telling each other. Now everybody knew my business, and it was weird.

'How's it going?' he said. Rubbish was practising his rock 'n' rolls. He hadn't got any better.

'Yeah, well. You know.'

I was doing a 5–0 grind in the Bowl, pretending I was concentrating on it more than I was.

'You're screwed, aren't you?'

'Thanks.'

'Sorry. But you are.'

'Thanks again.'

'Sorry. But . . .'

'You weren't going to tell me I'm screwed for a third time, were you?'

'So explain why you're not.'

'I can't explain why I'm not. Because I am.'

'Oh,' he said. 'Sorry. Again. I've just realized.'

'What?'

'I don't know. When somebody tells a kid our age that he's screwed, he's usually not, is he? Not really. I mean, maybe it will end up with him getting a slap. Or a bollocking from a teacher. But it isn't going to ruin their life, is it? Something little happens and it's over. But you becoming a father . . . That's serious, isn't it? I mean, you really are . . .'

'Don't say it again. Really. Otherwise you're screwed. Old-school. In other words, I'll have to give you a slap.'

I never hit anyone, but he was doing my head in.

'Sorry. I mean, sorry I nearly said it again. And I'm sorry for all that's happened.'

'Why, was it your fault? Was it actually you that got Alicia pregnant?'

I was joking, but because I'd just offered to give him a slap he looked worried.

'I've never even met her. I just meant, you know. Bad luck.'

'Yeah. Well.'

'What are you going to do?'

'About what?'

'I dunno. About anything.'

'I haven't got a clue.'

I was enjoying the feeling of the decks mashing against the concrete, mostly because I knew what I was doing. It was the first time I'd known what I was doing for ages. Rubbish was rubbish at grinds and rock 'n' rolls and pretty much everything, but I still wanted to be him. I wished that skate tricks were all I had to worry about. I used to be like Rubbish, except I could do the tricks. From where I was standing, that looked like the perfect life. I'd had the perfect life, and I hadn't realized it, and now it was over.

'Rubbish,' I said.

He ignored me. The trouble with being called Rubbish is you don't always know when someone's talking to you.

'Rubbish. Listen to me.'

'Yeah.'

'Your life is perfect. Did you know that?'

Right at that second, he bailed. He smashed his knees right into the concrete bench, came off the board, and lay on the ground swearing and trying not to cry.

'Did you know that?' I said again. 'Perfect. I'd give anything to be you right at this second.'

He looked at me to see if I was laughing at him, but I wasn't. I meant it. I'd slammed too. I'd never had a slam like this, though. The wheels had come off the trucks, the trucks had come off the deck, and I'd shot five metres into the air and gone straight into a brick wall. That's what it felt like, anyway. And there wasn't even a mark on me.

'Andrea called,' Mum said later. I stared at her.

'Alicia's mum,' she said.

'Oh. Yeah.'

'She said you and Alicia are planning to live together at her house when the baby's born.'

I looked at my shoes. I hadn't ever properly noticed that the holes for the laces were red round the outside.

'You didn't want to talk to me about this?'

'Yeah. I was going to.'

'When?'

'Today. Now. If you hadn't got in first. You beat me to it by ten seconds.'

'You think this is all a joke?'

It's true I was joking about when I was going to tell her. But the point of my joke was that nothing was funny, really, and I was trying to be brave. I was taking everything so seriously that making a joke seemed like the nearest I could get to being a hero. I thought she'd see that, and love me for it.

'No,' I said. 'Sorry.' There was no point in explaining it all. She wasn't going to think I was being heroic.

'Do you want to live at Alicia's house?'

'It's gone past what I want, hasn't it?'

'No,' she said. 'You mustn't think that. You're a kid. You've got your whole life in front of you.'

'Is that what you felt when you got pregnant?'

'No. Course not. But . . .'

'But what?'

'Nothing.'

'But what?'

'Well. I didn't have a choice, did I? I was carrying you around with me. I couldn't escape.'

'You mean blokes can get out of it?'

I couldn't believe what I was hearing. My mum! Telling me I should run!

'I'm not saying you can get out of it. I'm not

suggesting that you run away to Hastings. That would be pathetic.'

'Thanks.'

'You can't have it both ways. You can't go all high and mighty about blokes not getting out of it five minutes after you tried to do exactly that.'

There wasn't much I could say.

'I'm saying, you know, go there every day. Look after your kid. Be a father to him. Just . . . don't live in Alicia's bedroom.'

'She wants me to. And there's a lot of getting up in the night and burping and all that, isn't there? Why should she have to do that on her own?'

'Has she seen your bedroom? You can't hardly live with yourself, let alone someone else. You going to throw your dirty underwear all over her floor? Have you thought about all of that?'

I hadn't thought of any of it. And there wasn't any point anyway.

I talked to TH again last thing that night.

'What am I going to do?' I said. 'Don't go on about your life. I'm fed up of hearing about your life. Tell me about my life. Say, "Sam, this is what you've got to do about Alicia and the baby," and then just give me some answers.'

'Riley demanded a change in our lifestyles, and Cindy and I figured out a way to make it all work,' he said.

Riley was his son. I wasn't interested in his son.

'What did I just tell you?' I said. 'It's no use to me, all that business about Riley. I'm not a world-famous skater. You're not listening to me.'

'How the park locals stopped themselves from beating me up I'll never know. I could be the biggest idiot without realizing it.'

We'd been here before. I realized he said this when he was frustrated with me, when he thought I was being an idiot. And when he was frustrated, he whizzed me.

I went to bed. But I didn't know when I was going to wake up.

12

Mum woke me by banging on my bedroom door. I knew I was in trouble when I started looking around for something to wear. I picked my jeans up off the floor and then went to get a shirt out of my wardrobe and found a load of stuff I hadn't seen before – Hawk cargo pants and a couple of cool Hawk T-shirts that I'd wanted for a while – that one with the hawk emblem, and the other one with the Hawk logo in flames. I knew it was the future straight away. And the first thing I noticed about the future was that I wasn't living at Alicia's place. I put on the burning hawk T-shirt and went out into the kitchen.

Mark was there with a baby. It looked like a girl. And she wasn't a tiny baby. She was sitting up in a baby seat and eating what looked like mashed-up Weetabix with a spoon.

'Here he is,' said Mark. 'Here's your big brother.'

I was prepared. I knew who she was, and where I was, and everything like that. I'd been in the future before. But when Mark said that, I felt quite emotional. I was a big brother. She was my little sister. I'd been an only child all my life, and suddenly there was this new person. And she liked me too. She started smiling and then opened her arms like she wanted me to pick her up. I went over to her.

'She hasn't finished yet,' said Mark.

He didn't know it was a big deal for me to meet my sister. He probably saw me last night and I probably saw her last night and for Mark this was just a tiny moment, one of a million tiny moments. Not for me, though. This wasn't a tiny moment at all.

It was different, meeting this baby. Meeting Roof had been a shock, in a lot of ways. I didn't know about being whizzed then, so that was a shock. And I didn't know for sure that Alicia was pregnant, so meeting your own son even before you were a hundred per cent that your girlfriend or even ex-girlfriend was going to have a baby . . . That would be a shock for anyone. Plus, I didn't know what I felt about having a son. Or rather, I did know how I felt, and how I felt was bad. But this baby wasn't my baby, she was my little sister, and nothing about her was going to make me feel sad or worried.

I wanted to know her name.

'Come on, dumpling. Eat up. Daddy's got to go to work.'

'Where's Mum?'

I suddenly remembered that kid at school who didn't know anyone he lived with. Maybe Mum had gone, and I lived with Mark and a baby whose name I didn't know.

'She's in bed. This one was up half the night.'

'Roof'. 'This one'. 'Dumpling'. Why didn't people ever call babies their real names?

'Is she all right?' I said.

'Yeah. Fine. Just a menace.'

'Can I feed her?'

Mark looked at me. I guessed that I didn't offer to do things like that very often.

'Course. You got time?'

I remembered now the thing I hated most about the future, apart from being scared that I'd never get back to my own time. In the future, you never knew what you were supposed to be doing when.

I shrugged.

'What you got on?'

I shrugged again.

'College? Roof?'

He was still called Roof, then. He seemed to be stuck with it.

'The usual,' I said.

'So you haven't got time.'

'Will I see her later?' I said.

'She'll be here,' said Mark. 'She lives here.'

'And so do I,' I said.

It was more of a question, really, but he didn't know that.

'You've woken up sharp,' said Mark. 'If you

already know where you live, there'll be no stopping you today.'

I smiled, to show I knew he was joking. There wasn't much else I knew.

Mum came into the kitchen in her dressing gown looking sleepy, and older, and fatter. I'm sorry if that sounds rude, but it's the truth. She walked over and kissed the baby on the top of her head. The baby didn't seem that bothered.

'Everything OK?'

'Yeah,' said Mark. 'Sam just offered to feed her.'

'Blimey,' said Mum. 'Are you broke again?'

I felt in my pockets. There was a note in there.

'No, I think I'm all right.'

'I was being sarcastic.'

'Oh.'

'Have you woken up daft?'

'Mark just said I'd woken up sharp.'

'I was being sarcastic too,' said Mark.

I hated being like this. It seemed to me that if TH was going to whizz me into the future, he should at least sit me down and tell me some things first. Like where I went to college, and what my sister's name was. Basic stuff. If you're sitting in a room with your sister and you don't know her name, you feel stupid, even if she is only a baby.

'That's your mobile,' said Mum.

I listened. All I could hear was a cow mooing.

'That's just a cow,' I said.

'Yeah, that was hilarious the first time,' said Mum.

I listened again. It really sounded like a cow. Except the mooing went, 'Moo moo, moo moo . . . Moo moo, moo moo . . .' Like a telephone. It wasn't a real cow, because what would a real cow be doing in my bedroom? I could see what had happened. What had happened was, I had downloaded a ringing tone that sounded like a cow, some time between the present and the future, for a laugh. I wasn't sure how funny it really was.

I found my phone in my jacket pocket.

'Hello?'

'It's Bee.'

'Oh. Hello, Bee.' I wasn't sure who Bee was, but it sounded a bit like Alicia. You couldn't be sure of anything, though, when you were in the future.

'Bee. Not Bee.'

'Bee not Bee? What does that mean?'

'It's Alicia. And I've got a cold. So I'm trying to say, you know, "It's Alicia," except I'm saying, "It's Bee," and it comes out as "It's Bee."'

'Me.'

'Yes. Bloody hell. Have you woken up stupid?'

'Yes.' It just seemed easier to admit it.

'Anyway. I know you were supposed to be going to college, but I'm really not well, and Mum and

Dad aren't around, and I was going to take him for his jab this morning. So can you do it?'

'Jab?'

'Yes. His thingy. Inoculation. Immunization. Injection.'

That sounded like a lot of stuff for a little kid.

'Anyway. Can you do it?'

'Me?'

'Yes. You. His father. We can't put it off again.'

'Where is it?'

'The health centre. Up the road.'

'OK.'

'Really? Thanks. I'll see you in a bit. He needs to get out somewhere. He's been up for hours and he's doing my head in.'

My mum had taken over the feeding now. The baby smiled and stretched out her arms to me again, but Mum told her she had to wait.

'How old are kids when they have their jab?'

'What jab?'

'I don't know.'

'Well, it depends what jab, doesn't it?'

'Does it?'

'Are you talking about Roof?'

'Yeah.'

'Alicia said she wanted to take him for his jab now. He should have had it months ago, but she wasn't sure.'

'So how old are they normally?'

I was trying to find out how old my son was. And also how old I was.

'Fifteen months?'

'Right.'

So Roof was a few months older than fifteen months. Fifteen months was a year and three months. He might be nearly two, or more than two, even. So I was eighteen. I was going to buy a paper on the way to Alicia's, so I could see the date, and then I'd know whether I could drink in a pub legally.

'I've got to take him this morning. Alicia's not well.'

'Do you want me and Emily to come with you?'

'Emily?'

'What, you want me to leave her here?'

'No, no. Just . . . Anyway,' I said. 'No. You're all right. I'll take him to the swings or something.'

Kids of nearly or just over two could go on swings, couldn't they? That's who those little swings were for, wasn't it? What else could a two-year-old do? I didn't have a clue.

'Mum. Is Roof good at talking? In your opinion?'

'He could talk for England.'

'That's what I thought.'

'Why? Has someone said something?'

'No, no. But . . .'

But I didn't know whether he could talk, or two-year-olds could talk, or anything. And I couldn't tell her that either.

'I'll see you later,' I said. 'See you, Emily.'

And I kissed my baby sister on the head. She cried when I left.

Alicia looked terrible. She was in a dressing gown, and her eyes were streaming, and her nose was red. It was quite good, really, because I was getting the impression that we weren't together any more, what with me living back at home and so on, and I was sad. Back in the present, we'd been getting on OK, and I was starting to fancy her again, just like I did when we first met. Her looking like this . . . It made the break-up easier.

'I've actually got a cold,' she said, and laughed. I looked at her. I didn't know what she was talking about.

'Maybe I caught it off you,' she said, and laughed again. I was worried that she'd had some kind of nervous breakdown.

'He's watching TV,' she said. 'I haven't had the energy to do anything else with him.'

I walked into the living room, and there was this little blond boy with long curly hair like a girl, watching some Australian people singing with a dinosaur. He turned round and saw me, then came running at me and I had to catch him or he would have smashed his face against the coffee table.

'Dadda!' he said, and I swear, my heart stopped beating for a couple of seconds. Dadda. It was all too much, meeting my sister and my son all on the same day. It would be too much for anybody. I'd met him before, last time I'd visited the future, but he wasn't much, then, and I'd hardly gone anywhere near him. He'd done my head in last time. He was doing my head in now, but in a good way.

I swung him round for a bit, and he laughed, and when I'd stopped swinging him I had a look at him.

'What?' said Alicia.

'Nothing. Just looking.'

He looked like his mum, I thought. Same eyes and mouth.

'I can have a ice cream if I'm a good boy.'

'Is that right?'

'After the doctor.'

'OK. And then we'll go on the swings.'

Roof started crying, and Alicia looked at me as if I was an idiot.

'You don't have to go on the swings,' she said.

'No,' I said. 'Not if you don't want to.'

I didn't have a clue what that was all about, but I could tell I'd made a mess of something.

'Did you just forget?' Alicia hissed at me.

'Yeah,' I said. 'Sorry.'

You really need to live your life, and not just zoom in and out of it. Otherwise you never know what's going on.

'Anyway. Just keep him for as long as you can. I feel terrible.'

We put Roof in the buggy to go to the health centre, except of course I couldn't do the straps up, so Alicia had to help me, but she didn't seem surprised at how useless I was. She asked me when I was going to learn how to do it. I was quite pleased to realize that I was usually useless, because then I didn't have to explain why I could do it one day and not the next. When we got out of the house, though, he started kicking up a fuss and trying to wriggle out. I knew he could walk, because I'd seen him run across the room when he jumped at me, so I fiddled around with the straps until something clicked, and let him run up the street. Then I realized he was going to charge straight into the road, so I had to catch him up and stop him. After that I made sure I was holding his hand.

My mum was right. He could have talked for Brazil, let alone England. Everything we passed, he said, 'Look at that, Dadda!' And half the time you couldn't see what the hell he was talking about. Sometimes it was a motorbike or a police car; sometimes it was a twig or an old Coke can. At first I tried to think of something to say about these things, but what is there to say about a Coke can? Nothing much.

There were loads of people in the health centre. A lot of the people in there were parents with sick-looking kids, kids with coughs, kids with a fever, kids who were just slumped over their mothers' shoulders. I was glad Roof wasn't sick like that. I'm not sure I could have handled it. I waited at the reception desk while Roof went off to look through a box of toys in the waiting area.

'Hello,' said the woman behind the desk.

'Hello,' I said. 'We've come for the inoculation and jab and immunization.'

The woman laughed. 'Probably just one of them today, eh?'

'If that's OK,' I said.

'Who's "we", anyway?'

'Oh,' I said. 'Sorry. Him.' I pointed at Roof.

'Right. And who's he?'

Oh, bloody hell, I thought. I don't really know my kid's name. I was sure I wasn't the best dad in the world, but the feeling I'd got from Alicia and Roof when I went to pick him up was that I wasn't the worst, either. Not knowing your kid's name, though . . . That wasn't good. Even the worst dad in the world knows his kid's name, which made me worse than the worst dad in the world.

If Roof was his name, then his initial was 'R'.

And his second name was either my second name or Alicia's second name. So it was either Jones or Burns.

'R. Jones,' I said.

She looked on a list, and then looked on a computer screen.

'Nothing here for that name,' I said.

'R. Burns,' I said.

'May I ask who you are?'

'I'm his dad,' I said.

'But you don't know his name?'

'Yeah,' I said. 'No.'

She looked at me. She obviously didn't think that was a good enough explanation.

'I forgot we used his mum's second name,' I said.

'First name?'

'I call him Roof,' I said.

'What does everyone else call him?'

'We all call him Roof.'

'What's his name?'

'I think I'd better come back tomorrow,' I said.

'Yeah,' said the woman. 'When you've got to know him a bit better. Spend a little quality time with him. Have a father–son bonding session. Ask him his name, stuff like that.'

On the way to the park, I asked Roof his name.

'Rufus,' he said.

Rufus. Of course it was. I wish I'd asked him on the way there, instead of on the way out. He didn't seem surprised that I'd asked. He just seemed pleased that he got the answer right. I suppose kids are always being asked stuff they already know.

I couldn't wait to find out how I'd ended up agreeing to call my kid Rufus. I still had my heart set on Bucky.

'Rufus,' I said. 'If Mummy asks whether the injection hurt, just tell her you were a brave boy, OK?'

'I was a brave boy,' he said.

'I know,' I said.

He still hasn't had that jab.

The reason Roof didn't like swings at the moment was that he'd been hit on the head by one, last time I took him to the park. I let him run in front of one, from the sound of it, and it had clonked him right on the nose. He told me all this as we were walking through the park gates. I felt terrible. He was such a beautiful little boy, and you'd think I could take better care of him than that.

I suppose that ever since I'd found out Alicia was pregnant, I'd only really worried about myself. I'd worried about how it was going to mess up my life, and what my mum and dad were going to say to me, and all that sort of thing. But I'd already had to stop Roof from running into the road, and

I'd seen all those sick kids at the health centre. And now I'd found out that he'd half knocked himself out in the park I wasn't old enough for all this worry, I didn't reckon. But then, who was? My mum worried all the time, and she was old enough. Being old enough didn't help. Maybe most people didn't have babies when they were my age because then there'd be one small part of their lives when they could worry about other things, like jobs and girlfriends and football results.

We played in the sandpit for a little while, and then he went down the slide a few times, and then he had a ride on one of those wooden horses that have a big spring coming out of the bottom of them so you can wobble around. I could remember sitting on them when I was a kid. I was pretty sure I could remember sitting on this one. I hadn't been in this park for about five years, but I didn't think anything had changed since I used to play in it.

I had twenty quid in my pocket. Roof had his ice cream, so then I had nineteen quid, and then we walked all the way from Clissold Park to Upper Street, just for something to do. And then he wanted to go in this toyshop, and I thought, Well, we can just look, can't we? And then he wanted this helicopter thing that was £9.99, and I told him he couldn't have it, and he just threw himself down on the floor and screamed and started banging his head. So then I had nine quid left.

And then we walked past the cinema, and they were showing this kids' film called *Dressing Salad*. From the poster, it looked like a kind of Wallace and Gromit rip-off about vegetables. So of course, he wanted see it, and when I looked, the first performance was just starting. And I thought, Well, it's a good way of killing a couple of hours. It cost £8.50 for the two of us, so I had fifty pence left.

We walked into the cinema, and up on the screen there was this giant talking tomato trying to run away from a bottle of mayonnaise and a salt-shaker.

'I don't like it, Dadda,' Roof said.

'Don't be silly. Sit down.'

'I DON'T LIKE IT!' he yelled. There were only about four people in there, but they all turned round.

'Let's just . . .'

The giant tomato ran straight at the camera shouting, and this time Roof just screamed. I grabbed him and we went out into the foyer. I'd spent twenty quid in about twenty minutes.

'Can I have some popcorn, Dadda?' Roof said.

I took him back to Alicia's. She'd got dressed while we were out, and she looked better, although she still didn't look good.

'That was all you could manage?' she said.

'He wasn't feeling well. After the jab and everything.'

'How did it go?' she said.

'How did it go, Roof?' I asked him.

He looked at me. He didn't have a clue what I was talking about. He'd forgotten what we rehearsed.

'At the doctor's?'

'They had a fire engine,' he said.

'Were you brave?' I said.

He looked at me again. You could tell he was trying to remember something, but he had no idea what it was.

'I was a brave fireman,' he said.

'Oh, well,' said Alicia. 'He doesn't seem too upset by it all.'

'No,' I said. 'He was good.'

'Do you want lunch with us? Or have you got to get off?'

'Yeah,' I said. 'You know.'

I was hoping she did, because I didn't.

'I'll see you soon, Roof.'

It was true, sort of. If I got whizzed back to the present when I went to bed that night, which is what happened last time, then I'd see him in a few weeks, when he was born. That made me feel weird. I wanted to hug him, and say something about looking forward to meeting him, but if I did that, then maybe Alicia would guess that I didn't really belong in the future, which of course wasn't the future for her. That would have been a hard thing to guess, but she'd still have thought that there was something not quite right about me telling my kid that I was looking forward to meeting him.

He blew me a kiss, and Alicia and I laughed, and I walked backwards down the path so that I could look at him for a bit longer.

I went home, and nobody was in, and I lay on my bed and looked at the ceiling and felt stupid. Who wouldn't want to visit the future and see what everyone was up to? But here I was, in the future, and I couldn't think of anything to do. The trouble was, it wasn't really the *future* future. If anyone ever asked me what the future was like, I could only tell them that I had a baby sister and a two-year-old kid, which wouldn't be the most amazing news anyone had ever heard.

I don't know how long I was lying there thinking, but after a little while Mum came in with Emily and a load of shopping, and I helped her put it away while Emily sat in her little rocking chair thing and watched us.

I suddenly needed to know something. Actually, I needed to know a lot of things, like what was I supposed to do all day. But what I ended up asking was this.

'Mum. How am I doing?'

'All right,' she said. 'You haven't dropped anything, anyway.'

'No, no. Not with the putting away. How am I doing in, like, life?'

'What do you want? Marks out of ten?'

'If you like.'

'Seven.'

'Right. Thanks.'

Seven sounded all right. But it didn't really tell me what I needed to know.

'You pleased with that?' she said. 'Too high? Too low?'

'It sounds about right,' I said.

'Yeah, I thought so.'

'Where would you say I lost the three points?'

'What are you asking me, Sam? What's this all about?'

What was it all about? What I wanted to know, I suppose, was whether the future was worth waiting for, or whether it was going to be a lot of trouble. There wasn't anything I could do about it one way or the other, but it would be useful to find out whether Rubbish was right. Had I screwed everything up?

'Do you think things will turn out OK?' I said. I didn't know what things I was talking about, or what OK meant. But it was a start.

'Why? What sort of trouble are you in?'

'No, no, it's nothing like that. As far as I know. I just mean, with Roof and all that. College. I dunno.'

'I think you're doing as well as can be expected,' said Mum. 'That's why I gave you seven.'

'As well as can be expected'? What did that mean?

And I suddenly saw that, even in the future, you still wanted to know what was going to happen. So as far as I could work out, TH hadn't helped me at all.

Later on I went down to the Bowl with my board, and nobody seemed too surprised, so I obviously hadn't given up skating. And I told Mum and Mark I didn't want to eat with them, even though I was starving, because I couldn't really talk to them about yesterday or today or tomorrow. I messed around in my room, played on my Xbox, listened to music and went to bed. And when I woke up, I didn't have Hawk cargo pants or a Hawk burning T-shirt any more, so I knew I was back in my own time.

13

So you know everything. There's nothing more for me to say. I don't know whether you thought I was making up that stuff about the future, or whether you thought I'd lost it, but it doesn't really matter now, does it? We had a baby called Rufus, in real life. So there you are. End of story.

So now you're probably thinking, If this is the end of the story, why doesn't he shut up, so that I can get on with something else? The truth is that, when I said that you knew everything . . . It's sort of true, in terms of the facts. I mean, there are a few dots to join up. But we had a baby, Mum had a baby, Alicia and I lived together in her bedroom and then stopped living together. It's just that there comes a point where the facts don't matter any more, and even though you know everything, you know nothing, because you don't know what anything felt like. That's the thing about stories, isn't it? You can tell someone the facts in ten seconds, if you want to, but the facts are nothing. Here are the facts you need for *The Terminator*: in the future, supercomputer robots want to control the earth and destroy the human race. The only hope we have in the year 2029 is the leader of the resistance. So the robots send Arnold Schwarzenegger, who is the Terminator, back in time to kill the leader of the resistance before he has even been born. That's pretty much it. Also, a member of the resistance travels back in time to protect the mother of the future leader. That's why there's so much fighting. So you've got defenceless mother of future leader plus resistance fighter against Arnold the Terminator. Did you enjoy those facts? No. Of course you didn't, because you felt nothing, so you didn't care. I'm not saying that the story of Alicia and Roof and me is as good as the Terminator. I'm just saying that if you stick to the facts, then the whole point of a story has disappeared. So here's the rest of it.

One thing you should know is that I had a bad slam, down at the Bowl. I never hurt myself down there, because it's only for messing about in, the Bowl. If I was going to hurt myself, you'd think it would be down at Grind City, where there's proper skating, by proper skaters, and not round the corner from my house, where you go for five minutes before your tea.

It wasn't really my fault, although I suppose I would say that, wouldn't I? I'm not even sure if it was officially a slam. What happened was this. The only way you can make skating at the Bowl even a tiny bit interesting is if you approach it from the side and do an air, or something even flasher if you feel up to it, over the three steps and straight into the Bowl. The Bowl needs to be empty, obviously, but even if it's dark you can see and hear anyone in there from a long way off. Or rather, you can see and hear them as long as they're not sleeping in the middle of the Bowl, using their board as a pillow. That was what Rabbit was doing, although I didn't know that until I was mid-air and about to land on his gut. Is that a slam? If someone's asleep like that?

Nobody in the world could have stayed on the deck in that sort of situation, so I wasn't blaming my skills. I was blaming Rabbit, though, and I did blame him, when the breath returned to my body, and the pain shooting up and down my wrist had eased off a bit.

'What the fuck are you doing, Rabbit?'

'What am I doing?' he said. 'Me? What about you?'

'I was skating, Rabbit. In the Bowl. That's what it's for. Who goes to sleep in the middle of a concrete bowl? Where people skate?'

Rabbit laughed.

'It's not funny. I might have broken my wrist.'

'No. Yeah. Sorry. I was laughing because you thought I was asleep.'

'What were you doing then?'

'I was just dozing.'

'What's the bloody difference?'

'I hadn't actually gone to bed there. That would be weird.'

I just walked away. You need to be in the right mood to talk to Rabbit, and I wasn't in the right mood.

My mum ended up taking me to get my wrist X-rayed, just in case. We had to wait ages, just to be told that there wasn't really anything wrong with it, apart from it hurting like hell.

'I don't think you can do this any more,' said Mum while we were waiting. I didn't know what she was talking about. Do what? Wait in hospitals? Go places with her?

I looked at her, to show that I didn't understand her.

'Skating,' she said. 'I'm not sure you can skate any more. Not for the time being, anyway.'

'Why not?'

'Because for the next two years, your life is going to be pushing and carrying. And Alicia won't thank you if you break a limb and you can't do anything.'

'It was just Rabbit being stupid,' I said.

'Yeah, like we've never been in casualty before.'

It's true there have been one or two broken bits and pieces, fingers and toes. Nothing that would stop me being able to cart a baby around.

'I'm not going to pack it in.'

'You're being irresponsible.'

'Yeah well,' I said. 'I never asked to have a kid.'

My mum didn't say anything. She could have said a lot, but she didn't. And I kept skating, and I didn't have any more falls. But that was only because I was lucky. And because Rabbit didn't use the Bowl to kip in after that.

Mark moved in not long before I moved out. Can a person be the opposite of another person? If he can, then Mark is the opposite of Dad, in every way, apart from they're both English guys of the same height and colour, with similar tastes in women. You know what I'm saying. They were opposite in every other way. Mark liked Europe, for example, and the people that lived there. And sometimes he turned the TV off and opened a book. And he read a newspaper with words in it. I liked him. I liked him enough, anyway. And I'm glad he was around for Mum. She was going to be a thirty-two-year-old grandmother – a *pregnant* thirty-two-year-old grandmother – which was a step backwards for her. And Mark was a step forwards. So she'd end up exactly where she was before, which is better than it could have been.

Mum got round to telling me she was pregnant, eventually. She told me not so long after she knew, but quite a long time after I knew. Sometimes I wish I could have said, 'Look, don't worry about it. I think I got whizzed into the future, so I know everything already.' That's how I felt when Mum was trying to get up the courage to tell me about her baby.

To be honest, I think I would have worked it out even if I hadn't been whizzed, because she and Mark were so useless at hiding it all. It began right before I moved out, and Mum stopped drinking her glass of wine with dinner. I wouldn't have known that a lot of women don't drink alcohol when they're pregnant, especially in the first few weeks, if it hadn't been for Alicia. But I did know, and Mum knew I knew, so she poured herself a glass of wine every night and didn't touch it, as if that would somehow fool me. The thing was, it was my job to clear away the supper things, so for about five evenings on the trot, I picked up her full glass of wine off the table and said, 'Mum, do you want this?' And she'd go, 'No, thanks, I don't really fancy it. Mark, do you want it?' And he'd say, 'If I must,' and sip it while he was watching TV. It was all mad. If I hadn't cottoned on, I would have said something – you know, 'Mum, why do you pour yourself a glass of wine every night and not drink it?' And she would have probably started drinking water with dinner. But because I knew what it was about, I didn't say anything.

And then one morning, Mark offered me and Mum a lift, because he had to take the car in to work, and he was going to drive past my school and her work. And we were late, because she was in the bathroom being sick. I could hear her being sick, and Mark could hear her being sick. And because he knew why, and I knew why, nobody said anything. Does that make sense? He didn't say anything because he didn't want to be the one to tell me. And I didn't want to say anything because I wasn't supposed to know. I looked at Mark, and he looked at me, and we might as well have been listening to a dog barking, or a DJ on the radio, anything that you hear all the time and never feel the need to say anything about. And then there was this really loud heave, and I made a face without meaning to, and Mark noticed, and he said, 'Your mum's not feeling so well.'

'Oh,' I said. 'Right.'

'Are you OK?' Mark said when she came out. And she gave him a shut-up look and said, 'I couldn't find my phone.'

And Mark said, 'I just told Sam you weren't feeling very well.'

'Why would you say that?'

'Because you were throwing up so loud that the walls were shaking,' I said.

'We'd better have a chat,' she said.

'I can't now,' said Mark. 'I really have to go to this meeting.'

'I know,' said Mum. 'Have a good day.' She kissed him on the cheek.

'Call me later,' he said. 'Let me know, you know . . .'

'I'll be fine,' I said when he'd gone. 'Whatever

you want to tell me, I won't be bothered.'

And then suddenly I had this terrible thought. Supposing that I was wrong, and the future was wrong, and Mum was about to tell me that she had some terrible illness? Cancer or something? I'd just told her I wouldn't be bothered.

'I mean, if it's good news I won't be bothered,' I said. 'If it's bad news, I'll be bothered.' And then that sounded stupid, because everyone's bothered by bad news, and people are usually pleased if it's good news.

'If it's good news I'll be pleased or not bothered,' I said. 'And if it's bad news I'll be bothered.'

My dad used to say that if you were in a hole you should stop digging. It was one of his favourite expressions. It meant that if you were in a mess, you shouldn't make it any worse. He was always saying it to himself. 'If you're in a hole, Dave, stop digging.' I stopped digging.

'Have you guessed?' said Mum.

'I hope so.'

'What does that mean?'

'If I'm wrong, then there's something really wrong with you.'

'No, there's nothing wrong with me.'

'Right then,' I said. 'So I've guessed.'

'You guessed before,' she said.

'Yeah. I guessed wrong that time.'

'But why did you keep guessing I was pregnant? I never thought I'd have another kid.'

247

'Man's intuition,' I said.

'Men don't have any intuition,' she said.

'This one does,' I said.

It wasn't really true, if you thought about it logically, and left the future out of it. I'd been completely wrong the first time, and the second time I'd watched her not drinking her wine and listened to her throwing up in the bathroom. You didn't need much intuition for that.

'Are you really not bothered?' she said.

'Really,' I said. 'I mean, it's all good. They'll be friends, won't they?'

'I hope so. They'll be the same age, anyway.'

'What will they be to each other?'

'I was working this out,' she said. 'My baby will be your baby's aunt or uncle. And my grandchild will be a few months older than my child. I'm four months, and Alicia's eight.'

'Mad, isn't it?' I said.

'Must happen a lot,' Mum said. 'I just didn't think it would happen to us.'

'How do you feel about it?' I said.

'Yeah. Good. I mean, at first I didn't think I'd want to keep it. But then I don't know . . . This is the time, isn't it?'

'For you, maybe.'

And I laughed, to show I was joking.

Suddenly, my mum wasn't my mum any more. We were friends who'd got themselves into the same stupid place in the same year. It was a weird time in my life, really, if you threw the trips to the future in there as well. Nothing was fixed properly. Things could happen whenever they wanted to, instead of whenever they were supposed to, like in some science-fiction movie. We can all laugh about it now, but . . . Actually, that's not true. We can only laugh about it on a really, really good day.

I worked out that there were two futures. There's the one I got whizzed to. And then there's the *real* future, the one you have to wait to see, the one you can't visit, the one you can only get to by living all the days in between . . . It had become less important. It had nearly disappeared, in fact. One bit of it had, anyway. Before Alicia got pregnant, I used to spend a lot of time thinking about what was going to happen to me. Who doesn't? But then I stopped. It felt like, I don't know . . . Last year, some kids at a school down the road went on some climbing holiday in Scotland, and it all went wrong. They'd stayed out too late, and the teacher wasn't an experienced enough climber, and it got dark, and they were stuck on this ledge, and they had to be rescued. So how many of those kids on the ledge that night were thinking, Shall I do English literature or French for A-level? Do I want to be a photographer or a web-designer? I'll bet none of them. That night, their future was, you know, a bath, a toasted sandwich, a hot drink.

A phone call home. Well, having a pregnant girl-friend when you're still at school is like that all the time. Alicia and I were on a ledge, sort of, and we were thinking about Roof coming (but we didn't call him Roof then), and sometimes about the first week of his life, but not much more, not much further than that. We hadn't given up hope. It was just a different kind of hope, for different sorts of things. We hoped that everything would somehow sort of maybe turn out not too bad.

But the thing was, we still had to do something about the future, because that's how you spend half your time when you're sixteen, isn't it? People – schools and colleges and teachers and parents – want to know what you're planning to do, what you want, and you can't tell them that what you want is for everything to be OK. You can't get any qualifications for that.

Alicia was five months pregnant when it was time to take our GCSEs, and seven months preg-nant when we got our results. Hers were terrible, really, and mine were OK, and none of it mattered much to us either way by then. But I still had to listen to Alicia's mum going on about how badly everything had affected her, and how unfair it was that the boys just float through everything as if it wasn't happening. I didn't bother telling her that when I first met Alicia she'd told me she wanted to be a model. That wasn't what her mum and dad wanted to hear. That wasn't the picture of her they wanted to see.

So we spent the summer working out what we were going to do, and waiting. The working out what we were going to do took about ten minutes. I enrolled in a sixth-form college, and Alicia decided to take the year out, and go back to studying when the baby was a year old. The waiting, though . . . That took up the entire two months. We couldn't do anything about it.

14

I was skating down at the Bowl on my own, and suddenly my mum appeared. She was all out of breath, but that didn't stop her from yelling at me for not having my mobile switched on.

'It is switched on,' I said.

'So why don't you answer it?'

'It's in my jacket pocket.'

I pointed at my jacket, which was on the stone bench right by the Bowl.

'What's the use of that?'

'I was going to have a look at it in a minute,' I said.

'That's a fat lot of use when you've got a pregnant girlfriend,' she said.

We were both of us wasting time arguing about how often I should look at my mobile, except only Mum knew we were wasting time, because she had information that she hadn't yet passed on.

'What are you doing here anyway?'

I must have known why she'd run from the house all the way down to the Bowl, but for some reason I was blocking it out. Actually, we can all guess the reason. I was scared to death.

'Alicia's in labour!' Mum shouted, as if I'd not

been letting her tell me for the previous two minutes. 'You've got to run!'

'Right,' I said. 'Right. OK.'

I picked up my board and I sort of started running, except I was running on the spot. It was like I was revving up my engine. The thing was, I didn't know where to run.

'Where shall I run?'

'Alicia's house. Quick.'

I can remember feeling a bit sick when she said I had to run to Alicia's. I'd been having these little daydreams and nightmares about the birth in those last four weeks. My nightmare was that Alicia's mum and dad weren't around when she went into labour, and she'd have the baby on a bus or in a minicab, and I'd be with her, not knowing what to do. My daydream was that I was out somewhere, and I got a message to say that Alicia had had the baby, and they were both safe and well, and I'd missed the whole thing. So when Mum told me I had to run to Alicia's, I knew that I hadn't missed the whole thing, and there was still a chance that the baby would be born on the top deck of the number 43.

As I ran past Mum, she grabbed me and kissed me on the cheek.

'Good luck, sweetheart. Don't be scared. It's an amazing thing.'

I can remember what I was thinking when I was pelting along Essex Road towards Alicia's house.

I was thinking, I hope I don't get too sweaty. I didn't want to be stinky while I was doing whatever it was I had to do. And then I was thinking, I hope I don't get too thirsty. Because even though we had a bottle of water in the emergency bag we'd packed to take to the hospital, I couldn't start chugging out of that, could I? That was Alicia's water. And I couldn't ask the nurses for a glass of water, because they were supposed to be looking after Alicia, not me. And I couldn't sneak off to the toilets and stick my mouth under the tap, because Roof would almost certainly choose those five minutes to be born. So you could say that I was worrying about me, not about Alicia and the baby, except the reason I was worrying about me was that I knew I wasn't supposed to worry about me.

Alicia's mum answered the door. Andrea. Andrea answered the door.

'She's in the bath,' she said.

'Oh,' I said. 'Right.' And I walked past her and sat down in the kitchen. I mean, I didn't sit down like I was making myself at home. I was nervous, so I just sat sideways on one of the kitchen chairs and started drumming my foot on the floor. But Alicia's mum still looked at me as if I'd gone mad.

'You don't want to see her?' she said.

'Yeah. But she's in the bath,' I said.

Andrea started laughing.

'You're allowed to go in,' she said.

'Really?'

'Oh, my God,' she said. 'The father of my daughter's baby has never seen her naked.'

I blushed. I was pretty sure I'd seen all of her. I just hadn't seen it all at once.

'You're about to see an awful lot,' she said. 'I really wouldn't worry about seeing her in the bath.'

I stood up. I still wasn't sure.

'Do you want me to come with you?'

I shook my head and went upstairs. Even then I was hoping the bathroom door might be locked.

Alicia and I still hadn't had sex since we'd got back together. So over the last few months I'd sort of lost touch with what she looked like under her baggy T-shirts and her brother's jumpers, if you know what I mean. I couldn't believe it. She just wasn't the same person. Her stomach looked like she had a two-year-old in there, and her breasts were about five times the size they'd been the last time I'd seen them. Just about every part of her looked like it was going to burst.

'Eight minutes,' she said. Her voice was all funny too. It sounded deeper and older. In fact, she suddenly looked like she was about thirty, and I felt as though I was seven. We were going in opposite age directions fast. I didn't know what the eight minutes bit was all about, so I ignored it.

'Will you time them now?'

She nodded at her watch. I didn't know what to do with it.

We had been to pregnancy classes, although you'd never have thought it to look at me. After the disaster in Highbury New Park, where all our classmates were teachers or grey-haired people, Mum found us something more suitable at the hospital. There were people there our age, more or less. That's where I met the girl who showed me how to change a nappy in the McDonald's toilets. And that's where I met all those girls she talked about that day, Holly and Nicola and them. There weren't that many dads. Anyway, the teacher at the hospital told us about timing contractions and all that. But first of all Mum comes down the Bowl to tell me that Alicia's gone into labour, and then I charge round to Alicia's house, and then I go into the bathroom to find a nude woman who looks nothing like Alicia in the bath . . . For a little while, everything went right out of my head. She could tell I didn't understand what she wanted, so she shouted at me.

'Time the contractions, you fuckwit,' she said. She didn't say it in a nice way, either. She was angry and frustrated, and I nearly chucked the watch into the bath and went home. Over the next twelve hours, I nearly went home about five hundred times.

Suddenly, she made this terrible, terrible noise. She sounded like an animal, although I couldn't tell you which animal, because I don't know much about wildlife and all that. The closest to it I've ever heard was a donkey, in a field next to our hotel in Spain. The watch nearly ended up in the bath again, this time because I nearly jumped out of my skin.

'What was that?' she said.

I looked at her. She didn't know? She thought there was someone else in the room? Or a donkey?

'It was . . . It was you,' I said. I didn't like saying it. It sounded rude.

'Not the noise, you fucking fucking moron,' she said. 'I know that was me. The timing. How many minutes?'

I was relieved that I hadn't understood, because that meant she wasn't going mad. On the other hand, I didn't know how many minutes it was, and I knew she'd be angry with me.

'I don't know,' I said.

'Oh, for Christ's sake,' she said. 'Why the bloody bastard hell not?'

They warned us in the classes about the bad language. The woman said that our partners might call us names and say things they didn't mean, because of the pain and all that. I'd got the idea that she wasn't going to start swearing until the pushing bit, though, so this wasn't a good sign.

'You didn't tell me when the last one was,' I said. 'So I can't tell you.'

She started to laugh then. 'I'm sorry,' she said. 'You're right.'

And then she reached for my hand and squeezed it, and she said, 'I'm glad to see you,' and she started crying a bit. 'I'm really scared,' she said.

And I know it sounds stupid, but one of the things I'm most proud of in my life is that I didn't say, 'Me too.' I felt like saying it, of course. It was already frightening, and it hadn't even started yet. I just said, 'It'll be fine,' and squeezed her hand back. It wasn't much use, what I said. But it was better than saying, 'Me too,' and bursting into tears and/or running away to Hastings. That wouldn't have been much use to her.

Her mum took us to the hospital, and Alicia didn't have the baby in the car. She wanted her mum to go at ninety miles an hour, and nought miles an hour over the speed bumps. If you have ever been in a car in London, or anywhere else, probably, you will already know that you can't even drive ninety miles an hour at three o'clock in the morning, partly because of the traffic, and partly because there are speed bumps every six inches. And it wasn't three o'clock in the morning anyway. It was three o'clock in the afternoon. In other words, we travelled at about three miles an hour, which was too slow when we weren't going over the speed bumps and too fast when we were. I wanted to tell Alicia to stop making the donkey noise, because it was making me nervous, but I knew I couldn't.

I needn't have worried about being thirsty. There was a sink in our cubicle at the hospital, and anyway, we had plenty of time. At one point, there was so little happening that I went out the hospital and down the road to buy a Coke and a bar of chocolate. I was expecting everything to be, you know, 'Push! Push! I can see the head!', with me running around from . . . Actually, I didn't know where I'd be running from or to. One side of Alicia to the other, I suppose. Anyway, I needn't have worried about not having time to go to the Gents for some water, and I needn't have worried about having to stop the car and deliver the baby outside a post office or somewhere. How many babies are born in this country every year? About six hundred thousand, is the answer. I just looked it up on the Internet. And how many of those are born on a bus, or by the side of the road? About two or three. (That's a guess. I tried to look it up. I put 'Babies born on buses in UK' into Google, but my search did not match any documents.) That's why you read about them in the paper sometimes: because they're special. It's slow, labour. Slow and then fast. Unless you're having one of the babies born on the bus.

Anyway, the nurse came to meet us at the door

of the maternity unit and showed us to our cubicle, and Alicia lay down on the bed. Her mum gave her a massage, and I unpacked the bag we'd got ready ages ago. They told us at the classes to pack a bag. I'd packed clean underwear and a T-shirt, and Alicia had packed some clothes too. And we had a load of crisps and biscuits and water. We'd also put in a portable CD player and some music. The woman at the pregnancy class said that music was good for relaxing you, and we'd spent ages choosing songs and burning CDs. Even Alicia's mum had made one, which we thought was a bit weird, but she said we might thank her for it. I plugged the CD player in and put on my CD, which probably seems a bit selfish to you. But my thinking was that nobody would mind my music too much at the beginning, so I could get it out of the way. And as it was all loud and fast skate music, it might give Alicia some energy. The first song was 'American Idiot', by Green Day.

'Turn that off before I kill you,' she said. 'I don't want to hear about American idiots.' So that was the end of my music. I put her CD on.

'What is that shit?' she said. 'It's horrible.'

Her CD was mostly R&B, with a bit of hip-hop thrown in. And the very first song was Justin Timberlake, 'Sexy Back', which she'd got into when she went to these pregnant dance classes. Nobody wants to hear the word 'sex' while they're having a baby, just like you don't want to watch a McDonald's advert when you're throwing up, and I'd told her not to choose it. We'd had an argument about it.

'I told you this wouldn't be any good,' I said. I couldn't resist it. I knew it wasn't the right time, but I knew I'd been right to tell her.

'This isn't mine,' said Alicia. 'You must have put this on.'

'That is such a lie,' I said. I was really angry. I didn't like Justin Timberlake (and I still don't), so I wasn't happy about her saying that he was my choice. But it was the unfairness that got me most of all. I'd told her it was shit! I'd told her it wouldn't be right for her labour! And now she was telling me it was all my idea.

'Let it go,' said Andrea.

'But she was the one who wanted it!'

'Drop it.'

'It wasn't me,' said Alicia. 'It was you.'

'She's not dropping it,' I said. 'She's not letting it go.'

Andrea came up to me and put her arm around my shoulder and whispered in my ear.

'I know,' she said. 'But you have to. For the next however many hours we're in here, we all do what she says, and agree with what she says, and get her what she wants. OK?'

'OK.'

'This is good practice,' she said.

'For what?'

'Having a kid. You have to let things go about fifty times a day.'

Something clicked when she said that. I knew that Alicia was about to have a baby. I'd even met the baby, kind of. But when we were in the hospital, having the baby seemed like the whole point of everything, and once it was out, then our jobs were done, and we could eat any crisps we had left over all at once and go home. But that was just the beginning, wasn't it? Yes, we'd be going home. But we'd be going home with the baby, and arguing with each other about Justin Timberlake and with the baby about whatever, all the time, for ever. It was easy to let the Justin Timberlake thing go when I thought about that.

'Shall I put my CD on?' said Andrea.

Nobody said anything, so she did, and it was perfect, of course. We didn't know what anything was, but it was sweet, and quiet, and sometimes there was what I would call classical music mixed in, and if any of it was about sex and booty and all that, then they were singing about it in ways we didn't understand, which was fine. Neither of us was sure about having Alicia's mum at the birth. But we would have been in trouble without her. I'd have stomped off home in a rage before Roof was born, leaving Alicia with the stupid music that she chose driving her mental while she was trying to have a baby. The truth was, we needed a parent, not a kid.

The contractions stayed the same for a bit, and then slowed down, and then they stopped altogether for a couple of hours. The nurse was cross with us for coming in too early, and told us to go home, but Alicia's mum wasn't having any of that and shouted at her. We wouldn't have shouted at her. We would have gone home, and Alicia would have ended up having the baby on the bus. When the contractions stopped, Alicia dozed off, which is when I went for a walk and bought my Coke.

She was still asleep when I got back. There was one chair in the room, and Alicia's mum was sitting on it. She was reading a book called *What to Expect When You're Expecting*. I sat down on the floor and played the bricks game on my mobile. We could hear a woman having a really hard time next door, and the noise made whatever was in my stomach turn to mush. Sometimes you know you will remember moments for ever, even if there's nothing much happening.

'It's OK,' said Alicia's mum after a while.

'What?'

'Everything. The waiting. The noise next door. It's all life.'

'I suppose.'

She was trying to be nice, so I didn't tell her that was what was bothering me. I didn't particularly want life to be like that. I didn't want the woman next door to be making those noises. I didn't want Alicia to have to make those noises, whenever it was she started again. I didn't even know if I wanted Roof.

'It's funny,' said Andrea. 'The last thing you want when you've got a sixteen-year-old daughter is a grandchild. But now it's happening, it's really OK.'

'Yeah,' I said, because I didn't know what else to say, apart from, Well, I'm glad it's OK for you. Except I couldn't think of any way to say it that wouldn't have sounded sarcastic.

'I'm fifty,' she said. 'And if Alicia had her baby when I had her, then I'd be sixty-eight. And I'd be old. I mean, I know you think I'm old now. But I can run, and play games, and . . . Well, it will be fun. So there's a part of me that's glad this has happened.'

'Good.'

'Is there a part of you?'

I thought about it. It wasn't like I didn't know what I wanted to say. What I wanted to say was, No, not really. Even though I met my son when I got whizzed into the future, and he seemed like a really nice kid, and so it feels terrible to say that I don't want him. But I don't feel like a dad, and I'm too young to be a dad, and I don't know how I'm going to cope with the next few hours, let alone the next however many years. But I couldn't say that, could I? Because how could I explain about the future and TH and all that?

Maybe that's why I got whizzed. Maybe Tony

Hawk was just stopping me from saying something I might have regretted one day. I know why Andrea wanted to talk. The waiting made everything seem like we only had a little bit of time to say what was on our minds, as if we were going to die in this room. And if it had been a film, I would have told her how much I loved Alicia, and loved our baby, and loved her, and we would have cried and hugged, and Alicia would have woken up, and the baby would have popped out, just like that. But we weren't in a film, and I didn't love hardly any of those people.

I don't know what to say about the rest of it. Alicia woke up soon afterwards, and the contractions started again, and this time they were for real. There's a lot of counting, when you have a baby. You count the time between the contractions, and then you count the centimetres. The mother's cervix dilates, which means the hole gets bigger, and the nurse tells you how big it's got, and when it gets to ten centimetres, then you're off. I'm still not sure what the cervix is. It doesn't seem to come up in normal life.

Anyway, Alicia got to ten centimetres without any trouble, and then she stopped sounding like a donkey and started sounding like a lion which is having one of its eyes poked out with a stick. And it wasn't just that she sounded angry, either. She actually was angry. She called me names and her mum names and my mum names, and she called the nurse names. It sounded to me like the names she was calling me were worse than the names she was calling the others, which is why Andrea kept having to stop me from walking out the door, but to be honest I might just have been looking for an excuse to leave. It didn't seem like a place where a happy thing could be happening. It seemed more like a place where bombs explode and legs came off and old ladies dressed in black started screaming.

For a long while, you could see the baby's head. I didn't, because I didn't want to look, but it was there, Andrea said, which meant the baby would be coming soon. But then it didn't come soon, because it got stuck, so then the nurse had to cut something. I'm making it sound as though it all happened quickly, but it didn't, until that part. But when the nurse cut whatever it was she cut, the baby just slithered straight out. It looked terrible. It was covered in stuff, blood and slime and I think even some of Alicia's shit, and its face was all squashed. If I hadn't seen it already, I would have thought there was something wrong with it. But Alicia was laughing, and Andrea was crying, and the nurse was smiling. For a moment, I felt nothing.

But then Alicia said, 'Mum, Mum. What's this music?'

I hadn't even noticed there was anything playing. We'd had Andrea's CD on repeat for hours, and

I'd sort of blocked it out. I had to look at the CD machine to hear a man singing a slow song and playing the piano. It wasn't the sort of thing I'd normally listen to. But then the sort of thing I normally listened to was good for skating to, and absolutely useless for having a baby to.

'I don't know the name of the song,' she said. 'But the singer's name is Rufus Wainwright.'

'Rufus,' said Alicia.

I don't know why that got me more than the part where he came slooshing out, but it did. I lost it, then.

'What are you crying for?' said Alicia.

'Because we've just had a baby,' I said.

'Der,' she said. 'You've only just noticed?'

And the truth was, I had.

My mum came in about an hour after Roof was born. Andrea must have called her, because I hadn't. I'd forgotten. She came in puffing and panting because she'd been too excited to wait for the lift. 'Where is he? Where is he? Let me at him,' she said.

She said it in a funny voice, pretending to be desperate, but she was only pretending to be pretending. She really was desperate, you could tell. She didn't look at Alicia or me or Andrea – not at our faces, anyway. Her eyes were going all over the room looking for any small bundle that might have been a baby. In the end she found the bundle on my chest, and she snatched him away from me.

'Oh my God,' she said. 'It's you.'

I didn't understand what she meant at first. I thought she was saying 'It's you!' like you do to someone you've never met before but you've heard a lot about, or someone you haven't seen for a long time and didn't expect to see. So I thought she was being all emotional about meeting him. But what she meant was that Roof looked just like me. Andrea had already said he looked just like Alicia and Rich and about fifteen other people in her family, so I'd have been pretty confused if I'd thought that any of them were worth listening to. They weren't, though, not then. They'd pretty much gone mad. They spoke fast, and they laughed a lot, and sometimes they'd start crying almost before they'd finished laughing. So you weren't really going to get an honest opinion about anything.

My mum held him close and then held him at a distance so that she could look again.

'How was it?' she said, without taking her eyes off the baby's face.

I let Alicia explain about the contractions going away and painkillers and the baby getting stuck, and I just listened. And as I listened, I watched them, and I started to get all muddled up as to who was who. Alicia seemed older than my mum, all of a sudden, because she'd had her baby, and my mum was still a few months away, and my mum was asking her questions, and Alicia had all the answers. So my mum was Alicia's younger sister, and my mum was my sister-in-law. And that made sense, because Andrea seemed so much older than my mum, so it was hard to think of them as Roof's two grandmothers. Andrea seemed more like my mum's mum. And I didn't really know who I was. That's a weird feeling, not knowing what you are to anybody in the room, especially if you're sort of related to all of them.

'He's called Rufus,' I said.

'Rufus,' said my mum. 'Oh. Right.'

She didn't like it, you could tell.

'Someone called Rufus was singing when he was born,' I explained.

'Could be worse, then, couldn't it? He might be called Kylie. Or Coldplay. Coldplay Jones.'

At least my mum was the first to do it. Over the next few weeks, I heard that joke about ten thousand times. 'Could have been worse, then, couldn't it? He might have been called Snoop. Or Arctic Monkey. Arctic Monkey Jones.' Or Madonna, or Sex Pistol, or 50 Cent, or Charlotte. They usually choose the name of a woman singer and the name of a band, although sometimes they change the woman for a rapper. And they always put the surname on after they've said the name of the band, just to show how funny it would be. 'Or Sex Pistol. Sex Pistol Jones.' They don't put the surname after the name of the woman singer, because that's not so funny. 'Or Charlotte. Charlotte Jones.' Charlotte Jones is just a normal girl's name, isn't it? There's no joke there. Anyway, they always say it, and I always feel I have to laugh. In the end, I stopped telling people why he was called Rufus, because I was afraid I was going to end up stoving someone's head in.

It was the surname, though, that got Andrea's attention.

'Or Burns,' she said.

My mum didn't get it, I think because 'burns' is a normal word, like 'runs' or, you know, 'pukes'. When you hear the word 'Burns', you think of stuff burning before you think of any member of Alicia's family. We don't, not now, but we used to, and most normal people would.

'Sorry?'

'Burns,' said Andrea. 'Coldplay Burns.'

Andrea was being serious about Roof's second name. We'd never had this conversation, and we were going to have it sooner or later, although an hour after his birth seemed to be too much on the sooner side. But even though it was a serious conversation, it was hard not to laugh. It was the way she said it. She was concentrating on the surname, so she said the first name as if it was normal.

'You said Coldplay *Jones*, but he's going to be Coldplay *Burns*, isn't he?' Andrea said.

I caught Alicia's eye. She was trying hard not to giggle too. I don't know why we thought we couldn't. Maybe it was because we could tell that they were both so serious. But if we'd giggled, we could have stopped them.

'Unless Alicia and Sam get married in the next few weeks, and Alicia takes Sam's name. Either of which scenario seems highly unlikely.'

My mum smiled politely.

'I think in these cases you can choose the surname, can't you? Anyway. We don't want to argue about it now.'

'I don't think there's anything to argue about, is there? I'm sure we all want to give this child the best possible start in life, and . . .'

Oh, man. Alicia and I have had arguments about her mum. Alicia says that she's really OK, but she just speaks without thinking, sometimes. I don't know if that makes sense. I mean, a lot of people speak without thinking, I can see that. But whether they're a nice person or not really depends on what comes out, doesn't it? Because, you know, if you say something racist to someone without thinking, it must mean you're a racist, mustn't it? Because that means you've got to think all the time to stop yourself saying racist things. In other words, the racism's in there all the time, and you need your brain to stop it. Andrea's not a racist, but she is a snob, because she needs to think long and hard to stop herself saying snobby things. What did that mean, that stuff about Roof needing the best possible start in life? The obvious answer is, it didn't mean anything. It didn't really matter whether he was called Coldplay Jones or Coldplay Burns. You'd have thought that being called Coldplay anything would be the problem, ha ha. But there's no difference in the surnames, is there? You've got no idea whether Mr Burns is posher than Mr Jones just from reading their names on a list.

But that wasn't what she meant. It was all about the families, wasn't it? She was trying to say that Rufus Jones would leave school at sixteen to be a dad and get some rubbish job and no GCSEs and probably start taking crack. But Rufus Burns would, I don't know, go to university and become a doctor or a prime minister or whatever.

'I'm sorry,' said my mum. 'Can you explain that?'

'I would have thought it's obvious,' said Andrea. 'No offence, but . . .'

'No offence?' said my mum. 'How do you work that out? How can what you're about to say not be offensive?'

'I'm not offering an opinion about your family,' said Alicia's mum. 'I'm just talking about the facts.'

'And what are the facts about this baby?' said my mum. 'He's not an hour old yet.'

It was like a horror movie, or something out of

some Bible. Two angels, one good and one bad, fighting over the soul of a tiny baby. My mum was the good angel, and I'm not just saying that because she was my mum.

Just then, even before Andrea could tell us the facts about this baby, Alicia's dad walked in. He could tell there was an atmosphere, because he said 'Hello' quite quietly, as if even that one word might set someone off somewhere.

'Hi, Robert,' said my mum. And she stood up, kissed him on the cheek, and handed him Roof. 'Congratulations.'

Robert held him for a moment and got a bit teared up.

'How was it?' he said.

'She was brilliant,' said Andrea.

'It's you,' said Robert, and I knew what it meant this time. It meant that the baby looked exactly like Alicia.

'Has he got a name yet?'

'Rufus,' I said. 'Roof.'

'Roof?' said Alicia. And she laughed. 'I like that. Where did you get that from?'

'I dunno,' I said. 'I thought . . .' I was going to say, I thought everyone called him that, but I stopped myself.

'Rufus,' said her dad. 'Yeah. Good. It suits him.'

'Rufus Jones,' said Alicia.

You don't need to know about the rows and

the tears that came after that. But she stuck to it, and Rufus Jones he was and still is, from that day on. It was Alicia's way of saying something to me, and to my mum. I'm not sure what, exactly. But it was something good.

15

Rufus was born on September the twelfth. If Alicia's contractions hadn't stopped, he would have been born on September the eleventh, which wouldn't have been great, really, except loads of people must have been born on September the eleventh since September the eleventh. Anyway, there was enough to worry about, without worrying about things that didn't happen.

On September the thirteenth, I moved into Alicia's house. She went home after lunch, and I went back to my house and got some stuff, and Mum and Mark gave me a lift round the corner. I felt sick for more or less the whole day. I suppose it must have been homesickness, but how would I know, seeing I'd never really been away from home for very long? I'd gone on a few holidays with Mum, and I'd spent a night in Hastings, and that was about it.

'You just have to see how it works out,' Mum said. 'It's not for ever, is it? Nobody's expecting you to stay there until, you know . . . until, well . . . for long.' I didn't blame her for giving up on the sentence. There wasn't a way of finishing it.

She was right. I knew that, somewhere inside. But how long was not for ever? A couple of days? A week? A year?

I remembered what my dad said when he gave up smoking. He said, 'What you have to ask yourself all the time is, Do I want a fag now, this second? Because if you don't, then don't have one. And if you think you can survive that second, then you're on to the next second. And you have to live like that.' That's what I'd tell myself. Do I want to go home now, this very minute? And if I think I can stick it out for one more minute, I'll move on to the next one. I'd try not to worry about tomorrow, next week, next month.

It wasn't a very relaxing way to live, though, was it? Not in your own home.

Andrea let us all in, and we went into Alicia's bedroom. We'd decorated it a bit over the summer, just like I knew we would. We'd taken down the Donnie Darko poster, and put up the pink alphabet thing, so the room wasn't as purple as it had been. Alicia was lying on the bed feeding Roof.

'Look, Roof,' she said. 'It's Daddy. He's come to live with us.'

She was trying to sound cute, I suppose, but it didn't make me feel much better. It wouldn't have been so bad if Roof had looked round and gone, you know, 'Hooray! Daddy!' But he didn't, because he was one day old.

'Stay with you,' said my mum.

'Live with us,' said Alicia.

A lot of things don't seem worth arguing about to me. At school, you hear rubbish about who's going to mash who all the time. Arsenal will mash Chelsea. Chelsea will mash Arsenal. And I think, you know, just let them play each other. And then it's a draw half the time anyway. It was the same here. Nobody knew. Let the future just happen, I thought. Which was a new thing for me to think, seeing as I'd spent half my life wondering and worrying about what was going to happen.

There wasn't room for everyone, but nobody moved. Mum and I sat down on the end of the bed. Andrea hovered in the doorway. Mark leaned against the wall next to the door. Nobody said anything, and we all pretended to watch Roof feed, which meant looking at Alicia's breasts. I suppose that didn't matter if you were Mum or Andrea, but it was more difficult if you were a guy. I'd had a bit of practice at avoiding breasts in that NCT class, but then it was a poster. Alicia's were real. Obviously. I looked at Mark. He didn't seem bothered, but I couldn't work out whether that was just an act, and really he was embarrassed. The thing was, if you looked away – like I had just done, to see where Mark was looking – it showed that you were thinking about it, which was just as embarrassing. So either way you ended up feeling you were doing something wrong.

'He's all restless now,' said Alicia. 'I think there are too many people around.'

'I'll wait outside,' said Mark quickly, so I knew he'd had enough of staring at the ceiling. My mum and Andrea didn't seem to have heard her.

'Me too,' I said.

'You don't have to go,' said Alicia. 'You live here.'

Mum didn't say anything, but I could see she was thinking about it. That was all she was thinking about, though. She obviously wasn't thinking about whether Alicia was dropping a subtle hint about who should go and who should stay.

'I said, YOU LIVE HERE,' Alicia said again.

'So do I,' said Andrea.

'Not here you don't,' said Alicia. 'Not in this room.'

'Neither does Sam,' said Mum. 'He's just staying for a while.'

'I think what Alicia is saying,' I said, 'is she wants everyone to go apart from me.'

'And Roof,' she said in a baby voice.

'I can take a hint,' said my mum, which was funny, seeing as she'd had to be told that she'd missed one. 'Call me later,' she said and kissed me on the cheek.

And then Mum and Andrea left and closed the door behind them.

'So,' said Alicia. 'Here we are, Roof. Mummy and Daddy. This is your whole family.' And she laughed. She was excited. My lunch started to shift around in my stomach, as if it wanted to go home with Mum and Mark.

I hadn't brought much with me, just a couple of bags full of jeans and T-shirts and underwear. I did bring my TH poster with me, though, and I could see that was a mistake as soon as I put it down on the bed.

'What's that?'

'What?'

'On the bed?'

'This?'

'Yeah.'

'Oh, just, you know. Is he feeding OK?'

'Yeah. And no, I don't know.'

'You don't know what?'

'I don't know what that is. The poster.'

'Oh, just . . .' I'd already asked about Roof feeding OK. There didn't seem to be much else to say, apart from what she wanted to know.

'It's my Tony Hawk poster.'

'You want to put it up in here?'

'Oh. In here. I hadn't thought of that.'

'So why did you bring it?'

What could I say? I never told Alicia I talked to Tony Hawk. She still doesn't know. And that day, the day I moved in with my girlfriend and my son, wasn't the day to tell her either.

'Mum said she was going to throw it away if I left it at home. I'll put it under the bed.'

And that was where it stayed, apart from when I needed it.

16

I woke up in the middle of the night. I wasn't in my own bed, and there was someone in the bed with me, and there was a baby crying.

'Oh, shit.' I recognized the voice. The person in bed with me was Alicia.

'Your turn,' she said.

I didn't say anything. I didn't know where I was or even when I was, and I didn't know what 'Your turn' meant. I'd been dreaming about entering a skate tournament in Hastings. You had to skate up and down the steps outside the hotel I'd stayed in.

'Sam,' she said. 'Wake up. He's awake. Your turn.'

'Right,' I said. I knew what 'my turn' meant now, and I knew where and when I was. Roof was about three weeks old. We couldn't remember a time when he wasn't with us. Every night we slept as though we hadn't slept for months; every night we were woken up after one or two or, if we were lucky, three hours, and we didn't know where we were or what was making the noise, and we had to remember everything all over again. It was weird.

'He can't need feeding,' she said. 'He had one about an hour ago, and I've got nothing left. So he either needs winding or he has a dirty nappy. He hasn't been changed for hours.'

'I keep making a mess of it,' I said.

'You're better at it than me.'

This was true. Both things were true. I kept making a mess of it, but I was better than Alicia. I liked being better than Alicia. I just sort of presumed that she'd be better than me, but she can't ever seem to get the nappy tight enough, and Roof's poo always leaks through the nappy and on to his all-in-one vest. I lay there feeling pleased with myself and went straight back to sleep.

'Are you awake?' she said.

'Not really.'

She whacked me with her elbow. She got me right in the ribs.

'Ow.'

'You awake now?'

'Yeah.'

The feeling of the pain in my ribs was familiar, and for a moment I couldn't think why. Then I remembered that she'd whacked me like that the night I got whizzed into the future. This night was that night. I'd caught myself up. Everything was the same, but everything was different.

Alicia put the bedside light on and looked at me to see if I was awake. I remembered that when I'd seen her the night I got whizzed, I'd thought she looked terrible. She didn't look terrible to me now, though. She looked tired, and her face was puffy, and her hair was greasy, but she'd been like that for a while, and I'd got used to it. She was different, I could see that. But so was everything else. I don't think I'd have liked her so much if she'd stayed the same. It would have been like she wasn't taking Roof seriously.

I got out of bed. I was wearing a T-shirt of Alicia's and the pair of boxer shorts I put on that morning, or whatever morning it was. The baby was sleeping in a little cot at the end of the bed. He was all red in the face from crying.

I bent down and put my face near him. The last time, when I knew nothing, I was breathing through my mouth to stop myself from smelling anything, before I knew that baby poo smells nice, almost. 'Yeah, he needs changing.'

In the future, I'd pretended he hadn't needed changing, even though I was sure he did. But I didn't need to now. I put him on the changing table, unbuttoned his sleep suit and his vest, pulled them both back above his bum, opened the nappy and wiped him. Then I folded the nappy up, put it in a bag, put a new one on and buttoned him back up again. Easy. He was crying, so I picked him up and put him against my chest and jiggled him, and he went quiet. I knew how to hold him without his head jerking about. I sang to him a bit too, just made-up stuff. He liked it, I think. At least, he seemed to go back to sleep quicker if I did my singing.

Alicia went back to sleep, and I was alone in the dark with my son on my chest. Last time, I was confused, and I stood in the dark asking myself all those questions. I still remember what they were. Yes, I lived here now, and we were just about surviving. We got on each other's nerves, but the baby distracted us. What sort of a dad was I? Not bad, so far. How did Alicia and I get on? Pretty good, although it was sort of like we were at school, working together in pairs on some biology project that went on all day and all night. We never really looked at each other. We just sat side by side, looking at the experiment. Roof wasn't like a dissected frog or whatever, though. For a start he was a living thing, and he changed from minute to minute. And also, you can't really go all gooey over a dissected frog, unless you are a sicko.

I put Roof back in his cot and climbed into bed, and Alicia put her arms around me. She was warm, and I pushed into her. Roof suddenly made this sort of stuttering breathing noise and then started snoring. Something I've noticed is that Roof's noises make the room seem more peaceful. You wouldn't think it would work like that, would you? You'd think that the only way a bedroom can seem peaceful in the middle of the night is if nobody is making any noise. I think what it is, though, is that you're so frightened a baby's going to suddenly stop breathing that all his snuffles and stutters sound like your own heartbeat, something that tells you all is right with the world.

'You do love me, Sam, don't you?' Alicia said.

I remembered the last time, back in the future, and how I'd said nothing. I knew more now.

'Yeah,' I said. 'Of course.'

I still didn't know whether that was true. But I did know it was more likely to come true if I said it, because she'd like me more, and I'd like her more, and eventually we might love each other properly, and life would be easier if that happened.

Here's a funny thing. You go into the future, and afterwards you think, Well, I know about that now. But like I said before: if you don't know how something feels, then you don't know anything. The future looked terrible when I went there before. But once I was on the inside of it, it really wasn't so bad.

And then about three hours after I'd decided that, all the wheels started to come off.

That morning, I went to college, for about the third time in three weeks. The last time I'd been, a week or so after Roof was born, I'd got into a fight. I never get into fights. I never got bullied, and I never bullied anyone, and I never cared enough about anything at school to want to thump anyone.

I was talking to another kid from my old school outside a classroom, and this kid with gelled hair came up to us and just stood there listening to us. I nodded hello, but he didn't seem to want to be friendly.

'What are you fucking nodding at?' he said, and then did an impersonation of me nodding, which was actually more like an impersonation of a special-needs person headbutting someone. 'What's that supposed to be?'

And I knew, straight away, that I was going to have to fight him. I knew I was going to get hit, anyway. I didn't know whether I was going to hit him back, which is something I'd have to do if there was going to be a fight, as opposed to just me getting a beating. I didn't know why he was going to hit me, but there was no doubt where this conversation was going. You could smell it. He couldn't have calmed down even if he'd wanted to, which he didn't.

'Anyway,' he said. 'Thanks for looking after my kid. Saved me a few quid.'

It took me a while to work out what he was talking about. Who's his kid? I was thinking. When was I looking after someone's kid?

'It is mine, though, you know that, don't you?'

'Sorry. I don't know what . . .'

'Yeah, well you don't know fucking much, do you?'

I wanted him to ask me an ordinary question, one I could say yes or no to. I mean, I could have said no to that last one, because it was obviously true that I didn't know much. But saying no, I could tell, wasn't going to do me a lot of good.

'He doesn't even know what I'm talking about,' he said to the kid I used to go to school with. 'Alicia's baby, you mug. She told you it was yours.'

Ah. Right.

'Who are you, then?' I said.

'Doesn't matter who I am,' he said.

'Well,' I said, 'it does matter if you're the father of Alicia's baby. I'm sure Alicia would be interested, for a start. And me. What's your name?'

'Wouldn't mean anything to her, probably. She's such a slag she wouldn't remember.'

'So how come you're so sure he's your kid, then? Could be anyone's.'

For some reason, this seemed to make him angry, even though I was just pointing out the obvious. There wasn't much logic to anything he said, and there wasn't much logic to what pissed him off.

'Come on, then,' he said, and he started towards me. Seeing as he wasn't very bright, I was pretty sure that he was going to be good at fighting, and that I was going to get a pasting. I thought I'd get one in first, just so that I could tell Alicia I'd fought back. I lifted my foot, and as he got near I got him in the balls. It wasn't a kick, really. It was more like a mid-air stamp, because I got him with the sole of my shoe.

And that was it. He went down holding his crotch and swearing, and he rolled around on the floor for a bit, like a World Cup footballer. I couldn't believe it. Why would you pick a fight with someone if you were that rubbish?

'You're dead,' he said, but he was lying on the ground when he said it, so it wasn't very scary. And by then a few people had come to see what was going on, and a couple of them were laughing at him.

There was another reason why I wanted to kick him, to tell you the truth. It wasn't just that I wanted to tell Alicia that I'd had a go back. I also wanted to kick him because I believed everything he'd told me. I reckoned this was the guy that Alicia had gone out with right before we met, and when I thought about it, everything seemed to fit together. She hadn't dumped him because he was putting pressure on her to have sex. That didn't make sense. Why would you split up with someone because he wanted to have sex with you, and then have sex with someone else right away? And then . . . Shit! Bloody hell! What a sucker I'd been . . . It was her idea for us to make love without me putting a condom on straight away, right? Why? Where did that come from? She said she wanted to feel me better, but the truth was, she was already worried she was

288

pregnant. And that guy had already dumped her! So she had to find some sucker to take the blame as soon as possible! It all made complete sense now. I couldn't believe how blind I'd been. This happened all the time, blokes finding out that their girlfriends' kids weren't theirs. It probably happened *every* time. Look at *EastEnders*. Hardly anyone has ever had a baby in *EastEnders* without changing their mind about who the father is.

So I went straight home after classes to have a row with her.

'How was college?' she said. She was lying on the bed, feeding Roof and watching TV. That was pretty much all she did, in those first few weeks.

'How do you think?' I said.

She looked at me. She could tell I was in a mood, but she didn't know what about.

'What does that mean?'

'I had a fight,' I said.

'You?'

'Yes, me. Why not me?'

'You're not like that.'

'I was today.'

'What sort of fight? Are you OK?'

'Yeah. I didn't start it. He just came at me and I kicked him and . . .' I shrugged.

'And what?'

'And nothing. That was the end of it.'

'One kick?'

'Yeah.'

'And who was he?'

'I don't know his name. You might. He says he's Roof's dad.'

'Jason bloody Gerson.'

'So you know what I'm talking about.'

Part of me felt like I wanted to throw up. That was the stomach part of me, most probably. And another part of me thought, That's it, I'm out. It's someone else's baby, and I can go home. That was probably more connected with my brain.

'Would you mind explaining who Jason bloody Gerson is?' I said it quietly, but I didn't feel quiet. I wanted to kill her.

'The guy I was seeing before you. The one I stopped seeing because he kept going on about wanting to have sex with me.'

Any other time, that might have sounded funny. How long ago had that been? Less than a year? And now the girl telling me that she stopped seeing Jason bloody Gerson because he wanted to have sex with her was lying on a bed, breastfeeding a baby.

'How did you know it was him?'

'Because I know he goes to your college, and he's a wanker. It's just the sort of thing he would say. I'm sorry, sweetheart. That must have been horrible.'

'Quite neat, though, isn't it?'

'What is?'

'The way it all fits in.'

'The way what fits in?'

'I don't know. Say you got pregnant. And say the bloke who made you pregnant dumped you. You'd need another boyfriend quick, so you could make out it was his baby. And you start sleeping with him straight away, and then you say to him, Go on, let's try without a condom, just once, and . . .'

She looked at me. She'd started crying even before I'd finished. I couldn't look back at her.

'That's what you think?'

'I'm just saying.'

'What are you just saying?'

'Nothing.'

'It doesn't sound like nothing.'

'I'm just pointing out the facts.'

'Really. How about these facts? When did we meet?'

I thought. I could see what she was getting at. I didn't say anything.

'About a year ago, right? Because we met at my mum's birthday party, and it's her birthday next week.'

Why hadn't I worked things out like this on the way home? Why hadn't I done the sums? Because if I'd done the sums, I could have saved myself a lot of trouble.

'And how old is Roof?'

I sort of shrugged, which must have looked to her as if I didn't know.

'He's three weeks old. So unless I've just had an eleven-month pregnancy, he can't be Jason's, can he? Unless you think I was sleeping with him and you at the same time. Is that what you believe?'

I shrugged again. Every shrug was making things worse for myself, but the trouble was, I was still angry about Jason, and the fight, and the things he'd said, and I didn't want to back down. Even though it was now obvious to me that I'd got everything wrong, it was as if I couldn't change direction. My steering had gone. That thing with the months should have done the trick, really, but it didn't.

'So when would I have been sleeping with him? Before breakfast? Because I was seeing you every afternoon and evening.'

One more shrug.

'Anyway,' said Alicia. 'If that's how little you trust me, then everything's pointless, isn't it? That's the thing that gets me the most.'

That would have been a good place to say sorry too, but I didn't.

'I think you want everything to be pointless.'

'What does that mean?'

'Gets you off the hook, doesn't it?'

'What does that mean?'

I understood everything, really. But asking what things meant all the time gave me something to say.

'I know you don't want to be here. So what you want is for me to tell you to go home to your mummy. I'm surprised you even bothered fighting Jason. You probably wanted to kiss him.'

'I'm not bloody . . .'

'OH FOR GOD'S SAKE!' she shouted. 'I KNOW YOU'RE NOT GAY!'

'Are you all right in there?' said Andrea's voice outside the door.

'GO AWAY! I'm not talking about your gayness, you fool. God. I so knew you were going to say that. Pathetic. You probably wanted to kiss him because, if he was the father, you didn't need to be here any more.'

Oh. That was pretty much exactly what I thought. I didn't explain that I only kicked Jason bloody Gerson, or did a mid-air stamp on his balls, because he was coming for me, not because he said he was Roof's dad.

'That's not true,' I said. 'I'm glad Roof's my kid.'

I didn't know what was true and what wasn't. It was all so complicated. Every time I looked at our beautiful baby, I was amazed that I'd had anything to do with him. So yes, I was glad Roof was my kid. But when Jason bloody Gerson said those things, I did want to kiss him, in a not-gay way. So no, I wasn't glad Roof was my kid. I'd never really had arguments like this before, arguments I couldn't understand properly, arguments where both sides were right and wrong all at the same time. It was like I'd suddenly woken up to find myself on TH's skateboard at the top of one of those huge vert ramps. How did I get up here? you'd think. I haven't been trained for this! Get me down! We went from arguing about which film we wanted to see to arguing about what our lives meant in about ten seconds.

'You think it's only your life that's been fucked up, don't you? You think I wasn't really going to have a life, so it doesn't matter one way or the other if I've got a baby,' she said.

'I know you were going to have a life. You told me you were. You told me you were going to be a model.'

When you kick someone in the balls, or do a sort of mid-air stamp, there's a moment when you think, What did I do that for? Well, I felt exactly the same at that moment. What did I say that for? I knew why she'd told me she wanted to be a model. She'd said it because she wanted to find out if I fancied her. Plus, that was a long time ago, when we were just getting to know each other, and trying to be nice to each other. We'd said all kinds of rubbish then. You should never drag stuff out of a nice conversation and chuck it back in the middle of a nasty one. Instead of one good memory and one bad memory, you're left with two shitty ones. When I remember how pleased I was when I worked out what Alicia was saying when she told me that . . . Well, that's the trouble, isn't it? I don't want to remember any more.

I didn't mean anything by it. Or rather, I knew it was a bad thing to say, and I said it to hurt, but it was only after it had come out of my mouth that I started to think about why it was nasty. And as Alicia was lying there crying, I came up with a few reasons.

– It sounded like I was taking the piss. It sounded like I thought she was never pretty enough to be a model.

– It sounded like I thought she was thick, because that's all she could come up with when we were talking about what we wanted to do.

– It sounded like I was laughing at her for being all podgy and greasy now, and not like a model in any way.

'It's funny, isn't it?' she said when she could speak again. 'My mum and dad think you've messed me up, and dragged me down, and all that. And I've tried to stick up for you. And you and your mum think I've messed you up and dragged you down. And I know I wasn't ever going to be, you know, a rocket scientist or a great writer or any of the things my parents think I can do. But I was going to be something. I don't mean something incredible. Just something. And what chance do you think I've got now? Look at me. So you had a fight at college. Big deal. At least you went to college today. Where have I been? The kitchen and back. So stop it, OK? Stop it with how I've messed up your life. You've got half a chance. What chance have I got?'

It was the most she'd said to me for weeks. Months, probably.

After much too long, I calmed down, and I said sorry a lot, and we hugged, and we even kissed a bit. We hadn't done anything like that for ages. That was the first row, though. It made it much easier to have all the others.

Alicia and Roof went to sleep, and I took my skateboard out for a little while, and when I came back, my mum was there, sitting at the kitchen table with Roof on her lap.

'Here's Dadda,' she said. 'Alicia let me in, but she's gone for a walk. I made her go out. I thought she was looking a bit peaky. And there's no one else here.'

'Just the three of us, then,' I said. 'That's nice.'

'How was college?'

'Yeah, good,' I said.

'Alicia told me about your bit of trouble.'

'Oh,' I said. 'That. It was nothing.'

She looked at me. 'Sure?'

'Yeah. Honest.'

And I was being honest. That really was nothing.

17

A couple of days after the fight at college and the row, my dad called and offered to take me out for something to eat. He'd called me on the day Roof was born, but he still hadn't bothered to come over and see the baby or anything. He reckoned he had a lot on at work.

'You can bring the baby if you want,' he said.

'To the restaurant?'

'Son,' he said. 'You know me. I've learned almost nothing from anything I've ever done, so I can't pass much on in the way of advice or anything. But one thing I remember from when we had you is that, if you're a young dad, it's easier to get served in pubs and that.'

'Why wouldn't anyone serve you in a pub?'

'Not me, you pillock. You. You're underage. But if you've got a baby with you, nobody asks you anything.'

I didn't bother telling him that I could get a drink in a restaurant anyway if an adult was with me. Mum was always making me drink a glass of wine with my dinner, in order to teach me about responsible drinking. If he only had one piece of advice for me, it would break his heart to find out it was useless.

I waited until nobody was around, and then I got Tony Hawk out from under the bed and stuck him on the wall with the old bits of Blu Tack that were still on the back. He curled up a bit, but he stayed up long enough for me to tell him that my dad was coming round.

'It came naturally for my dad to do everything to help his kids, but he outdid himself when he started the National Skateboard Association (NSA),' said Tony.

Tony didn't often make jokes when we were talking, but this was a good one. I mean, it's not a joke in the book. His dad really did start the NSA, just because his son was a skater. But it was a joke in this conversation. My dad wouldn't have started a fire if I was cold.

'Yeah, well,' I said. 'My dad's not like that. My dad . . .' I didn't know where to begin, really. I was embarrassed to say that my dad hated people from Europe and all that.

'For Frank and Nancy Hawk – thank you for the undying support,' said Tony. That's what it says right at the beginning of *Hawk – Occupation: Skateboarder*. And TH's dad died, so the 'undying support' bit shows how much he still thinks of him.

'If I wrote a book, I wouldn't mention my dad, even if it was an autobiography,' I said. 'I'd say, "I was born with just a mum."'

'I was an accident; my mom was forty-three

years old and my dad forty-five when I popped out,' said Tony.

He knows I was an accident too. He also knows that my mum and dad were sort of the opposite of his.

'My dad won't be forty-five until I'm ...' I added it up on my fingers. 'Twenty-eight!'

'Since my parents were fairly old when I came around, they'd outgrown the strict mom-and-pop rearing and slipped into the grandparent mentality,' said Tony.

'My dad's not even old enough to be a dad, let alone a granddad,' I said.

'We spread his ashes in the ocean, but I kept some for later,' said Tony. 'My brother and I recently sprinkled the rest throughout the Home Depot.'

Tony's dad died of cancer. It's the saddest part of his book. But I couldn't understand why he was telling me that when we were supposed to be talking about how useless mine was.

'I'm sorry,' I said. And I didn't know what else to say, so I took the poster off the wall, rolled it up, and put it back under the bed.

So Dad came round, said hello to Alicia, told everyone who would listen that the baby looked exactly like me, and then we put Roof in his basket and took him to the Italian restaurant on Highbury Park. There was a booth at the back with a long leather seat, and we put the basket down there, out of the way. Lots of people came over to look at him.

'They probably think we're a couple of poofs who've adopted him,' said my dad. This was his way of saying that we looked the same age, even though we didn't, and we still don't.

He ordered two beers and winked at me.

'Well,' he said when they came. 'I'm drinking a beer with my son and his son. My son and my grandson. Bloody hell.'

'How does that feel?' I said, for the sake of something to say.

'Not as bad as I thought it would,' he said. 'Probably because I'm not even thirty-five.' He looked over to the next table, where two girls were eating pizzas and laughing. I knew why my dad was looking.

'Have you seen those two?' he said. 'I wouldn't climb over either of them to get to you.'

If you were visiting Earth from another planet, you wouldn't have a clue what my dad was talking about half the time, even if you'd learned the language. You'd catch on pretty quickly, though. He was either saying he was skint, or that he'd seen someone he fancied, or he was saying rude things about Europeans. He had a million expressions for either, and almost no words for anything else.

'Oh,' he said. 'That's my other piece of advice. There's nothing better than a baby for pulling.'

'Right,' I said. 'Thanks.'

Neither of the girls seemed the slightest bit interested in us, or in Roof.

'I know what you're thinking,' he said. 'You're thinking, silly old tosser, what do I want to know that for? I've got a girlfriend. But it will come in handy. One day.'

'Roof might not be a baby by then,' I said.

He laughed. 'You reckon?'

'Thanks,' I said.

'Don't get me wrong. She's a lovely girl, Alicia. And her family seem very nice, and all that. But . . .'

'But what?' He was really pissing me off.

'You haven't got a cat in hell's chance, have you?'

I banged my beer glass down on the table, because I was annoyed with him, and one of the women – the one I'd pick, with big brown eyes and long wavy dark hair – turned round to see what was going on.

'What is the point of taking me out to tell me all this?' I said. 'It's hard enough as it is.'

'It's not just hard, son,' he said. 'It's impossible.'

'How do you know?'

'Oh, I'm just guessing. I haven't got a clue about any of this really. Der.'

'Yeah, but how do you know about me and Alicia? We're different people.'

'Doesn't matter who you are. You can't sit in one room with a baby without doing each other's heads in.'

I didn't say anything to that. The day of the row, we'd started to do each other's heads in.

'Me and your mother, we ended up like brother and sister. And not even in a good way, either. There was no incest or anything like that.'

I made a face. His jokes were horrible, most of the time. Incest, gay adoption, he didn't care.

'Sorry. But you know what I mean. We were just watching this thing. You. And going, you know, Is he breathing? Has he pooed? Does he need changing? That's all we ever said. We never looked at each other. When you're older, it's OK, because there was usually a time before all that, and you can see a time after. But when you're sixteen ... I'd only known your mum five minutes. It was mental.'

'Where did you live?' I'd never asked either of them before. I knew we hadn't been in our house for ever, but I'd never been interested in what had gone on before I could remember anything. Now that time seemed worth knowing about.

'With her mum. Your Gran. We probably killed her off. All the crying.'

'Mum was saying the other day I was a good baby. Like Roof.'

'Oh, you were as good as gold. No, it was her that was doing all the crying. We got married when we found out about you, so it was different. More pressure, sort of thing. And your Gran's place was tiny. Do you remember it?'

I nodded. She died when I was four.

'But, you know. It wasn't so different really. A room's a room, isn't it? All I'm saying is that nobody is expecting you to stick at it. Stick at being a dad, or you'll have me to answer to . . .' I tried not to laugh at my useless dad telling me to be a good dad or else. 'But the other thing . . . Don't let it kill you. Relationships don't last five minutes anyway at your age. When you've got a kid as well, that should cut it down to three minutes. Don't try and make it last the rest of your life if you can't even see how you're going to get through till teatime.'

My dad is probably the least sensible adult I know. He's probably the least sensible *person* I know, apart from Rabbit, who doesn't really count as a person. So how come he was the only one who said anything that made any sense in that entire year? Suddenly I understood why TH had told me that story about his dad's ashes. He was trying to get me to treat my own dad as if he was a proper dad, someone who might have something interesting to say to me, someone who might actually be useful. If TH had tried to do that on any other day of my life, it would have been a complete waste of time. But then, that's why TH is a genius, isn't it?

On the other hand, maybe if my dad hadn't said

all that, Alicia and I wouldn't have had an argument when we got home. She wanted to know where we'd put Roof in the car, and I said we'd put his basket on the back seat and driven really slowly, and she went nuts. She said things about my dad, which normally I wouldn't have minded, but because he'd been helpful, I stuck up for him. And sticking up for him meant saying a load of things about Alicia's mum and dad that I probably shouldn't have gone into.

I don't think my dad had anything to do with the row we had a couple of days later, though. That was about me sitting on the remote control and not moving, so the channels just changed all the time. I can't remember why I did that. It was probably because I could see it was driving her mad. And my dad definitely didn't have anything to do with the row we had the day after that, which was about a T-shirt that had been on the floor in the bedroom for about a week. That one was all my fault. The T-shirt part of it was, anyway. It was Alicia's T-shirt, but I'd borrowed it, and I was the one who'd chucked it on the floor when I took it off. But because it was her shirt, I just left it there. I wasn't thinking, Oh, that's not my shirt. And I wasn't thinking, Oh, I'm not picking it up, even though I've been wearing it, because that's not my shirt. I just didn't see it, because it wasn't mine, in the same way that you never see shops that aren't interesting, dry cleaners and estate agents and so on. It didn't register. In my opinion, though, it didn't need to end up the way it did, with every single item of clothing in the room being thrown on the floor and trampled on.

Everything was getting out of hand. It was like a teacher losing control of a class. It was all right for a while, and then one thing happened, and another, and then things started happening every day, because there was nothing to stop them happening. They were easy.

When I went back home, it wasn't anything to do with the rows. That's what we told ourselves, anyway. I went down with a heavy cold, and I was coughing and sneezing half the night, and I kept waking Alicia up when she needed all the sleep she could get. And she wasn't happy about me picking Roof up and passing my germs on to him, either, even though her mum said it was good for his immune system.

'I'll sleep on the sofa in the living room if you want,' I said.

'You don't have to do that.'

'I'll be fine.'

'Wouldn't you prefer a bed? What about sleeping in Rich's room?'

'Yeah,' I said. 'That might work.' I know I wasn't sounding very enthusiastic.

'It's next door, though, isn't it?' I said.

'Oh. You mean I'd still hear you.'

'Probably.'

We both pretended to think hard. Was anyone going to be brave enough?

'You could always go back to your old room,' said Alicia. And she laughed, just to show what a mad idea it was.

I laughed too, and then pretended that I'd seen something she hadn't.

'It wouldn't kill us for one night,' I said.

'I see what you mean.'

'Just till I've stopped coughing half the night.'

'You sure you don't mind?'

'I think it makes sense.'

I left that day, and I never went back. Whenever I go round to see Roof, her family always ask me how my cold's coming along. Even now, after all this time. Do you remember when I got whizzed into the future that second time? When I took Roof for his injections? And Alicia said, 'I've actually got a cold,' and laughed? That was what she was laughing at.

The first night back was sad. I couldn't get to sleep, because it was too quiet in my bedroom. I needed Roof's breathing noises. And it didn't seem right, him not being there, which meant that my own bedroom, the bedroom I'd slept in just about every night of my life, didn't seem right either. I was home, and I wanted to be home. But home was somewhere else now too, and I couldn't be in both of the places at once. I was with my mum, but I couldn't be with my son. That makes you feel weird. It's felt weird ever since.

'Did your father say something to you when you went out for a pizza?' my mum said when I'd been home a couple of nights.

'Like what?'

'I don't know,' she said. 'It just seems like a bit of a coincidence. You go out with him and then suddenly you're back home.'

'We had a talk.'

'Oh Gawd,' she said.

'What?'

'I don't want you listening to him.'

'He was all right. He said I didn't have to live there if I didn't want to.'

'He would say that, wouldn't he? Look at his track record.'

'But that's exactly what you said.'

She was quiet for a bit.

'I was saying it from a mother's point of view, though.'

I looked at her to see if she was joking, but she wasn't.

'What point of view was he saying it from?'

'Not a mother's, that's for sure. I mean, obviously. But not a father's, either. A bloke's.'

I suddenly thought about Roof and Alicia and me, all arguing like this one day. Maybe it was all a mess that just went on for ever. Maybe Alicia would always be angry with me about my cold, so that even if we agreed – like my mum and dad agreed now – she wouldn't ever agree that we agreed.

'Anyway,' she said. 'You're only here because you've got a cold.'

'I know.'

'So it's nothing to do with what your dad was on about.'

'I know.'

'So.'

'Yeah.'

On the night I went home with a cold, I went straight into my room to talk to Tony Hawk. I'd taken the poster home with me, of course.

'I just had a bit of a cold,' I told him. 'So I've come home for a few days.'

'I knew that, even though I still loved Cindy, we lived in two separate worlds that were not uniting,' said Tony. 'In September of 1994 we split up. Unfortunately it took this event to make us realize the importance of parenthood.'

I looked at him. Fair enough, he'd seen right through the cold straight away. But I really didn't need him telling me about the importance of parenthood. What else was there in my life, apart from Roof? I went to college about once a bloody month, I never had time to go skating, and all I ever talked about was the baby. I was disappointed in him. He wasn't making me think at all.

'It was never an ugly separation,' he said. 'We were both dedicated to creating the best possible life for Riley.'

'Thanks for nothing,' I said.

But the thing about TH is, there's always more to what he says than you can see.

18

There's loads of stuff about teenagers having babies on the Internet. I mean, there's loads of stuff about everything on the Internet, isn't there? That's the great thing about it. Whatever your problem is, it's on there somewhere, and it makes you feel less alone. If your arms have suddenly turned green, and you want to talk to other people your age who've got green arms, you can find the right website. If I decided I could only have sex with Swedish maths teachers, I'm sure I could find a website for Swedish maths teachers who only wanted to have sex with English eighteen-year-olds. So it wasn't really surprising that you could find all the information you wanted about teenagers and pregnancy, if you think about it. Having a kid when you're a teenager isn't like having green arms. There are more of us than there are of them.

Most of the stuff I found was just kids like me complaining. I couldn't blame them, really, because we had a lot to complain about. They complained because they had nowhere to live, no money, no work, no way of getting work without paying someone more than they could ever earn to look after their kids. I didn't feel lucky very often, but I felt lucky when I read this stuff. Our parents would never chuck us out.

And then I found this little book full of facts that the Prime Minister had written some of. Most of them were pointless – for example, it said that most teenagers got pregnant by accident, DER!!!!!!! And some of them were funny – like, one in ten teenagers couldn't remember if they'd had sex the night before or not, which is pretty incredible if you think about it. I think this meant that one in ten teenagers had got so blasted the night before that they didn't know what had gone on. I don't think it meant they were just forgetful, like when you can't remember whether you packed your games kit. I wanted to run and tell Mum about this one. You know, 'Mum, I know I shouldn't have done it. But at least I remembered I'd done it the next day!'

I learned that Britain had the worst teenage pregnancy rates in Europe, which by the way means we have the highest. It took me a while to realize that. For a moment I thought they might mean it the other way, that our teen pregnancy rates were low and the Prime Minister wanted us to do better. And I learned that after fifteen years or so, eighty per cent of teenage fathers lose touch with their kids completely. Eighty per cent! Eight out of ten! Four out of five! That meant that in fifteen years' time, the chances were that I wouldn't have anything to do with Roof. I wasn't having that.

I was angry when I left the house, and I was still angry when I got to Alicia's. I knocked on her door way too hard, and Andrea and Rob were angry with me even before they let me in. I probably shouldn't have gone, but it was already about nine or so, and she was asleep by ten, so I didn't have time to calm myself down. The way I looked at things, it wasn't going to be me who stopped seeing Roof. The only way I was going to lose touch with him was if Alicia stopped me from seeing him and moved away and didn't tell me where she'd gone. So it was all going to be her fault.

'What on earth is all the racket about?' said Andrea when she came to the door.

'I need to see Alicia,' I said.

'She's in the bath,' said Andrea. 'And we've only just got Roof off to sleep.'

I didn't know whether I was allowed to see Alicia in the bath any more. On the day Roof was born, Andrea more or less made me go into the bathroom. Since then, I'd lived with her and then moved out again, although we hadn't actually split up, or even talked about splitting up, even though I think we both knew what was going to happen. So what did all that mean? Was it OK to see Alicia naked or what? This was the sort of thing the Prime Minister should be writing about on the Internet. Never mind whether you could remember whether you'd done it the night before or not. The night before was over. It was too late for the night before. We wanted to know about all the nights after, the nights when you wanted to talk to a naked girlfriend or ex-girlfriend and you didn't know whether there should be a door in the way or not.

'So what shall I do?' I said to Andrea.

'Go and knock on the door,' she said.

It was, I had to admit, a pretty sensible answer. I went upstairs and knocked on the door.

'I'll be out in a second,' said Alicia.

'It's me.'

'What are you doing here? Is your cold better?'

'No,' I said. Except I was quick enough to make it sound more like 'Doe', to show I was still blocked up. 'I need to talk to you.'

'What about?'

I didn't want to talk about not knowing Roof in fifteen years' time through a bathroom door.

'Can you come out? Or can I come in?'

'Oh, bloody hell.'

I heard her get out of the bath, and then the door opened. She was wearing a dressing gown.

'I thought I was going to get ten minutes to myself.'

'Sorry.'

'What is it?'

'You want to talk in here?'

'Roof's asleep in our room. My room. Mum and Dad are downstairs.'

'You can get back in the bath if you want.'

'Oh, what, so you can have a good look?'

I'd only been here two minutes, and she was really getting on my nerves. I didn't want to look at anything. I wanted to talk about whether I was going to lose touch with my son. I asked her whether she wanted to get back in the bath because I felt bad about interrupting it.

'I've got better things to look at than you,' I said. I don't know why I chose those particular words. I think I may even have got it wrong, and missed out some words, like, 'do than'. 'I've got better things to do than look at you,' I might have meant. I was angry with her, and she was sounding cocky. It was my way of saying, you know, You're not all that.

And then I said, 'People.' I said 'people' because Alicia isn't a thing.

'What does that mean?'

'What I said.'

I didn't think she could have taken it another way, you see.

'So you're already seeing someone else? Sleeping with another girl?'

I didn't say anything straight away. I couldn't understand how she'd got from there to here.

'What are you talking about?'

'You little shit. "Oh, I've got a cold." You liar. Get out. I hate you.'

'Where did you get that from?' We were both shouting now.

'You've got better people to look at? Well, go and bloody look at them.'

'No, I . . .'

She wouldn't let me speak. She just started pushing me out of the door, and then Andrea came running up the stairs.

'What the hell is going on here?'

'Sam came round to tell me he was going out with someone else.'

'Charming,' said Andrea.

'You can forget all about seeing Roof,' said Alicia. 'I'm not letting you near him.'

I couldn't believe it. It was all completely insane. Half an hour ago I'd been worried about losing touch with Roof in fifteen years' time, and I'd come round to talk to Alicia about it, and I'd lost touch with him straight away, on the first day of the fifteen years. I felt like strangling her, but I just turned round and started to walk away.

'Sam,' said Andrea. 'Stay here. Alicia. I don't care what Sam has done. You are never to make threats like that unless something extremely serious has happened.'

'And you don't think that's serious?' said Alicia.

'No, said Andrea. 'I don't.'

It all got sorted out. Alicia got dressed, and Andrea made us both a cup of tea, and we sat down at the kitchen table and talked. That makes it sound more intelligent than it really was. They let me speak, and I was finally allowed to tell them that I wasn't going out with anyone else, and I didn't want to go out with anyone else, and all that stuff about better people to look at came from nowhere and meant nothing. And then I explained that I'd come round angry because of what the Prime Minister had said in his report or whatever it was, that I was going to lose touch with Roof and I didn't want to.

'So it was sort of ironic that Alicia tried to stop you seeing him tonight,' Andrea said. And Alicia sort of laughed, but I didn't.

'How does it happen?' I said. 'How do all those dads lose touch with their kids?'

'Things get hard,' said Andrea.

I couldn't imagine how hard things would have to get before I stopped seeing Roof. It felt like I couldn't stop seeing him, like it wouldn't be physically possible. It would be like not seeing my own feet.

'What things?'

'How many of those rows do you think you could have before you gave up on Roof? Rows like the one you had tonight?'

'Hundreds,' I said. 'Hundreds and hundreds.'

'OK,' she said. 'Say you have two of those a week for the next ten years. That's a thousand. And you've still got five years to go before you get to fifteen years. Do you see what I mean? People give up. They can't face it. They get tired. One day, you might hate Alicia's new boyfriend. You might have to move to another part of the country for work. Or abroad. And when you come home to visit, you might get depressed that Roof doesn't really recognize you . . . There are loads of reasons.'

Alicia and I didn't say anything.

'Thanks, Mum,' Alicia said after a while.

Like I said, there's nothing you can do about the real future, the one you can't get whizzed into. You have to sit around and wait for it. Fifteen years! I couldn't wait fifteen years! In fifteen years' time I'd be a year older than David Beckham is now, two years younger than Robbie Williams, six years younger than Jennifer Aniston. In fifteen years' time, Roof might make the same sort of mistake that I made and my mum made, and become a dad, and I'd be a grandfather.

The thing was, though, I had no choice but to wait. There wouldn't be any point in hurrying it up, would there? How would that work? I couldn't cram fifteen years of knowing Roof into two or three, could I? It wouldn't help. I still wouldn't necessarily know him in fifteen actual years.

I hate time. It never does what you want it to.

I asked to see Roof before I went home. He was fast asleep, hands up near his mouth, and he was making his little snoring noises. The three of us watched him for a while. Hold it there, I thought. Everybody stay like this. We'd have no problem getting through the fifteen years if we could just stay here, saying nothing, watching a kid grow up.

19

I'm telling you all this as if it's a story, with a
beginning, a middle and an end. And it is a story,
I suppose, because everyone's life is a story, isn't
it? But it's not the sort of story that has an end.
It doesn't have an end yet, anyway. I'm eighteen,
and so is Alicia, and Roof is nearly two, and my
sister is one, and even my mum and dad aren't old
yet. It's going to be the middle of the story for a
long time, as far as the eye can see, and I suppose
there are lots of twists and turns to come. You
may have a few questions, though, and I'll try to
answer them.

*What about your mum's baby? How did all that
turn out?*

Mum's baby Emily was born in the same hospital
as Roof, but in the room next door. Mark was
there, of course, and I took Roof in on the bus a
couple of hours later.

   'Here's Grandma,' I said when we went in. 'And
here's your auntie.' Mum was used to being
Grandma by then, but not so many people get
called Grandma while they're breastfeeding a baby.

And not many people get called Auntie when they're two hours old.

'Bloody hell,' said Mark. 'What a mess.' He was laughing, but Mum wasn't having it.

'Why is it a mess?' she said.

'She's been alive for five minutes, and she's got a nephew who's older than her, and two half-brothers with different mothers, and a mum who's a grandmother, and God knows what else.'

'What else?'

'Well. Nothing else. But that's a lot.'

'It's just a family, isn't it?'

'A family where everyone's the wrong age.'

'Oh, don't be so stuffy. There's no such thing as a right age.'

'I suppose not,' said Mark. He was agreeing with her because she was happy, and because there was no point in talking about all that in a hospital room just after a baby had been born. But there is such a thing as a right age, isn't there? And sixteen isn't it, even if you try to make the best of it when it's happened. Mum had been telling me that ever since I was born, pretty much. We'd had babies at the wrong age, with the wrong people. Mark had got it wrong the first time, and so had Mum, and who knew whether they'd got it right this time? They hadn't been together that long. However much Alicia and I loved Roof, it was stupid to pretend that he'd been a good idea, and it was stupid to pretend we were going to be together when we were thirty or even when we were nineteen.

What I couldn't work out was whether it mattered that we'd all chosen the wrong people to have kids with. Because it all depended on how we all turned out, didn't it? If I got through all this and went to university and became the best graphic designer the world had ever seen, and I was an OK father to Roof, then I'd be glad that Mum and Dad were my parents. If I'd had some other mum or dad, then everything would have been different. It might have been my dad that passed on the graphic-design gene, even though he can't draw to save his life. We learned about recessive genes in biology, so his graphic-design gene might have been like that.

There must be loads of famous people whose mum and dad should never have got together. Well, would they have been famous if they hadn't? Prince William, say? OK, bad example, because if he'd had the same dad he'd still be Prince William. Prince Something, anyway. The William might have been Diana's idea. And he might not want to be a prince. Here's one: Christina Aguilera. She's written songs about how her dad was abusive and all that. But she wouldn't be Christina Aguilera without him, would she? And she wouldn't have been able to write those songs if her dad had been nice.

It's all very confusing.

That day in the future when you took Roof for his injections ... Was there really a day like that?

Yes, there was. It's clever, the future. It's clever the way Tony Hawk does it, anyway. When I get to those bits in my life, the bits I've visited before, then pretty much the same things happen that happened first time round, except for different reasons, and with different feelings. On that day, for example, Alicia did call me because she had a cold, and I did have to take Roof to the doctor's. But I did know his name when we got there, so nobody could say that I'd learned nothing in all that time, ha ha.

He didn't have his injections, though, so that part was true. What happened was, he started crying in the waiting room when I told him it wasn't going to hurt. I think he worked out that, as I never normally told him that something wasn't going to hurt, then something was going to hurt, otherwise I wouldn't have bothered. And I thought, She can take him. I don't want to deal with this.

I think I can remember Ms Miller telling us in religious studies once that some people believe you have to live your life over and over again, like a level on a computer game, until you get it right. Well, whatever religion that is, I think I might believe in it. I might actually be a Hindu or a Buddhist or something, without really knowing it.

I've lived through that day at the doctor's twice now, and I've got it wrong both times, except I'm getting better at it, very slowly. The first time I got it completely wrong, really, because I didn't even know Roof's proper name. And the second time I knew his name and I knew how to look after him properly, but I was still not good enough to make him go through with it. I'm not going to get a third shot at it, probably, because it's not in the future any more. It's in the past. And Tony Hawk hasn't whizzed me back anywhere yet. He's only whizzed me forward. So on the way home I was thinking about whether I'd ever have another kid, when I was older. And maybe I'd have to take him or even her to the doctor's for his or even her injections, and this time I'd do it all perfectly – get the kid's name right, tell him or even her that it wasn't going to hurt and that he could cry all he wanted, he still had to have it done. That would be the perfect day. Then I could move on, and stop having to live my life over and over again.

Oh, one other thing. I didn't take him to the toyshop to waste time afterwards, so I saved myself £9.99 on that helicopter thing. I do learn. It's just that I learn very slowly.

Do you still talk to Tony Hawk? And does he still talk back?

You'll see.

College OK?

Fine, thanks. I mean, I can do the work. And the teachers are understanding and all that. I'm not sure I can get everything done, though, not in the time I have. You know I told you about my mum, and my granddad, and how they slipped off the first step? Well, I got halfway up the staircase. I can't see a way of getting up much further than that, though. And I may have to come down again unless I can find a way of staying here.

Maybe Roof will get further up. That's the thing in our family. You know that if you mess up, there'll be another kid along in a minute who might do better.

And what about you and Alicia?

I knew you'd ask me about that.

A while ago – it was just after Alicia got rid of her cold – we had sex again, for the first time since Roof was born. I can't really remember how it happened, or why. It was a Sunday night, and we'd spent the day with Roof, together, the three of us, because we'd decided that he liked having both of his parents around. We usually took it in turns at weekends. I'd go round to Alicia's and take Roof out, or bring him back to mine so that he could spend time with his baby aunt. I'm not sure he was that bothered. I think we just felt guilty about something. Probably we felt guilty about making him live in a sixteen-year-old girl's bedroom, and about how he was stuck with a mother and a father who didn't have much of a clue. Being in the same park or the same zoo together was something we could do. It was hard, but it was hard in the way that holding your breath for five minutes is hard, not in the way that maths exams are hard. In other words, any idiot can at least have a go at it.

We took him to Finsbury Park, which has been done up since I was a kid, so you don't sit there thinking that it was only four or five years ago that you were swinging on those monkey bars. Andrea and Robert had given Alicia twenty quid, so we had lunch in the cafe, and Roof had chips and ice cream, and about four goes on those machines full of bouncy balls in see-through plastic eggs. We didn't talk about anything. I mean, we didn't talk about life and all that. We talked about bouncy balls, and ducks, and boats, and swings, and boys who had Thomas the Tank Engine scooters. And when Roof was on the swings or playing in the sand, then one of us had a sit down on the benches.

My mum once asked me what Alicia and I talked about when we looked after Roof together, and I told her that we didn't talk about anything, that I kept out of the way. Mum thought that was a sign of maturity, but the truth was, I was scared of her. If she wanted a row, she didn't care where we were, so I found it was safer to sit on a bench and watch her pushing Roof on a swing than it was to stand next to her. If you did that, then you could suddenly find yourself in the middle of a playground being called all the names under the sun while a small crowd gathered to watch. I'm not saying it wasn't my fault, half the time. It was. I forgot arrangements, equipment, food and drink. I made stupid jokes about things she didn't want me joking about, like her weight. I was joking because I'd started to think of her as a sister, or a mother (mine, not Roof's) or a friend I used to go to school with or something. She wasn't laughing at these jokes because that wasn't how she thought of me.

The day we went to Finsbury Park was nice, really. No rows, Roof was happy, the sun shone. We kept it going. I went back to Alicia's to help her with Roof's tea and bedtime, and then Andrea asked me if I wanted to stay for dinner. And after dinner we went into her room so that I could see Roof asleep before I went home, and she put her arm round me, and one thing led to another, and we ended up going into her brother's bedroom. The funny thing was, we still didn't have any condoms. She had to go and pinch them from her parents again.

It had been a long time since I'd done anything like that. I'd kept myself to myself, if you know what I mean. Up until that night, I hadn't wanted to sleep with Alicia, because I didn't want her to think we were together. But I couldn't sleep with anyone else, could I? That would have been the row to end all rows, if she found out. And I was still scared. What if I got someone else pregnant? That would be the end of me. I'd just be walking one endless circle from child to child, with the occasional visit to college, for the rest of my life.

So I slept with Alicia, and what happened? She thought we were together. We lay there on her brother's bed afterwards, and she said, 'So what do you think?'

And I said, 'About what?'

I swear I'm not leaving anything out. 'So what do you think?' were her first words on the subject.

'About giving things another go?' she said.

'When were we talking about that?'

'Just now.'

When I say I'm not leaving anything out, I'm telling the truth. But I'm telling the truth as far as I can remember it, which I suppose is a different thing, isn't it? We had sex, and then we were quiet for a little while, and then she said, 'So what do you think?' Did she say it when we were having sex? Or when we were being quiet? Did I fall asleep for a little while? I've got no idea.

'Oh,' I said, because I was surprised.

'Is that all you can say? "Oh"?'

'No. Course not.'

'So what else can you say?'

'Isn't it a bit soon?'

I meant, Isn't it a bit soon after the sex? Not, you know, Isn't it a bit soon after I moved out? I knew that the moving out had happened a long time before. I wasn't that out of touch.

Alicia laughed.

'Yeah,' she said. 'Right. How old do you want Roof to be before you make up your mind? Fifteen? Is that a good age?'

And then I realized that I hadn't missed anything. I hadn't missed anything little, anyway. I'd just missed the whole thing, that's all, everything that had been going on in the last few months. She thought I'd been trying to make my mind up ever since my cold, and I thought I had.

'You wanted me to go when I did, though, didn't you?'

'Yeah. But things have changed since then, haven't they? It's all settled down. It was difficult when Roof was a baby. But we've got it all worked out now, haven't we?'

'Have we?'

'Yeah. I think so.'

'Well,' I said. 'That's good, then, isn't it?'

'Is that a yes, then?'

A lot of the last couple of years has seemed like a dream. Things happened too slowly, or too quickly, and half the time I couldn't believe they were happening anyway. Sex with Alicia, Roof,

Mum getting pregnant . . . Getting whizzed into the future seemed as real as any of it.

If I had to say when it was that I woke up, I'd say it was then, when the door to Rich's bedroom opened and Alicia's mother came into the room.

She screamed. She screamed because the room was dark, and she wasn't expecting to see anybody. And she screamed because the people in there had no clothes on.

'Out,' she said, when she'd finished screaming. 'Out. Dressed. Downstairs in two minutes.'

'What's the big deal?' said Alicia, but she said it in a quivery voice, so I knew she wasn't being as brave as she sounded. 'We've had a baby together.'

'I'm going to tell you what the big deal is when you're downstairs.' And she slammed the door hard as she went out.

We got dressed without speaking. It was weird. We totally felt as though we were in trouble, and I felt much younger than I was when we found out Alicia was pregnant. We were nearly eighteen, our son was asleep next door, and we were about to get yelled at for having sex together. One thing I can tell you, something I learned from those couple of years, is this. Age isn't like a fixed thing. You can tell yourself that you're seventeen or fifteen or whatever, and that might be true, according to your birth certificate. But birth-certificate truth is only a part of it. You slide around, in my experience. You can be seventeen and fifteen and nine and a hundred all on the same day. Having sex with the mother of my son after a long time without any made me feel about twenty-five, I'd say. And then I went from twenty-five to nine in two seconds, a new world record. I didn't have a clue why I felt nine years old when I'd been caught in bed with a girl. Sex is supposed to make you feel older, not younger. Unless you're old, I suppose. Then it might work the other way round. See what I mean about the sliding around?

Andrea and Robert were sitting at the kitchen table when we got downstairs. Andrea had a glass of wine in front of her, and she was smoking, something I'd never seen her do before.

'Sit down, both of you,' she said.

We sat down.

'Can we have a glass of wine?' said Alicia. Andrea just ignored her, and Alicia made a face.

'Will you answer my question now?' said Alicia.

'Which question?' said Robert.

'I asked Mum what the big deal was,' said Alicia.

Neither of them said anything. Robert looked at Andrea as if to say, This is all yours.

'You can't see it?' said Andrea.

'No. We've had sex before, you know.'

I'd stopped feeling nine years old. I was somewhere around fourteen, but heading towards my actual age and maybe even past it quite quickly. I was on Alicia's side. Now I'd stopped feeling like a naughty boy, it was hard to see what the big problem was. OK, nobody wants to think about members of their family having sex, but if I ever think about that, I just feel a bit sick. I don't get angry. We were under the covers, so there was nothing showing. Plus, we'd finished. We weren't in the middle of anything. And like Alicia had just said, Roof was living proof that this was old news. Maybe it was because we were in the wrong room. Andrea would never have given us such a hard time if she'd caught us in Alicia's bedroom, I didn't think. She wouldn't even have gone in there. I thought I'd try that, seeing as nobody else seemed to have any ideas about what we'd done wrong.

'Was it because we were in Rich's room?' I said.

'What the hell difference does that make?' said Andrea. So it wasn't that. 'Say something, Robert,' she said. 'Why should it only be me that waves the big stick?'

Robert blinked, and fiddled with the stud in his ear.

'Well,' he said. And then he dried up.

'Oh, you're a great help,' she said.

'Well,' he said again, 'I share your mother's, ah, embarrassment. And . . .'

'It's a bit more than bloody embarrassment,' she said.

'In which case, I'm at something of a loss,' said Robert. 'We know that Sam and Alicia have a, a sexual relationship, so . . .'

Did we? I thought. I wasn't sure.

'Do you?' said Andrea.

'Not really,' I said.

'Yes,' Alicia said, at exactly the same time.

'Well, why do you?' said Andrea.

'Why?' said Alicia.

'Yes, why?'

This was turning into the worst conversation of my life. If I had to choose between telling my mum that Alicia was pregnant and talking to Alicia's parents about why we had sex, I'd definitely have chosen the talk with my mum. That was terrible, but she got over it. I'm not sure I'd ever get over this one.

'Do you love him? Do you want to be with him? Do you think this relationship has a future? You can't imagine ever sleeping with anyone else?'

I didn't love Alicia, not really. Not like I loved her when I first met her. I liked her, and she was a good mum, but I didn't really want to be with her. I could easily imagine sleeping with someone else, one day. I didn't know whether that meant we shouldn't be together now, but I did know that we had enough to worry about without all that. As I listened to Andrea, I felt sick, because

I knew I'd have to put a stop to it, if Alicia didn't put a stop to it first.

'Mum, he's Roof's dad.'

'That doesn't mean you have to screw him,' Andrea said. She was really steaming now. I didn't get it.

'Well,' said Robert. 'She obviously has to at some stage.'

'What?' Andrea looked at him like she was going to get a bread knife out of the drawer and cut out his tongue.

'Sorry. Silly joke. I just meant . . . you know. If he's to be the father of her baby.'

Alicia sniggered.

'And you think that joke is in good taste, do you?'

'Well. Good taste and humour don't always go together.'

'Spare us a bloody lecture on the theory of comedy. Don't you see what's happening, Robert?'

'No.'

'I'm not having her wreck her life in the way I wrecked mine.'

'I'm not wrecking my life,' said Alicia.

'You don't think you are,' said Andrea. 'You think you're doing the right thing, sleeping with the father of your children, because you want everyone to be together. And then one decade goes past, and another, and you realize that nobody else would ever want you, and you've wasted all this time sticking with something that any sane person would have got out of years before.'

'Bloody hell, Mum,' said Alicia. 'We were only thinking of giving it a go for a while.'

'I'm not sure you've got the point, Alicia,' said Robert quietly. Andrea couldn't look him in the eye. She'd said way too much, and she knew it.

There were a lot of tears that night. I went upstairs with Alicia and said my bit, in as nice a way as I could. I didn't have to say very much, really. Once I launched in she just said, 'I know, I know,' and started crying. I hugged her.

'It's not fair, is it?' she said.

'No,' I said, but I didn't really know what wasn't fair, or why.

'I wish we could start all over again. We didn't have the same chances as everyone else,' she said.

'What sort of chances?'

'To be together.'

It seemed to me as though we'd had at least two chances. We had one chance before Roof, for example, and we messed that one up. And then we had another chance after he'd arrived, and that one didn't go much better. It was hard to see what would be different if we started all over again. Some people just aren't meant to be together. Alicia and I were two of them. In my opinion, she didn't believe what she was saying. She was just trying to be romantic. I didn't mind. I searched around for something that would do, something right for the moment.

'Even though I still love you,' I said, 'We live in two separate worlds that are not uniting. I don't want this to be an ugly separation. I think we should both be dedicated to creating the best possible life for Roof. Try and make it as easy as possible for him.'

She pushed me away and looked at me.

'Where did all that come from?' she said.

'Tony Hawk,' I said. 'When he split up with Cindy.'

On my way downstairs I could hear Andrea and Robert going at it. I didn't poke my head into the kitchen to say goodbye.

You know when you got whizzed into the future, and you asked your mum to give you marks out of ten for how you were doing? Well, how many would you give yourself?

OK. Good question. But I can see why my mum didn't know how to answer it. I'll give you two different scores. First, the mark for how I'm getting on with what I've got to do every day – college, Roof, all that. I'll give myself eight out of ten for that. I could do better, but mostly I'm all right. There's nothing Alicia does with Roof that I can't do. I can cook for him, and I can put him to bed, read him stories, give him his bath. I work hard, I'm not late, I do as much college work as I can, and so on. I look after Emily sometimes, and I get on all right with Mark and his son. But if you're asking me to give my life marks out of ten . . . I'm afraid I couldn't go any higher than a three. This isn't what I had in mind. How could it be?

20

I'm woken up by my mobile bleeping. I seem to have woken up on the top deck of a bus going down Upper Street. There's a pretty girl, nineteen or twenty years old, sitting next to me. She smiles at me, and I smile back at her.

'Who's that?' she says. She's talking about my mobile, which must mean she knows me.

Oh, man. It looks like he's whizzed me again. This girl knows me, and I don't know her, and I don't know where I'm going on the bus, and . . .

'I dunno,' I say.

'Why don't you look?'

I reach in my pocket and bring out my mobile. I don't recognize it. It's tiny.

It's a text from Alicia.

'WHERE R U?' it says.

'What shall I say?' I ask the girl

'Why don't you tell her where U R?' she said. She made a funny face when she said the last bit, so that you knew she was talking in letters, not words.

'Upper Street,' I said.

'Brilliant,' she said, and she messed up my hair with her hand.

'Shall I say that, then?'

'God,' she said. 'If you're like this now, what are you going to be like when you're sixty?'

OK. So I wasn't sixty yet. That was something.

'I'll just text "Upper Street", then.'

'There's not much point,' said the pretty girl. 'We're getting off now anyway.'

She got up, pressed the buzzer and went downstairs. I followed her. I couldn't think of one question I was allowed to ask. It sounded to me as though the pretty girl and I were going to meet Alicia. Whose idea was that? If it was mine, I wanted shooting. Did Alicia know the pretty girl was coming? Or was that going to be a surprise?

We got off at the Green and walked back up the road to a Chinese restaurant I had never seen before, possibly because I'd never been to this part of the future before. It was beginning to feel like I'd been to most other parts.

There was hardly anyone in the restaurant, so we could see Alicia straight away. She stood up and waved. She was with a guy about her age, however old she was.

'We thought you'd crapped out,' Alicia said, and she laughed.

'Sorry we're a bit late,' said the pretty girl.

The guy stood up then too. Everyone was smiling like people in a toothpaste advertisement. In other words, their teeth were smiling, but nothing else.

Even I was smiling, and I didn't know what the hell was going on.

'This is Carl,' said Alicia. 'Carl, Sam.'

'Hello,' I said. We shook hands. He seemed OK, this Carl, although he looked like he might play in a band. He had long, dark, side-parted hair and a goatee.

The girls stood and smiled at each other. They were waiting for me to say something, but as I didn't know the pretty girl's name, there wasn't much I could say.

'No use waiting for him,' said Alicia, and she rolled her eyes. 'I'm Alicia.'

'I'm Alex,' said the pretty girl. And we all sat down. Alex squeezed my knee under the table, I think to tell me that everything was going to be OK.

I started getting nervous then. I suppose if I hadn't been in the future, I'd have been nervous all the way down on the bus, thinking about Alex meeting Alicia for the first time. So in a way I'd saved myself half an hour of nerves by not knowing what was going on.

'How was he?' said Alicia. She was looking at me, and I didn't even know who he was, let alone how he was, so I sort of waggled my head, something between a nod and a shake. Everyone laughed.

'What does that mean?' Alex asked.

I shrugged.

'As Sam seems to have gone temporarily mad,' said Alex, 'I'll answer. He was lovely. He didn't want us to go out, though, which is why we're five minutes late.'

'He' must be Roof, I thought. We had left Roof somewhere. Was that right? Should we have done that? Nobody seemed to mind, so I had to believe that it was OK.

'I don't know how Sam's mum manages bedtimes when she has both of them on her own,' said Alex.

'No,' I said, and shook my head. 'No' was pretty much the first word I'd said, and it seemed safe enough. You couldn't go wrong with 'no'. I started to feel cocky. 'I couldn't do it in a million years,' I said.

'What are you talking about?' said Alicia. 'You've done it loads.' Bollocks. Wrong again.

'Well, yeah, I know,' I said. 'But . . . It's hard, isn't it?'

'Not for you,' said Alex. 'You're really good at it. So shut up, or it'll sound like you're boasting.'

I felt like boasting. I could do bedtimes for two kids on my own? Roof stayed with me sometimes?

I shut up then, and listened to what the girls were saying. Carl hardly said a word anyway, what with being in a band and everything, so it looked like I was doing a spot of male bonding by keeping quiet with him. I listened to the girls talking about Roof, and about what they were studying. I'd met Alex on my course, so she did the same as me, whatever that was. Alicia was doing a part-time fashion course at Goldsmiths. She looked great. She looked happy and healthy, and for a moment I felt sad that I'd made her unhappy and unhealthy. I really liked Alex. I'd done well for myself there. She really was pretty, and she was friendly and funny too.

Every now and again, I learned bits about my life. I learned these things.

– It sounded like I'd gone part-time at college. Alicia was doing her course now, so I had to do my share with Roof. Plus, I had some kind of job. Plus, I looked after Emily sometimes. What with work, Roof, Emily and college, I didn't get out much.

– I'd given my skateboard away. Carl was a skater too, and Alicia told him that I'd been good at skating until I'd packed it in. I was sorry. I was sure I must be missing it.

– Roof was up at 5.15 that morning. Alex stayed in bed. So Alex must sleep at mine sometimes. I hoped we used at least three condoms every time we had sex.

– I was in a rush every single minute of every day, and this was my first evening out for ages. And the same went for Alicia, except she didn't have to look after Emily. Alex seemed to be feeling a bit sorry for me. Maybe Alex only went out with me because she felt sorry for me, I didn't know. I didn't care, either. I'd take what I could get. She was gorgeous.

All of it made me feel tired. Things looked OK in this Chinese restaurant with these people, but it was a long way from where I was, way back in the present, to here. There was a lot of work to do, and arguments to have, and kids to take care of, and money to find from somewhere, and sleep to lose. I could do it, though. I could see that. I wouldn't be sitting here now if I couldn't do it, would I? I think that's what Tony Hawk was trying to tell me all along.